I0761272

DEATH STALKS GLEVUM

Also by Rosemary Rowe

The Libertus Mysteries of Roman Britain

THE GERMANICUS MOSAIC
A PATTERN OF BLOOD
MURDER IN THE FORUM
THE CHARIOTS OF CALYX
THE LEGATUS MYSTERY
THE GHOSTS OF GLEVUM
ENEMIES OF THE EMPIRE
A ROMAN RANSOM
A COIN FOR THE FERRYMAN
DEATH AT POMPEIA'S WEDDING *
REQUIEM FOR A SLAVE *
THE VESTAL VANISHES *
A WHISPERING OF SPIES *
DARK OMENS *
THE FATEFUL DAY *
THE IDES OF JUNE *
THE PRICE OF FREEDOM *
A PRISONER OF PRIVILEGE *
A DREADFUL DESTINY *
THE REWARDS OF TREACHERY *

* *available from Severn House*

DEATH STALKS GLEVUM

Rosemary Rowe

SEVERN
HOUSE

First world edition published in Great Britain and the USA in 2026
by Severn House, an imprint of Canongate Books Ltd,
14 High Street, Edinburgh EH1 1TE.

severnhouse.com

Cover and jacket design by Nick May at bluegecko22.com

British Library Cataloguing-in-Publication Data
A CIP catalogue record for this title is available from the British Library.

ISBN-13: 978-1-4483-1443-0 (cased)
ISBN-13: 978-1-4483-2139-1 (paper)
ISBN-13: 978-1-4483-1697-7 (e-book)

All Severn House titles are printed on acid-free paper.

Typeset by Palimpsest Book Production Ltd., Falkirk, Stirlingshire, Scotland.
Printed and bound in Great Britain by TJ Books, Padstow, Cornwall.

The manufacturer's authorised representative in the EU for product safety is Authorised Rep Compliance Ltd, 71 Lower Baggot Street, Dublin D02 P593 Ireland (arccompliance.com)

Praise for the Libertus Mysteries of Roman Britain

'Larger-than-life characters combine with a gripping plot to make this a fine choice for historical mystery fans'
Booklist on *The Rewards of Treachery*

'Ancient rituals, Roman politics, and brutal murders combine in a fascinating mystery'
Kirkus Reviews on *The Rewards of Treachery*

'Perhaps the finest installment yet in Rowe's excellent historical-mystery series'
Booklist Starred Review of *A Dreadful Destiny*

'Exceptional . . . Rowe's mastery of the period enable her to provide a vivid backdrop, and the riveting plot delivers more than one emotional gut punch. Readers who miss Steven Saylor's Gordianus whodunits will be pleased'
Publishers Weekly Starred Review of *A Dreadful Destiny*

'Surpasses her own high standard . . . a welcome complement to Ruth Downie's Medicus mysteries'
Publishers Weekly Starred Review of *A Prisoner of Privilege*

'Meticulously researched historical details, well-drawn characters, and a clever plot, will keep even the most seasoned reader guessing'
Booklist on *A Prisoner of Privilege*

About the author

Rosemary Rowe also writes historical romances under her married name Rosemary Aitken. She has now resettled in her native Cornwall after having lived first in New Zealand for twenty years, and then for even longer in Gloucestershire, where this series is set.

To Ellen, Kathy, Paula, Stella and the team – with thanks for all you do.

FOREWORD

It is 200 AD and the province of Britannia is the northernmost outpost of a Roman Empire still reeling after the bitter civil wars. These, over succession to the Imperial throne, had finally concluded only a little over two years earlier with the defeat and brutal execution of one of the claimants, Clodius Albinus, erstwhile Governor of Britannia, and 'Emperor of the West.'

He had been given that title (and promised the succession) by the present Emperor Septimius Severus in return for his neutrality (if not actual support) against a third claimant to the purple, Pescinnus Niger, who had the good sense to take his own life in defeat. Unlike Clodius, who, on Pescinnus's death, was instantly denounced as an enemy of state, and forced to take up arms to try to claim what had been promised him.

His fate was dreadful. Vanquished in battle, he was stripped, whipped and Severus ordered the dying body to be laid before his horse where he trampled it to death – one rumour says until the limbs came off – beheaded it and had the pieces tossed into the nearby Rhine. His wife and children, who surrendered on promise of reprieve, were executed in the same manner, with the threat that known supporters would suffer the same fate.

Septimius was now firmly on the Imperial throne, but – as this tale suggests – he was not merciful in victory. Despite an oath which he had taken, he executed many Roman senators (one actually in the process of his 'trial') and actively sought out previous supporters of his rivals for punishment – usually death, but exile at best, if they did not simply 'disappear' before sentence could be passed. To this end he actively encouraged the role of 'delator' – essentially an Imperial spy and bounty hunter, paid to find eminent men who could be denounced.

Glevum (present-day Gloucester) had been staunchly loyal to its former governor, and was the home of one of the legions which inflicted early defeat on Septimius's troops, and humiliatingly captured and (honourably but foolishly) ransomed one of his commanders, Virius Lupus. Severus avenged himself for that defeat by making Lupus the new Governor of Britannia – whose suspicion and dislike of the colony, and of Glevum, in particular, must have been intense. It is against this background that this tale is set.

It is not clear from records what troops, if any, were assigned to Glevum at this time. After decimating the legions of his rivals (literally – killing one man in ten), and dispersing what remained, Severus was at this time short of numbers, but repairs to the inner tower wall, dating from this period, suggest that there was at least some presence at the fort. It was, however, much reduced in size, as there is evidence of civilian trades operating in part of the former area. (It is logical to suppose that this contraction happened following the wars, and – though some scholars argue it was earlier – this is the assumption in this book.)

Meanwhile, normal life attempted to go on. Britannia was the most far-flung of all the Roman Provinces, criss-crossed by Roman roads, subject to Roman laws and administered – again – by the provincial governor, appointed by and answerable to Rome. Latin was the language of the educated; local people were adopting Roman dress and habits; and citizenship, with the precious legal and social rights which it conferred, was still the aspiration of almost everyone.

(Almost everyone. At the perimeters there remained small groups who refused to yield to Rome, though Severus's merciless treatment of dissenting Celts meant that active resistance was becoming rare. And, of course – in the north and far south-west – there were areas which were not part of 'Britannia' at all.)

Glevum itself was an important town and river port, built as a colonia for retiring veterans, and all freemen born within its walls were citizens by right. Most inhabitants, however, did not qualify. Many were freemen born outside the walls, scratching a more or less precarious living from a trade. Hundreds more were slaves – mere chattels of their master, to be bought and sold, with no more rights or status than a domestic animal. Some slaves led pitiable lives, but others were highly regarded by their owners and might be treated well. A slave in a kindly household – with shelter, food and raiment guaranteed – might have a more enviable lot than many a poor freeman struggling to eke out an existence in a squalid hut.

Women, too, were virtually the property of their men. Although individual ones might inherit large estates, they were excluded from pubic office, could not make commercial contracts, and a woman of any age was deemed a child in law, under the official tutelage of first her father, then her husband (if she had one) or – if these failed – some other male relative or willing family friend. (If necessary, one could be appointed by the state.)

Being a wife and mother was the expected role. Respectable wives and daughters of rich Roman citizens did not work outside the home (and often not much in it, apart from genteel 'spinning' since she was likely to have slaves). The man under whose 'protection' (or 'potestas') she lived was expected to choose a spouse for her, usually for reasons unrelated to romance. The oldest, most complex and most binding form of marriage – the 'manus wedding' – was now vanishingly rare. Much more common was the 'usus' marriage which was easily dissolved – especially for men – and failure to produce an heir was grounds for a divorce.

However, the bride was entitled to take her dowry back, the husband enjoying the usufruct (control and profits) of it, only as long as she remained his wife. Therefore, legal severance was not always in his interests, and – however unhappy – she might lack the means to seek for one, since as a woman she could not bring a case herself.

All this of course related only to the wives and daughters of Roman citizens, who were thus officially of that rank themselves (though without the civic privileges afforded to the males). Most freeborn women, however, were not citizens at all. Marriage for them was a more casual affair, and more easily escaped. Tradesmen's women worked beside their men, and in the poorest households everybody toiled. There were even a few traditional 'female' trades, like midwifery, and at this time some working women were permitted to join guilds: the greengrocers' guild is known to have had some female membership, though, naturally, not enjoying most of the privileges of their male counterparts.

Most trades had such societies, partly social, involving convivial evenings of wine and food, and providing appropriate funerals for their members (one important service women members were entitled to) in return for regular payment of the fees. The more skilled the trade, the higher the dues and the more prestigious the guild, and the more it might offer, including sometimes even support in times of accident – think Masons, rather than the NUM. Most working freemen were very keen to join.

There is known to have been a mosaic-makers' guild in Rome, but it is not certain whether Junio and his (now-dead) adoptive father in this story would have belonged to such a thing, since there are only two such craftsman known of locally. There may have been a more general 'highly skilled artisan' *collegium*, but no woman would have been permitted to join that. There was however a guild for prostitutes and even one for slaves, whose owners sometimes paid the dues, though the membership of the latter seems to have been almost exclusively male.

Female slaves, of course, were available for use in any way their owner chose, the offspring of such pairings being either raised and sold for a profit when they were old enough or – since Romans considered that new-born infants did not yet have souls – simply disposed of at birth.

Medicine generally was in its infancy. Battlefield experience had resulted in good army surgery (for the period) and nearby Corinium was famous throughout the Empire for treatments of the eye, but other medicine might be of variable quality. The very rich, like Marcus Aurelius Septimus (Glevum's senior magistrate in this tale), might have a private Greek-trained doctor to attend the house, though this was expensive, and consequently rare. (Even Marcus does not have one at this date.) Glevum, like other important towns, had a public *medicus* – available to anyone who could afford his services – but there was no official training, far less an exam. One accompanied an experienced colleague for a year or two, then copied his prescriptions and procedures, which varied from the probably effective to the questionable at best. (Willow bark, source of aspirin, might be prescribed for pain, but carriage rides and cabbage diet were recommended for both 'lunacy' and what was clearly cancer.) Most households relied on home-made remedies.

But none of this was any help against the plague, outbreaks of which were endemic throughout the Empire ever since the Great Plague of Marcus Aurelius's time – the first recorded pandemic in history. It caused the death of millions and was almost certainly brought back to Rome by returning soldiers from the Parthian wars, though it is unlikely to have been caused – as many Romans thought – by the army's violation of a temple during the campaign. It was commonly believed to be a judgement by the gods, though whether it was communicated by an unseen miasma rising from the dead or by contaminated water was a matter of dispute.

The nature of the plague is not certain to this day. Many historians believe that it was smallpox, others say measles, or even both at different times (though Galen's description of the symptoms do not entirely match either of these diseases). Still others claim it as the first known outbreak of bubonic plague, or something similar to Covid. We simply do not know, and this story is consequently vague – relying simply on Galen's account.

Speaking of Covid, what interested me in the writing of this narrative was the similarity in many ways of how society reacted to the plague – instinctive 'social distancing', covering the nose and mouth, taking precautions when handling goods, avoiding public spaces when they could and cowering as far as possible indoors – except for the rich, who seem to have retired to country residences where they could be self-contained until contagion passed. There is evidence that shops and tavernas may have closed (possibly through the deaths of owners, possibly through fear). What I had not envisaged was the result of this – goods running short in markets, price rises and starvation following. It is alleged that in some towns more people died of hunger than of plague.

At the time when I began this story, I knew of no concrete evidence of any outbreak in Britannia at this period, merely that it tended to appear in twenty-year cycles (presumably as herd immunity was lost). However, the recent discovery of a plague-pit in Glevum dating from approximately 199 AD, containing a jumble of all ranks and ages, lends the narrative some verisimilitude.

The Romano–British background to this book has been derived from a variety of (sometimes contradictory) pictorial and written sources, as well as artefacts. However, although I have done my best to create an accurate picture, this remains a work of fiction, and there is no claim to total academic authenticity. Septimius Severus and happenings in Rome, as well as the events surrounding Clodius, are historically attested, as is the existence and basic geography of Glevum. (Several new fine pavements have recently been found during excavations around the bus station, suggesting an area of wealthy housing which is not accounted for in my description, but it was not known about when I began and the series must be consistent with itself.) The rest is the product of my imagination.

Relato refero. Ne Iupiter quidem ominibus placet. I only tell you what I heard. Jupiter himself can't please everybody.

PROLOGUE

Greetings to Libertus's loyal friend, from Junio, his adopted son. (I have not used your name, for fear this letter may fall into other hands.) I hope this finds you well, as I am myself – thank you for your kind message of concern. I have been fortunate to avoid the worst.

Remembering your former generous protection of my father, I write to crave similar sanctuary for two others, whom I commend herewith, and who are on their way to you. You will find an explanation in the following. Destroy this if it reaches you, and there should be no danger to you.

(Be so kind as to accommodate the courier overnight. No tip will be required. Send only a verbal message in reply; a written letter is too dangerous here.)

May all the gods be with you.

ONE

The first I heard of anything amiss was late one rainy afternoon shortly after the Nones of Aprilis. I was closing up my workshop in the town, as usual, and loading up my mule with some purchases I'd promised to my wife, when the woman from the tannery next door caught sight of me and hurried over from her premises at once.

When I saw her coming, I gave an inwards groan. She is always the first to know of any gossip, preferable of the more unpleasant kind, and is keen to share it (true or otherwise) with anyone prepared to lend an ear. Which, if I can avoid it, is not generally me.

But I could not escape by dodging down the alley or back into the shop, as I might otherwise have done, because I was encumbered by the animal. (You may remember Arlina, my father's mule?) My slave had already fetched her from the hiring-stables, where I have an arrangement to leave her for the day, and as she is so patient and used to the routine, I had not tethered her. I'd simply sent the boy off to fill the workshop's water jug, ready for tomorrow, while I held the reins with one hand and used the other to pack the panniers with things I'd purchased from the market earlier. There was quite a stack of them, and I had brought the trestle table out to make it easier.

So there was no escape from the tanner's wife tonight! I paused in the act of stuffing a brace of fresh eels into the bag, and forced myself to smile. 'Greetings, townswoman. What can I do for you?'

Although I knew, of course. Her gleeful expression told me everything. She had heard a rumour, somewhere, and had news to share.

I tried to forestall her. 'If you've come to tell me that Loftus the miller has been dragged before the courts and fined for putting grit and chalk into his wares, I'm afraid you're too late. I learned that when I was in town this afternoon. I had to cross the whole colonia to the docks and buy my flour at the other mill.' I nodded towards the dusty sack draped on Arlina's back. I was going to have to walk instead of riding her tonight. 'From some grumpy miller that I did not know at all.'

There are three such mills in Glevum. Small family concerns – respectable and busy, but on a smallish scale. (Quite unlike the owners of the vast estates who mill their own enormous crops, bake on a commercial scale, and send the excess into town to supply the street-vendors. Many flat dwellers have no legal means of cooking anything, though that does not always stop them trying. Which is why most building owners pay high fees to the firefighters' guild. Flails and buckets can sometimes save the worst.)

'Old Craithaw, eh? The one with a finger missing and the scar across his arm? Makes a few dozen loaves a day, so he can call himself a member of the bakers' guild?'

I made a vague noise of assent. I didn't really know – or care. I had been with my assistant, a freedman called Anylan Trovatus. He's always keen to come with me to the mill. Loftus has a dark-haired daughter of perhaps fifteen, whom I've seen him eyeing once or twice, though today she was nowhere to be seen. He was more dismayed than I was to have to go elsewhere. But I had more sense than say that to the tanner's wife!

She wasn't interested, in any case. 'Well, the flour won't be any better quality. Loftus is not the only one to slip chalk into the grain. Happens all round the Empire, I shouldn't be surprised. It makes the stuff look whiter and it adds a little weight. So does the grit, of course, but you can't help little bits of grindstone getting in the mix. Loftus told me so himself.'

I was surprised that she was defending him like this. She rarely had a positive thing to say of anyone. But I agreed politely. 'My wife used to complain of the same thing when we were young. She had more time than money, before the family arrived, and she would grind the grain herself. Always little bits left in the bottom of the groove. That's why the evening sweepings are so cheap, and why the poorest people wait till dusk to go and buy. But Loftus must have overstepped himself this time – tried to pass that inferior stuff to someone of rank and charge full price for it.'

That earned me a peculiar smile. 'You think so, citizen?'

'He must have done, or no one would have bothered with the case. I'm surprised that anybody did. It will have cost them more than the value of the flour to have had him dragged to court – even before the lowliest magistrate.' Even I knew that a man must be physically produced by his accuser, or there can be no trial. Only the state can prosecute *in absentia*. 'Loftus is no shrinking dwarf. He may be skinny but he's sinewy. He'd never have turned up for the case without some very burly men persuading him.'

She put her head on one side. 'So?' Something clearly was amusing her.

'Such things cost money – even if you already own a bodyguard. So it must have been somebody too rich to care about the cost.' I could still see the grin, so that clearly wasn't right. 'Or it might have been the garrison, I suppose. I know Loftus has supplied them once or twice, when their own system failed – the corn went mouldy or a cart-load was stolen by Celtic rebels on the road.'

'Not this time, citizen. You have but half the tale. His rival, Craithaw, made the charge. He's put it about that Loftus has been dallying with his wife. Though, if you ask me, I would say it is quite the opposite. I don't believe he cares a *quadrans* for his wife, and would be glad of an excuse for a divorce. He wants an heir and she's not provided one, so he wants a younger woman who might give him a son. Especially if she's pretty and can operate a mill . . . and may be in line to inherit one, some day.'

'Loftus's daughter?' I could take a hint when it was broad enough. 'But the father won't agree?'

'Says he needs the girl to help him, now his own wife is dead, and that Craithaw is too old and ugly, and most likely impotent, and only wants to get his hands upon the mill. Refuses to agree even to discuss a dowry for the girl – or the lack of one. Declares he'll give her nothing unless she marries someone he approves, and he'll leave the business to his brother's son.'

Little hope for poor Trovatus, then. 'So this case is merely an expensive way for Craithaw to revenge himself?'

I should not have shown a glimmer of curiosity. She nodded with delight. 'And it's not even likely to prevent the "crime" from happening again. No doubt Loftus will simply pay the fine – though Craithaw will ensure that it's a swingeing one – and go on putting chalk into the flour! Though perhaps in future he will have the sense not to publicly insult a rich competitor. But all this is hardly news. They dragged Loftus off at dawn and the story was all around the colonia by noon. Even you had heard it. But do you know the latest? There's sickness in the town.'

Loftus's woes were of some interest – to Trovatus anyway – but this, I thought, was not. Glevum is a big place – several thousand people pay the taxes here, and all of them have households, families and slaves. Among so many people there's always someone ill. But she always liked to be the bearer of bad news – the worse, the better.

I just said, 'Unfortunate,' and hoped she'd go away.

She didn't. Clearly, I did not sound sufficiently impressed. But she added nothing more.

In the end I was forced to speak myself, 'Who's fallen sick, then?' I said, mostly to be rid of her. My attention was really on where to put my piece of mutton, wrapped in its linen bag, where it would not be tainted by the eels. Deciding it was better in the other pannier, I switched hands with the reins and walked around the patient mule.

The woman followed me. My own fault – I had encouraged her. 'On the Street of the Fullers and the Feltmakers, several people in one family started falling ill, and by nightfall all of them were dead. Then the same thing happened to the neighbours either side.' She leaned a little closer, confidentially. 'I had it from a customer just this afternoon. She went over there to buy some felt to make a rug and found her usual supplier's premises were closed. Terrible business. Though good for me, of course, because she bought a skin from us instead.'

I put my meat away and went back to my stack. She followed me again. Clearly, I was going to have to listen to the end.

'I wonder if there's some infectious miasma from the gods,' I said. The Greeks, who know a thing or two about disease, believe an invisible miasma can descend on those who anger the deities in some way. 'Or perhaps there's something in the smell up there. Some people say that's where diseases lurk.'

I said 'smell', though 'stink' would be a better word. But it's a theory which sometimes causes me concern. My own workshop stands between a candlemakers and the tannery, both of which emit unwholesome stenches of their own.

A more alarming possibility occurred to me. 'I hope it's not the water. They no doubt use the public fountain that we use ourselves, and I've just sent my slave there to fill a jug for me.'

'There's nothing the matter with the water, citizen. I've drunk from it myself this very day. And this isn't mere sickness of the stomach, anyway.' A certain ghoulish satisfaction crept into her voice. 'There's talk of raging fevers and a dreadful rash. Vomiting and sweating and I don't know what. People falling over, close to death – and very suddenly.'

I did not actually believe it, even then. Indeed, I was inclined to question the whole tale. 'But how did your customer come to learn this? I thought you said the premises was closed?'

She was triumphant now. 'One of other traders further down the street came plucking at her sleeve, inviting her to come and see his merchandise – and when she said she'd rather wait and see her usual man, the fellow laughed. "You might be waiting for a long time, then," he said, and then explained what had been happening. But, thank Minerva, she decided not to go into his shop.'

'Because the infection might be lurking there?'

She looked at me a moment as though I were insane. 'Because otherwise she would not have come to us, I meant.' Her expression altered suddenly. 'But come to think about it, citizen, you're right. I'd better go and make a protective sacrifice. You mark my words, citizen, if it goes on like this, by the Ides it could be half the town. I must go and tell the candlemaker straight away. So farewell, citizen. And I wouldn't put those dates in with the eels, if I were you.'

I watched her go trotting down the street and stop a passing pie-man to tell him what she knew. No doubt announcing full-blown plague by now.

Perhaps I should have taken what she said more seriously (and not just about the dates!) but the woman is famous for being a harbinger of doom. So I thought no more about it, and turned my attention to my purchases.

I was just packing up the last of them when my slave Tenuis reappeared with the brimming water jug. I sent him to put it in the workshop and damp down the fire. He was in act of taking the trestle table in when Trovatus came hurrying down the street, full of apologies for having been delayed. He'd dashed away to check the final measurements for a dining-room pavement we were to repair, and it had taken longer than he thought.

'I'm sorry, citizen, the family are suddenly leaving for their country house today, and taking most of the household staff with them, so the master wanted to leave instructions with me before they went.'

I waved his apologies away. 'Tell me all that when we begin the work. No doubt they'll want it done before they all return. But tomorrow is an ill-omened *nefas* day, when every court and business in the town is shut, so we won't be starting then. No need for you to sleep above the shop for once. You can come home with us – and use that new stone dwelling that you've just built yourself.'

Trovatus had spent some years among the tribes in the south-west, where my father came from, and had learned the skill of making roundhouses from stone. (I would secretly rather he had not – my wife had dreams of a stone house of her own, in the Roman style, and inviting important visitors to dine, to show off the mosaics – which I would lay of course. But it would be a huge expense, not only to build but to equip with furniture and slaves. We could not afford it. So, I was not thrilled with having Trovatus's next door – on land which I had given him – even though it was a simple roundhouse in design. Though I suspect that his enthusiasm for making it owed something to an interest in a certain miller's girl.)

Up till now he'd rarely used the place. He took turns with Tenuis to keep a fire-watch in the shop – which had a sort of sleeping-space upstairs. We'd gained several customers by having someone there to open up the premises as soon as it was light.

'Tomorrow is nefas? I had forgotten that.'

'Lock the workshop door and bring the key with you. You'll dine with us tonight. I've warned my wife, and she's expecting you. I've bought some extra treats, as a surprise, as well as half a dozen of that vendor's awful pies, so there'll be plenty for us all. But we must be on our way. If we delay much longer we'll be walking part-way in the dark. And it's tricky on old track through the woods without a light.' Not to mention that there might be wolves or bears.

Besides, I was anxious to be home. I'd just been paid for a pavement that I'd laid, and to celebrate I was taking back these luxuries. I was looking forward to sharing my family's delight at mutton pies and dates and fresh-baked honey cakes. And it was all that I had hoped. My wife was pleased with the flour and eels and meat. I did not give the tanner's wife another thought.

There have always been rumours of the plague, ever since the Great Contagion swept the Empire in Marcus Aurelius's time. But after a day or two of panic, and perhaps the death of one or two unfortunates, there usually proves to be simply a dead dog in a well, or some family which has eaten a consignment of bad fish, and the problem is soon over.

But I was wrong to doubt. Within a day or two – by the time that we had finished with that small repair – there was outbreak somewhere else. Again, it was the tanner's wife who told me so.

She had been to the fountain and I saw her hurry by – in the early morning, this time, just as I was taking down the counter-shutters for the day. To my surprise, she did not seem inclined to stop, but when I hailed her she did pause to answer me.

'I can't linger, Master Junio. I don't think it is safe. People falling ill all over. I told you there would be.' She'd pulled a piece of cloak across her face and came to stand a good ten paces off.

'Worse, is it?' I said, concentrating on moving the heavy wood and letting light into the premises.

'You haven't heard?'

'We have been working in an almost-empty house, with just a doorkeeper and a couple of indoor slaves for company. The master's been away. We've not heard anything. Though Tenuis said that yesterday, in the workshop, there'd been no customers.'

'Well, there's been dozens ill, and there's starting to be more deaths. Several that I heard of only yesterday.' She was clearly edgy, but the temptation to tell me everything was too strong to resist. 'Two of them members of the *curia*, in fact. Julius Fortunatus – you might have heard of him. He and his family are dead, and all the slaves as well – so the curia had to bury everyone in haste. And Rufus, who used to be the *aedile*. Suppurating blisters head to foot, they say – so bad that the family had the funeral at once, without even laying the body out in state.' There was relish in her tone. 'They had to shroud his face before they put him on the pyre, because he looked so terrible. A handsome man, like that! They had to pay the undertakers double for their services – they're starting to be wary of dealing with the dead.'

I stopped and stared at her. 'Is this certain?' I enquired. Julius Fortunatus was a magistrate and just a name to me, but Rufus I had encountered many times. As aedile, he'd been responsible for the marketplace, though he'd now risen to a loftier rank. He was a patrician, and very proud of it. Normally a man like that would have his body laid in state for several days, then borne in procession round the town accompanied by his ancestral masks, with paid musicians and professional mourners hired to weep and wail. 'Rufus had no public funeral?'

She shook her head. 'I had it from one of the undertaker's slaves. They had to be paid handsomely to touch the corpse at all.'

I was shocked and sounded it. 'Real pestilence?'

She shifted her heavy water pot from hip to hip. 'It rather looks that way. No doubt why your recent customer decided to leave his house empty and flee town. People are simply dropping in the streets. I saw one this very morning, with my own two eyes. A woman near the temple of Minerva – probably wanting to go and make a preventive sacrifice – but she'd left it far too late. Just dropped down in the gutter and lay dead. Presumably the death-cart will come and get the corpse.'

I took a step backwards. Plague is said to hover in the air, and I had no wish to breathe it in. Just in case, I touched the lucky amulet I always wear. 'But if this is catching, as you seem to think, then surely the garrison will put itself at risk?' The death-cart is an army vehicle of course, charged with picking up the unknown dead from public places and disposing of them in the public pit.

She leaned forwards, pulling her veil a little closer round her face. 'They say the soldiers are not catching it. They must have special protection from the gods. They are picking up corpses every day, I hear, but they don't seem to be falling ill themselves. People are blaming them for bringing in the plague. All these fresh men the new governor brought in, to replace the ones that fought against him and the Emperor in Gaul.'

I nodded. That was possible. I knew that the eastern army brought the Great Pestilence to Rome, and thousands died of it – but the soldiers who survived it did not fall ill again. And it is true there is a fresh detachment here – brought in by the new provincial governor after Clodius Albinus, the previous one, was humiliatingly defeated in the Succession Wars.

It has made life in Glevum very difficult of late. People are afraid to speak their minds. Of course, the whole of Britannia has earned the Emperor's distrust because it supported Governor Clodius.

(With some justification, in my view. He had actually been promised by Septimius Severus that he would succeed and was given the title Emperor of the West in return for his support. But, naturally, as soon as Septimius was secure, Clodius was denounced and declared an enemy of state. After bitter fighting, much of it in Gaul, the legions from Britannia were defeated. Albinus was killed in an appalling way, and his legions – decimated as a punishment – were swiftly moved elsewhere. The new governor, Virius Lupus, has replaced them with his own, loyal to the new regime and extremely distrustful of the old.

(I dare not say that publicly, of course. People who do that are apt to be exiled, executed for treason – or just die suddenly, or simply disappear. Virius Lupus was appointed with a mandate to subdue dissent, and he hates Glevum in particular, because the local legions once defeated his in Gaul, and held him to ransom. He has not forgotten it.)

But Severus's army is depleted with the wars, so there are not so many soldiers at the garrison nowadays, and the quality of those is no longer what it was. People of quite lowly birth, who once could only have been auxiliaries at best, are proper legionaries now and even hold commands. Perhaps if they are tough enough to withstand the plague, they are tough enough for anything!

'From now on I'm going to keep a cloth around my face.' The tanner's woman was still wittering, 'I've seen other people doing that, to ensure they don't breathe contagion in – they say it hangs round you in a sort of cloud, though unfortunately it's invisible. I'm on my way now to the temple, to buy some doves and make a sacrifice. No doubt they're charging double by this time. But better to be safe. And best you do the same, though forgive me if in future I don't stop to speak.'

The tanner's wife, afraid to stop and gossip in the street! And Rufus, the proud patrician, buried without the proper rites! That's when I decided that Glevum was no place to be.

I called to my slave Tenuis, who was kindling the fire, and to Trovatus who was sorting stones. 'Close up the place again. There's plague in town. It isn't safe to stay. I'll chalk a notice on the door to say we're closed till further notice.'

And the moment that Arlina had been fetched, I ushered my little party hastily away.

TWO

Cilla would not be thrilled to see us come. I knew that the moment I saw the plume of smoke arising from the dye-house roof. She was obviously dealing with some wool that she had spun. It was not her favourite occupation. It made her hot and stressed.

I sent Trovatus and Tenuis to put the mule into the field, and went up the enclosure path alone. The dye-hut door was open and I could see my wife bending over something simmering in the pot which always hung above the central fire. The 'something' was giving off a powerful smell that I recognised. A pungent decoction of oak bark and galls, which reached me in great wafts as she stirred and lifted the yarn up with her stick.

I called to her and she came out at once, still carrying her dripping implement. She tried to force a smile, but her dark hair was bedraggled with the heat and her hands and wrists stained golden brown with dye. 'Husband! Whatever are you doing here at this hour? I thought you were Brianus returning with the pail.' (Brianus is our household slave.) 'I hope he isn't long. The yarn is almost ready for a rinse.'

'The children have gone with him, I suppose?' Not difficult to guess. If they were here, I would certainly have heard. This was not a time of day when even the toddler would be settled for a sleep.

'Of course! I don't want them round me while I am doing this.'

'I know,' I soothed. 'It's dangerous.' It was. I've known her tether the youngest to a tree when dye was being made – he is at the stage of crawling into everything, and tasting to see if it is edible! 'But we're here now, and you won't have to tether anyone!' That earned a rueful smile. 'In fact, we can help to keep the children occupied. It would be a good idea for me and Tenuis to take them to the woods – get in some piles of firewood – and Trovatus can come and set a squirrel trap or two.'

'That would be very welcome, certainly. I'm afraid I've got no food prepared to offer you beyond an apple or a piece of cheese. The nut loaf I am making isn't ready yet – it's baking in the embers in the roundhouse while I'm doing this – and there isn't any stew. There isn't even anything to drink till Brianus comes back.' She pushed her hair back with a brown-stained hand. 'But husband,' she added, 'why are you here at all at such an hour? Surely another tree has not come down and blocked the track again?'

A reasonable guess. That had happened once before. The shortest way to town is along the ancient track, though it's rocky, narrow and – in places – steep. Last winter an enormous oak was upended in a storm and next day we'd been forced to detour through the woods. Even with Arlina that was difficult, without a path, but we persevered because we had a waiting customer. We'd come the long way home that night – several extra miles along the military road, and several more along the gravelled lane that meets the old track just below our gate. The usual route remained impassable for days, till someone brought an ox to drag the tree away. (If I had an ox I would have done that, myself. Firewood is a valuable resource.)

'No trouble with the track. We've been to town, in fact. But . . .' I paused, wondering how best to break the dreadful news.

As I was dithering, Cilla spoke again. 'Then why . . .? Oh, great Mars, husband, you've not been taken ill?' I just had time to shake my head, before she hurried on. 'Tenuis, then? Or Trovatus, perhaps?'

'We are all three of us in the best of health,' I told her. 'And hope to remain so. That's why I've brought them home. But I fear it's not good news.' I outlined what the tanner's wife had said.

Cilla looked at me a moment. 'Plague?' She had turned as pale as milk. 'I suppose it's true? The tanner's wife isn't the most reliable of witnesses.'

'She would hardly have invented the stories about the

councillors – the fate of Rufus in particular, and his lack of any proper funeral. Things like that are too easily disproved. And the suppurating fevers. Too many people to contradict. I think we can assume it really is the plague.'

Cilla dropped her dye-stick and sat down heavily on the stool beside the door. (When dyeing, she keeps one ready alongside the iron pot which is used to rinse the wool.) 'Dear Mercury,' she muttered. 'No public rites at all? Rufus, of all people.' She ran a hand through her dishevelled locks. 'I still can't believe it.'

'I think it must be true. It tallies with a rumour that I heard before.' I didn't mention that the tanner's wife had told me that, as well. 'No doubt I'd have heard this sooner, if we had not been working in an empty house – virtually empty, though there was a slave or two. Probably left to keep an eye on us. But being indoor staff, even they knew little of what was happening outside. Their owners had left them with adequate supplies.'

Cilla understood at once. 'There'd be no visitors while the owners were away, so even the doorkeeper wouldn't speak to anyone. And no one would need to leave the premises – especially with you working there all day.'

'Lucky for them that they didn't,' I replied. 'And for us, perhaps. Otherwise I might have brought home more than rumours of the plague. I shan't be going to town again until the danger's over. Not if I can help it!'

Cilla looked up at me, and went to take my hand, then thought better of it – for fear of passing on the dye, rather than of catching contagion from my touch. 'So, what do we do now?'

'Wait here until it's over, and pray it passes as soon as possible.' Worry made me sharper than I meant. I tried to soften it with a smile. 'What else is there to do?'

'I don't know how we'll manage without someone going to Glevum now and then. Carus is growing out of his sandals as it is. Being the eldest there's no one to pass theirs on to him. Speaking of supplies, you didn't by any chance stop in the town as you were passing through, and bring home anything?'

She must have seen the answer in my face. 'Oh, I suppose you came the long way round, and kept outside the walls – to keep away from people?'

That was, of course, exactly what we'd done – though once or twice I had regretted it, because it's narrow, muddy, damp and – in places – overgrown. (If you don't know Glevum, you may be surprised at this. When the colonia began, the major road led from the eastern gate, but shortly afterwards they had to move the fort to higher ground because of floods, and the main road to Corinium and Londinium now starts – bizarrely – from beyond the northern gate. So the eastern road is unfrequented now, with the land around still boggy and very largely waste, and the track which runs that way outside the walls is not much used.) We had run into nobody except a group of peasants selling watercress – the fact that they were growing it gives you some idea about the nature of the land.

I had bought a large bunch – mostly to stop the hawkers crowding round us as we passed. Otherwise the thought of bringing home supplies had not occurred to me, although it should have done.

I was about to say this when Trovatus and Tenuis appeared from settling the mule. I saw the large green bunch that Trovatus was holding in his hand, and seized the chance to redeem myself – a little anyway.

'We're not quite empty-handed. See what Trovatus has.'

Cilla gave me a weary smile. 'Watercress? That won't go very far if we are stuck here for weeks. I suppose I can add it to the pot and make a tasty soup. In the meantime, he must eat with us, of course. It's much more economical with food.'

'Just as well we brought supplies the other day,' I said.

'I only wish we hadn't finished all the eels – I could have smoked one on a hook above the fire and eked that out to make another meal. And I've already put things in the stewpot for tonight. But we can make that last a bit – add whatever comes to hand from day to day and keep the mixture simmering. We'd still get a bit of flavour from the meat.'

I did my best to sooth her worries. 'Well, I'll help Trovatus set those squirrel traps. Not a patch on mutton, but it will have to do. He's skilled at catching birds, as well – another thing he learned while he was living with the Celts. We have a few things growing in the garden, too, though we may have to eat them before they're at their best.'

'I planted a few lentils by my roundhouse recently,' Trovatus put in. 'Nothing very much, but we could eat the leaves at least.'

I said, 'And there's that farmer from further up the lane, who comes this way to market now and then. Perhaps we could arrange to buy some things from him.'

Cilla nodded. 'I've got a sort of agreement with him as it is. If he doesn't manage to sell all his load in town, when he comes back he whistles at the gate, and I go out and bargain for whatever he has left. Extra turnips or things that we don't grow ourselves – depending on the season and what is on the cart. A bit bedraggled sometimes, and it often isn't much, but it all goes in the pot.'

'Since we're all here now, for a half a moon at least,' I said, 'we can help you watch for him. We'll try to stop him next time *before* he gets to town. Much safer that way and – even if it costs a little more – if this goes on, we will be glad of it. Though we'll have to keep our distance, even then. Perhaps we could contrive to leave payment at the gate, and he could leave his produce in return. Thank Jove that I have just been paid for that repair and we have some money in the house.'

'We could leave coins in a bowl of water to be safe, and he could leave his vegetables in it afterwards,' my wife agreed. 'They won't get soggy if we pick them up as soon as he is gone. Better be safe than sorry – we can barter by calling to each other through the fence. In the meantime, thank you for the cress.'

'You're welcome, mistress,' Trovatus murmured with a bow. He handed her the bunch.

She made a quick inspection and gave it back to him. 'That will do nicely. You can put that in the house. I'll deal with it later,' she said, as though Trovatus was a servant still, and not the freedman that he'd been for years. (She spoke that way to all of us – including me, sometimes!) 'There's some apple and a little cheese there, on the shelf, but you'd better leave it there. We will have it with the nut loaf later, and make a meal. From now on, we'll have to be careful what we eat. Meanwhile you, Tenuis, can come and help me stir this wool – I should not have left it this long. I must get back to it or it will spoil, and the dye will be much darker than I meant.' She turned to me again. 'Send Brianus to me, husband, as soon as he arrives. Then the slaves can help me with the rinse, and you two can take those children out into the woods until I've finished here.'

But it was quite a time before Brianus appeared. So long that I'd begun to be alarmed.

When he did come, all seemed quite as usual. He carried a heavy, brimming wooden bucket in one hand, while with the other he clutched our drowsing youngest to his chest. The other children were proudly carrying water of their own. Carus was struggling manfully, two-handed, with a full-size pail. His younger brother had a miniature version of the same, while their sister was attempting to copy women she had seen by balancing a half-full jug upon on her head.

Cilla was inclined to be furious, at first. She came out of the dye-hut, even more bedraggled in the steam, and waved her stick at Brianus as he put the water down. 'Where have you been all this time? That dye-batch has been in the pot for far too long without a rinse. It will be dark brown by now instead of tan, and I shall be lucky if it isn't spoiled. Brianus, I've a mind to put you on to bread and water for the day!' (She didn't use the stick, except to gesture with. Like me, my wife was once a slave herself, and rarely struck anyone, even when provoked.)

Brianus looked stricken, but he offered an excuse. 'Forgive me, mistress, and if the batch is spoiled I am sorrier than I can say. But – since I had the children with me – I thought it best to wait. There was a woman washing clothes in the pool up by the spring, slapping them against the rocks to get them clean . . .'

'Well?' my wife demanded. 'That did not stop you, surely? You could have waded past. There's room at the pool for several people to wash their clothes at once, and still leave space for you to reach the source.'

'Mistress, that is just the thing,' the slave replied. 'There was another woman, with her laundry, waiting on the bank. When she saw me coming, she shook her head at me. "I wouldn't go down there, right now," she said. "Especially with children. That woman washing has a husband ill – she told me yesterday – and now I hear there's talk of an outbreak of the plague. I'll wait until she's finished, thank you very much. I know it will offend her, she called me down just now, but she isn't looking well herself and I'm going nowhere near. It's up to you of course, but I should do the same."' He paused. 'I'm sorry, mistress, if I did wrong, but the woman doing washing did look very flushed, and for the children's sake I did not take the risk.'

I decided it was time the master took the lead. 'You did right,' I told him. 'The rumour is quite true. Let's hope the running water washed any plague away.'

Brianus looked gratefully at me. 'I made sure that I filled the pails directly from the spring, and I did not let the children get in the stream at all. The woman I was talking to allowed me to go first – she would not share the pool with anyone, not even me. When we were talking on the bank, she kept herself apart. She was genuinely worried, I could see.'

Cilla gulped and glanced at me. 'So, it is certain, then.' She turned to Brianus. Her manner was suddenly quite different. 'My husband is quite right. You did the proper thing, and far from chiding you I thank you for your care. But all the same, that dye-batch is still waiting for a rinse, and if we don't all want dark-brown tunics for a year, we'd better rescue it. So pour that water in the rinsing pot, then go and set that infant down to rest. He's half-asleep already. The other children can put their water in the butt, then their father and Trovatus will take them to the woods to get some kindling for the fire.'

'And if we see any fallen branches, we'll drag them back as well. We can cut them up and add them to the woodpile,' I said. 'There may be hard times coming.'

There were. Though I did not realise then just how hard they were to be.

THREE

I was right to restock the woodpile then. More and more people came to the forest every day, carrying off every piece of fallen timber they could find. Soon they started lopping growing branches too. It grew hard even to find kindling.

We quickly learned to be frugal with everything. Trovatus abandoned his smart stone abode and moved into our slave-hut, which saved a separate fire, and added the sparse contents of his larder to our own.

And, for a long time, that is how we lived. Exactly how long, I'm not certain even now. Three moons, perhaps, although it felt like more. I tried at first to calculate the days by cutting notches in a stick, but that was needed on the fire and I gave up in despair. Until I could go back to the forum and consult the calendar, I lost all track of time. I had no idea whether a day was nefas or otherwise, if we were nearer to the Kalends or the Ides – or even whether it was some holy day when sacrifice should be made to one or other of the gods. (We had little to offer them in any case!)

Life was becoming harder by the day. We had to choose our moment to go up to the spring, to fetch water or pick the bedding reeds – or even for Cilla to do the washing in the pool – for fear of meeting others doing the same thing. Even if one went a little before dawn, or after dark, with Tenuis carrying a burning taper to illuminate the task, you could still encounter people who'd had the same idea!

Food was the greatest worry. The mutton-flavour soon was just a memory, and it's surprising how quickly you can tire of squirrel stew! Yet even squirrel became a luxury. Suddenly, there were very few of them. Other households were clearly setting traps, and I'm convinced that someone was stealing things from ours!

Trovatus was running short of birdlime, too, which much reduced the number of birds that he could catch. (We quickly collected a store of holly bark – at some cost of scratches to ourselves – but it takes at least a moon to brew another batch.) We still had stone bird-traps, but these required berries to be used as lures – food we really wanted for ourselves – and they didn't always work. Sometimes the creatures simply tripped the stone and flew away.

Besides, our other stores were getting dangerously low – especially the grain pit. We began to worry about feeding the chickens and the geese. It was obviously possible to put them in the pot, but we were more and more dependent on their eggs. And, once the fowls were cooked, there was no replacing them. Even if we miraculously found anything for sale, there was simply no more money in the house. We had used up every coin in the money jar, and there was no prospect of earning any more.

Yet we had not spent a single bronze *as* of it, except on food. The farmer, who now came to whistle at the gate on his way to Glevum, as well as coming back, was demanding ever higher prices for his goods. He could easily obtain them in the town, he said, since fewer and fewer people from outlying farms were prepared to take the risk of taking produce into town. Everything was scarce.

Increasingly, on his return, there was scarcely anything at all left on the cart – beyond an odd squashed leek or wormy root. Certainly, there were no longer bargains to be had.

But we had to eat, so we resorted to paying him with goods: a set of wooden spoons, a handsome mixing bowl and then – reluctantly – a stool. Things, my wife declared, that I could replicate, since I now had time at home. But – what with setting traps and gardening, foraging in woods and lanes for anything which might be edible, and generally keeping the children occupied – opportunities for woodwork were limited until the sun had set. And we were short of tapers, too.

I contrived quite quickly to fashion some more spoons with help from Trovatus, who was skilled at whittling, but at mealtimes Tenuis was still squatting on the floor.

Finally, Cilla had been forced to swap that precious yarn for a sack of yellow carrots and a bag of turnip-tops.

But if the farmer ceased to bring us much to eat, he did at

least bring news. When he came back from Glevum he would whistle as before. I'd go out, and he would stand up in the cart and bellow out to me – even when he had nothing left to sell – while I kept a safe distance behind the palisade. I'd ask if the plague was passing. But the news got worse and worse. Dozens of new deaths every time we spoke, and scores – if not hundreds – of people falling ill. Meanwhile, the price of food was getting higher all the time.

Then one day he gave me a surprise.

'Streets all but deserted in the town,' he bawled to me from the enclosure gate. 'And hardly any buyers in the marketplace today. I've got some oddments left. First time for at least a moon, I haven't sold the lot.'

'Would you take a pair of ancient sandals?' I bellowed back at him. 'I've left them, just in case there was something to exchange.' I gestured to the pail. It was all that we had left to barter with, by now. They were rather worn, and they were not improved by having been immersed in water for an hour. He took them out, dripping, and looked doubtfully at them. But he put five welcome turnips and two onions in their place.

'Trade is that bad?' I shouted.

He shook his head despondently. 'Too many people sick or afraid to venture out. I don't know how apartment-dwellers manage to survive when they don't have anywhere to cook. Half the shops don't open any more. No street-vendors at all. Even most tavernas and hot-soup stalls have closed.'

'Thank all the gods that we don't live within the walls! Poor souls. Starvation will get them if the plague does not.'

'Then they'll be lucky to obtain a funeral! The undertakers are refusing to go to houses now, and people who don't have anywhere to build a private pyre are simply leaving bodies by the road. I saw one lying in the ditch today, outside the town – still there from the last time that I went that way.'

'And you didn't report it? Isn't that required? So the army can send the death-cart out for it and put it in the pit before it gives infection to anybody else?'

He shook his head again. 'I may be supposed to, but I certainly did not! Nor, quite clearly, has anybody else.'

'You're not afraid of vengeful spirits?' I was rather shocked.

'What was I supposed to do?' This whole conversation was a shout, but he managed to sound scornful. 'Go and report it and become a corpse myself? Only the army will approach the dead these days, so people avoid them whenever possible. Afraid to go near the sentry at the gate, let alone the garrison.'

He was tempting the spiteful Fates, I thought. Just as the souls of murdered people cannot rest until the killer can be found, so the souls of the unburied are condemned to stalk the earth till due respect is paid. Even dead soldiers on the battlefield are retrieved where possible to receive at least a sprinkling of dust, a piece of sacrificial pig and a respectful prayer.

A scornful laugh. 'Folks are more afraid of soldiers than of ghosts. They say the legions brought the plague with them – and I, for one, don't choose to take the risk. It's dangerous enough to mix with people in the marketplace. Though I'll have to go again. When I do, I'll try to trade these sandals. All the wealthy left the town as soon as plague began, so cash is very scarce. But there's sure to be someone who needs something on his feet. He won't be getting new ones – that's a certainty.'

'No shoemakers about?'

'Not one. They may well be dead by now. But I'll swap these somehow, though next time I'd like something easier to trade.'

I frowned at him. 'Such as?' We had little else to offer.

'Something, perhaps, which your youngest has outgrown? People with children are desperate for clothes. They are afraid to swap with neighbours for fear of handing on contagion in the cloth. And, as I said, money's running short, so it's hard to buy new cloth to make your own – even if you could find a trader selling it.'

'And the second-hand clothes stalls?'

He looked pityingly at me. 'All closed for want of trade. But children don't stop growing just because there is a plague.'

We had a little tunic, which was far too small, even for the toddler, so we parted with a smile and I promised to put out for him the next time that he called.

But there was no next time. He never came again. (I assumed

he'd decided that the risk had grown too great, but I learned later that he'd caught the plague and died.)

Without the farmer there was less and less to eat. We started to go hungry. It was hardest on Cilla who, I realised, was quietly giving much less to herself than to the children, to me, or even to the slaves. I had to insist that this must stop. If her milk dried up there'd be another mouth to feed, and that would make things worse.

There was very little in the kitchen garden now – there weren't even many laying geese and chickens left. As they'd grown ever scrawnier and had ceased to lay, one by one we had reluctantly put them in the pot. That sustained us for a day or two, of course, but each time meant fewer eggs and, with the garden being almost bare, every day we had to go further to forage and to hunt.

That was how I happened to be up the lane one afternoon. I had a basket and was searching for herbs or roots and leaves that we could eat – usually slaves' or women's work, but times were desperate – when I heard the sound of hooves and the rattle of an approaching cart. I wondered for a moment if, at last, it might be the farmer coming back from town. (I didn't know then that was impossible.)

Whoever it was, the problem was the same. The lane was narrow here, with high walls on either side. There would be people passing very close to me, and who knew what infection they might be carrying?

I looked around, but I could not simply dive into the woods. I had reached the point where the lane runs through Marcus's estate – the walls fringed his villa and his farmland opposite. In fact, the chervil I'd been picking had probably escaped from his herb garden, though it was thriving here.

I was shocked when I realised that the vehicle was his. I had not seen him since the plague began. But here he was, dressed in a travelling cloak, frowning like a bear and accompanied by a handsome-looking slave I hadn't seen before – perhaps a borrowed one, since he was not dressed in the distinctive scarlet uniform. Obviously some kind of bodyguard: young, strong and athletic, and armed with a cudgel that – as a thief – I did not care for much. But there was no chance to hide! Marcus had already ordered his gig driver to stop and was gesturing me imperiously across. I went unwillingly.

As I approached, the frown dissolved into a smile. 'Citizen Junio! I didn't recognise you – you have grown so thin. I am pleased to see you – I feared for you with all this contagion in the town. I'm glad that you escaped it.' But all the same he did not offer his ringed hand for me to kiss. With it he lifted a toga hem across his mouth, while the other clutched a bunch of hyssop to his face. (Everyone knows that hyssop helps against all sicknesses.)

I was debating how I should reply when Marcus spoke again. 'I think we were wise to keep away from it. As soon as it broke out, I took my family to Corinium – we have a house there, as I think you know.'

I did know, of course. Julia's previous husband had owned the property. When he died it came to her, and thus to Marcus when he married her. They kept a loyal household there and sometimes visited, or used it for important visitors. Julia was very fond of it. She returned there, once, when Marcus was obliged to go to Rome and she was close to giving birth. I might have guessed that she would want to use it now.

I was relieved. If Marcus had been away throughout, I could approach without much risk of catching anything. 'Extremely wise, Excellence.' I bowed.

His next question shattered my relief. 'But whatever are you doing with those leaves?' He was frowning. 'It looks like the chervil I imported years ago.'

'I believe it might be,' I replied. 'But I picked it from the lane.' I indicated the place, though since I had taken all the leaves there was no plant in evidence.

Marcus did not even deign to look.

That roused me sufficiently for me to add, 'My wife has sent me out to find some herbs to eat. We have a squirrel and two birds, which might last a day or two, but there's not much else remaining that we can put with them. We had some turnips but we've eaten all of those.' An excuse, but I expected a rebuke.

He was staring at me with an air of disbelief. 'A squirrel?' He spoke with the disdain of a man of privilege.

Perhaps that made me reckless. 'And two sparrows. And lucky to have that! Life has been difficult while you were away. More difficult than you might imagine, Excellence. We have no money and are short of everything – no oil, no flour, no anything, except what we can grow or catch or forage for. I've had no work for several moons.'

I had spoken with vigour and regretted it at once. It was not wise to be so impolite to any man of rank – let alone to Marcus, who is easily the most influential civilian in the town, if not half Britannia. And he was looking utterly appalled.

I bowed my head. 'Forgive me, Excellence. I did not mean to give offence.'

He was still frowning like a thundercloud, and I thought for a moment he was going to get down from the gig and seize the precious chervil from my hand.

'I promise you I found this growing by the wall.'

'Then, citizen, I am surprised at you.'

I braced myself, but His Excellence went on. 'Whyever did you not remove the plant and take it to your garden, and ensure a more continuous supply?'

I was about to confess I hadn't thought of it, when he surprised me even more.

'Anyway, if you wanted chervil, why not apply to me – or at least to the villa, since I was not here. We have plenty. They could have given some to you.'

It was more than I deserved and I could only mutter thanks.

Marcus waved my words aside. He had dropped the hyssop and the toga fold. 'I will see that a plant is dug up and sent to you at once. And some other things, perhaps. My wife will be quite horrified to think of you in want. If you insist, you may pay me later on – when you're employed again.'

I had no thought of insisting, but I nodded thankfully. 'It may be some time coming, Excellence,' I said. 'People do not think of pavements when there is a plague.'

'You haven't heard the latest news? The plague is dying down. Only a few deaths in the last few days, and fewer people are falling sick each day. I know because I asked the commandant-commander of the Glevum fort to keep me constantly informed while we were in Corinium.'

Of course, I thought, a man of Marcus's standing could request such things, and naturally the business of the Empire did not cease for anything as trivial as the plague. Though there was no legion stationed in Corinium, the courier of the Imperial post would have to go that way to reach the capital. And probably change horses at the staging-post. I stared at Marcus, scarcely able to believe the news. 'This improvement's certain?'

'Obviously. Otherwise I wouldn't have returned! I'd have left it for another half a moon, for preference, but I was needed here today. There was a meeting of senior magistrates to start calculating who is left and liable to tax – and how any shortfall should be met. That would fall on the curia of course, so we are planning to recall the councillors, and the courts as well.'

The world could fall, but Rome would want its tax. 'And your wife and family, Excellence?'

'Still in Corinium,' he said. 'Julia wanted to come with me, but I wouldn't take that risk. I have left her with the children and nursery slave, at least until full moon. After all, it's not quite over yet. In fact, since I have just come back from visiting the fort, I'm rather anxious to get home at once to go into the bathhouse to cleanse myself, and make a sacrifice, not merely to Vesta and the household gods, but to all the major deities. So, move on, driver!'

The gig driver – a skilful slave who'd kept the horses steady all this time – knew exactly how to move them on again. Marcus settled comfortably back and, with another wave of that ringed hand, was swiftly on his way.

FOUR

Cilla was pleased with the chervil. 'Every little helps! Makes the stew tastier and it goes slightly further, too. I'll keep the sparrows for tomorrow, though there's not much flesh on them. But I've got better news. That birdlime we fermented has turned out very well, so Trovatus has gone out to set it with the children now. Pray to Minerva that it works.'

'It will,' I said. 'Now we can be hopeful of something every day.'

She made a face. 'Though there's very little I can put with it – there's nothing in the garden fit to eat. I might have to join you foraging, myself – and teach Brianus and Tenuis what to pick.'

'Marcus has promised us a chervil plant,' I said. I explained about the meeting in the lane. 'We'll put it in the garden and start to grow our own.'

She was not especially impressed. 'Well, it's something, I suppose. And very kind of him. Though doubtless you'll have to pay for it sometime – if I know Marcus.'

I confessed that he'd mentioned something of the kind.

'Exactly! And be prepared to pay quite handsomely. Chervil is imported, so it always cost a lot – and just for a few leaves. If it had been leeks or onions it would be some proper help, though of course he'll now be needing those himself!'

'He did mention "other things",' I said in his defence. 'They've not been at the villa, so there'll be crops they haven't used. There may be something useful he can spare.'

But even I was not prepared for what arrived. Not an hour later, judging by the sun, as we were gathered in the roundhouse by the fire, we were astonished to look out of the door and see a group of slaves parading down the lane, each carrying a sack. We were more astonished still to see them turn in through our enclosure gate. They'd obviously been told to keep apart from us, because they did not come too close.

At first, I was puzzled. Who were they? They were dressed in sombre blue – surely they could not be Marcus's? But they obviously were – the leader was his bodyguard companion from the gig. The uniform of the Corinium house, perhaps?

I was still standing in the shadows, wondering, when he stepped further up the path and called doubtfully, 'We're looking for the citizen Junio?'

I understood why he was dubious. Roman citizens don't often live in roundhouses, nor spend the day in working tunics like the one I wore.

'You've found him. What do you want?' I shouted, ensuring that my family kept their distance too, though naturally the children wanted to come out and see.

'We have brought the chervil master promised you.'

It was rather more than that. He ushered the others forwards, one by one. Each came and laid an item at the door and swiftly stepped away. Marcus had been much better than his word.

Chervil, and a lot of 'other things': half a sack of barley (which could be ground and boiled to make several filling meals), one of yellow carrots, another full of leeks, onions, a large bag of ground spelt flour and – best of all – an amphora of oil. Now cooking, baking, heat and light would all be possible.

Cilla was mortified that she had been doubtful, earlier. 'I wish we had something to offer to his slaves,' she murmured, almost tearful in her gratitude. 'Refreshment, if no more. But there's not a morsel in the house. The stew's not ready yet. It takes hours for squirrel to be soft enough to eat.'

'They're not expecting it,' I said. 'They're already leaving.'

I spoke too soon, because even as I paused the leader reappeared, carrying a final offering. He hovered at a distance. 'Citizen Junio?'

I nodded my assent.

'The master says there is no hurry to repay, the mistress would've hated you to be in want, and would never have forgiven him if he did not send supplies.' He gave a little bow. 'But he would be glad to have the two amphorae back when you have done with them.'

I actually laughed. It was so like Marcus. He is famous for being careful with his wealth. Which made this unexpected kindness all the greater. I said, 'Of course! And your name is . . .?'

'Callidus!' He sounded proud, as well he might. The word means 'clever', so it was clear his master valued him.

'Then, Callidus, please convey our humble gratitude.' Pompous, but this bounty merited formal thanks.

'I will.' Callidus bowed, deposited his bag, and would have disappeared had I not opened it at once. It revealed – wonder of wonders – several assorted fragments of a pig, including the trotters, heart and ears, all of which Marcus has been known to serve at feasts.

A proper feast for us. I called the slave back. 'Pork?' I was astounded. 'Are you quite sure . . .?'

He misunderstood me. 'Ah, citizen, you guessed about the sacrifice? But you need not fear. It was indeed to be offered to the gods, but once its throat was cut, this pig proved inauspicious. One of its legs was crooked, so we had to start again. No point in insulting Jupiter, the master said, and no point in wasting this, so he sent it to the kitchen to feed the house tonight, with orders that the remnants should be sent to you. A perfect substitute was found and sacrificed, so there is no risk attached.' Callidus bowed farewell, then led his little procession hurriedly away.

I gazed at the bounty. Marcus had clearly noted everything I said, and sent exactly the things I'd said we lacked. I said as much to Cilla.

'In that case, husband, I wish you'd mentioned more!' She was joking, and I was glad that she'd got her twinkle back. Though the jest was half relief, she was as grateful as I was myself. 'All these supplies! I can hardly take it in. Of course,' she added, as we began to move the goods indoors, 'I'm sure we really have Julia to thank, but she isn't here so he had to think of it himself. Though how we shall repay him, I'm sure I do not know.'

'Not for many moons, in any case.' I picked up the barley sack, ready to refill the grain pit in the yard.

'Oh, he'll think of something. Marcus always does. A pavement someone wants, perhaps, where no doubt he'll also get a generous fee for introducing you.' She grinned tearfully at me. 'But at least you'll be alive to do it. And we shall have chervil in the garden from now on. Tenuis can go now and put it in the ground.'

If I should live to eighty years and dine with emperors, no feast could ever taste as wonderful as what we ate that night. Fresh flatbread smells like nectar to a hungry man, and it is quite astounding how much better squirrel stew can taste with the addition of an onion, a few carrots and some herbs. And for once we could eat till we were satisfied.

We slept a great deal better too. The children did not wake with hunger pains; though briefly, in the night, Cilla went missing from our bed of reeds. I went to find her and discovered her outside, saying she was feeling squeamish. (That surprised me till I remembered – to my shame – that she had quietly deprived herself for many days. Like a poor man at a banquet, she'd found the feast too rich, though happily she soon got over it.)

I woke next morning to the delicious smell of barley porridge. It had not all been a dream. (Recently, my sleep had been tormented by imaginings of food.) Cilla was busy with a pot above the fire, stirring with her longest spoon to stop the mixture sticking.

She saw me sitting up and flashed me a happy smile. 'Trovatus has taken the children to the traps and Brianus has gone with the bucket to the spring. I've used the last of the water making this, and he went early so as not to meet with anyone. When he brings it back I'm going to mix it with some flour, so it can sit out and ferment, and we can have a proper sourdough loaf again.'

'And Trovatus may bring something we can put into the pot. We shall be eating almost as we used to do.' I came up behind her and put my arms around her waist.

She shook me off. 'We'll have to be careful with things, all the same. I wish I had some salt. I could cure some pork and make it keep. Who knows how long this plague is going to last?'

'But you know what Marcus told me in the lane?'

'I know. Reports that the contagion may be slowing down. But slowing down is not the same as stopped.'

'Well, he must think it's safe enough.' I retreated to my stool. 'Or he wouldn't have returned. And his information ought to be reliable – it comes from the legionary commandant. Besides, the senior magistrates have already met and the courts and the curia will soon resume again.'

'That's as may be. Marcus takes his position seriously, I know. So he doubtless felt that "it was his duty to be here".' Cilla gave an imitation of his voice, at the same time making a mock-pompous face at me. (She's always had a gift for mimicry.)

I grinned, relieved to find her back to her familiar ways. 'Commendable, surely?'

'Of course. But he's not convinced enough to bring his wife and family back. He admits that there continue to be deaths – just somewhat fewer of them, and fewer people sick. So don't think of returning to the town, just yet, yourself.'

I could see that she was serious. I nodded dutifully. 'I suppose we must still be cautious, for the children's sake.'

'Oh, great Minerva! It's for your own sake too. What should I do without you?' She moved the porridge from the heat and gave my arm a squeeze.

She was obviously in earnest. She's not given to such displays. I put my hand on hers. 'But we can't stay here for ever, with me not earning anything, turning into beggars at Marcus's expense. I'll have to go back sometime and – with the farmer gone – how are we to learn if the plague is truly over?'

She looked up at me. Her eyes were suspiciously bright. 'Marcus talks of going back to the curia again. He would tell you, if you sent to him, I'm sure. But in the meantime, promise me that you won't even try. Not until the moon has waxed and waned again. We have enough provisions to last us up till then, thanks to His Excellence! Especially as Trovatus has his birdlime now. Speaking of which, look who is just coming up the path!'

It was Trovatus, with Tenuis and the children trailing after him. Carus was proudly holding a fat pigeon they had caught. (Quite a prize, though like the chervil it may have escaped from Marcus's estate.)

'We'll say no more about this now,' my wife murmured. 'But promise me you won't go back to town. One cycle of the moon. It isn't much to ask.'

I knew when I was beaten. I gave her waist a friendly squeeze, then dropped my arm. 'Very well. You have my word. One cycle of the moon. Unless something happens to persuade us otherwise.' Then, as the hunting party came into the hut, I raised my voice enthusiastically. 'Carus, what a splendid bird you have. We'll add him to the pot to cheer the stew tonight. Oh, and I see my clever girl has got a sparrow too.'

'Trovatus couldn't carry it, Papa,' she piped up, with a laugh, 'He's got little Gracchus, who is half asleep.'

'So he is. Tenuis, you lie him down to sleep. The rest of you can come and help me pluck the birds. We'll add the feathers to your mother's pile – she'll have enough to make another pillow very soon.'

Cilla flashed me a sideways glance. She said no more – not even thanks for keeping the children occupied! But I'd learned to pluck birds when I was a slave and I was good at it – and now the youngsters were acquiring the skill. That might be useful later in their lives – especially for the girls. Plucking fowl is generally a woman's task, if no slave is available. But this plague had altered everything, including who did what.

I was beginning to hanker for the workshop – proper work earning money for my wife and family. Especially as there was now Marcus to repay! But I'd promised that I wouldn't go into town for a moon – 'unless something happens to persuade us otherwise'. Though, already I was regretting that. Without our farmer to inform us, how could we be certain that the plague had passed? I could hardly send to Marcus for an update every night!

But I needn't have worried. Only a few days later 'something' did occur.

FIVE

I was up my home-made ladder one morning a few days later, patching the old thatch on the servants' sleeping-hut. It's a skilled job I don't entrust to slaves. (Though Trovatus, who also learned from my father, might have helped, but he was in the forest with the children setting traps.) Now that every hour was not spent scavenging for food, there was time to turn to some neglected tasks. The roof had been leaking steadily for days.

I did have Tenuis assisting me – steadying the steps and handing up the bundles of cut reeds. I'd just called to him to pass me up some more when I noticed a figure at the enclosure gate. That sombre blue again. Clearly a member of Marcus's household staff – and he was coming here! That meant me climbing down. Cilla had gone cutting bedding reeds with Brianus – I couldn't leave Tenuis alone to greet His Excellence's messenger.

I felt for the crosspiece with my foot, and realised the visitor was Callidus again. And whatever his mission, he was not bringing food.

Just as well, I thought, ungratefully. I was already more in debt to Marcus than I could easily repay. Besides, if plague was truly on the wane, food would soon be available in town – if I could somehow earn enough to pay for it. When times are hard, mosaics are not anyone's priority, so it might be some time before I could settle what I owed. Perhaps that was what Callidus was sent to talk about?

He didn't call up to me, but politely waited till I'd reached the ground and dusted off my hands.

'Greetings, citizen.' He gave the slightest of slight bows.

I knew what he was thinking. He was trying to gauge how formal he should be. I must seem little better than a beggar, after all. Had he not brought alms to me a day or two before?

And if he'd looked smarter than me then, it was ten times worse today. I was in the oldest patched tunic I possessed.

I tried to cover my embarrassment. 'You want me, Callidus? I'm working, as you see.'

He managed not to smirk. 'As I am myself. I bring a message from His Excellence.'

'You? What has happened to the usual courier?' It sounded slighting, though I'd simply been surprised. But Callidus was stung, I saw it in his face.

I tried to make amends. I have been a slave myself, and it wasn't his fault that he had me at a disadvantage here. Marcus's usual courier was a boy I knew, whom I'd once saved from savage punishment. Was he in disgrace again? Or was it merely that Marcus preferred this better-looking boy? Indeed, now that I came to think of it, I hadn't recognised a single one of the villa slaves who'd called with food that day. 'Please, Mercury, there has not been plague in your household, after all? Or has Marcus simply been disposing of his slaves?'

'The latter, citizen. He brought a new contingent in Corinium, and sold the staff here as soon as he got back. All to one person, as I understand.'

'Whatever for?' Surprise deprived me of propriety. It wasn't for a slave to question his master's actions, as I had just invited Callidus to do.

But he took it as encouragement. 'I don't know, citizen. He does not confide in me. Perhaps he feared they may have been in touch with pestilence. Whatever the reason, he has sold them all. Though not the courier, as it happens,' he added with a smile. 'He came with us to Corinium. He's an expert horseman and he's been carrying messages to and fro. It's simply that he's not available. He is on his way to the mistress as we speak.'

I had unwittingly made a friend, it seemed. 'Then Marcus is lucky that he has a substitute in you,' I said. 'And if he sends to ask if we're now provided for, please tell him that we are, thanks to his handsome generosity.'

'Citizen, I will convey your message, naturally, but I'm not here concerning that.' He glanced at Tenuis (who had been loitering with the reeds) as if reluctant to say more in front of witnesses.

That was alarming. Private messages from Marcus are never likely to contain good news.

Ever since my father left for exile, years ago, His Excellence has made a point of calling on my help whenever there is trouble at the villa – usually when he thinks his staff are cheating him – though only once has it ever been a serious affair. A tribute to his old protégé, he says, but it is much less of a compliment than he appears to think. It is often time-consuming, which keeps me from my work, and it would not occur to him to offer a reward.

He can be casually generous (as I had cause to know), but Marcus is Marcus, and he is not a man to cross. If something had happened at the villa while he was away, and he wanted my assistance, I could not well refuse. Especially when I was already in his debt.

I nodded to Tenuis that he should withdraw. He looked reproachfully at me, but obediently tossed the sheaf of reeds back on the pile and stomped into the roundhouse. Sounds of vigorous brushing with a besom-broom began.

Callidus waited till my slave was safely gone. 'I am to tell you that His Excellence requests your presence at the villa as soon as possible.'

I could not help a sigh. 'This afternoon, he means?'

Callidus grinned. 'I think he meant at once, but it might be wise to change.' That was strictly an impertinence – commenting upon my state of dress – and Cilla would have rebuked him instantly. But I myself had blurred the difference in our ranks, and my dismay at the summons must be obvious. He added confidentially, 'I think there's a commission he's hoping you'll fulfil.'

He clearly thought I would be pleased. But it was exactly as I'd feared. A summons to the villa – and now, of all moments, when there was plague about! And I had been assiduously avoiding contacts of all kinds! But of course Marcus knew that. I had told him so, myself – perhaps that was my mistake!

'Surely . . .' I was desperately searching for a way to be

polite. 'In the current circumstances a call would not be wise? I would not wish to pose a threat to His Excellence's health.'

The handsome courier gave a little smile. 'Oh, don't worry citizen. He has no fear of you. He knows that you have kept yourself apart from contagion of all kinds.'

I nodded glumly. 'I told him so when I met him in the lane the other day.'

'Oh, he knew it anyway. He'd already made enquiries about you in the town and learned that you had not been seen for moons.'

'Enquiries about me?' I was surprised. Marcus had mentioned that he'd heard I'd not been seen in town, but I'd not supposed that he had asked specifically. It was quite a compliment. 'How do you know that?'

'I was sent to make discreet enquiries myself. So, he knew you were either keeping well away or you were dead. And then, of course, he met you in the lane and you were clearly thin but well. He is confident that you don't carry plague – otherwise he would not have stopped to speak, or risked us coming here.'

He was talking as though I were an equal, once again. But it occurred to me that if I was to be investigating problems in the villa (was that why Marcus had disposed of all his slaves?) it would be useful to have an inside confidant.

'But he warned you all to keep your distance, nonetheless?'

Callidus grinned. 'He did, indeed. For our sake, as well as his. Since we came back from Corinium he insists we all wear one of these . . .' He reached into his tunic-neck and showed me a twist of something green suspended from a cord. 'A talisman of hyssop and other scented herbs, to keep dangerous smells at bay. Though *we* don't have personal protection from the gods.'

'But Marcus does?'

Another grin. 'He has an amulet – a most expensive one – personally blessed by the priest of Mars himself. He wears it constantly.'

'It seems to be effective,' I said with a wry smile. 'Since he went to Glevum and took no harm from it.'

'You sound doubtful, citizen? Though – forgive me – I think you are wearing such a charm yourself?'

I was. I'd put it on in Glevum, and had not removed it since. One cannot be too careful with the gods. But they do expect one to behave with common sense. 'It would be foolish not to wear it when it's available, but I never place my confidence entirely in these things.' All the same, I touched it reverently three times. It's better to be sure.

'But mine is not under the especial auspices of Mars.' I went on, 'I suppose your master is now doubly safe. If he'd caught the plague by mingling with other councillors, it would have struck by now. It's said to manifest symptoms very fast. And I know he had a meeting with all senior magistrates.'

'And private conversations afterwards with one or two of them! While standing very close.'

Perhaps, I thought, he'd been asking about me. But Rufus, the ex-aedile, was the only one of them (apart from His Excellence himself) who was even likely to recognise my name. And Rufus was long dead. So where had Marcus been to ask these questions about me? And why? He must have been already planning to ask me for my help. Perhaps there'd been a worrying message to Corinium.

This was not something to ask Callidus about. I attempted an oblique approach. 'Doubtless your master visited the temple too? Presumably that's where he bought the charm?' You can get them in the market, naturally, but even if they claimed to have been specially blessed, you could not be sure of it.

'He bought it at the temple in Corinium, in fact,' Callidus corrected. 'And now he will be awaiting my return. Can I tell him to expect you soon?'

Here was a dilemma. I did not want to go. I was needed here – to finish the thatch before it rained, at least, and probably to help with the little ones as well. But I owed Marcus more than duty and he wanted help. (Cilla would no doubt say that's why he'd been so generous!) But the idea of entering another person's house – even if that person was His Excellence himself, and the staff had not been exposed to plague – seemed most alarming. But it was evident that I could not refuse.

'Very well,' I murmured. 'But first I'll have to make a cleansing sacrifice – a quick protective one – to keep both households safe. Then I will be with him as soon as possible. You think I should be togate?'

Callidus looked surprised. (I think he had forgotten that, as a citizen, I'd have a toga to put on.) 'If that is practical,' he said, 'I think it would be wise.'

'I have one folded somewhere in the house, though I haven't worn the wretched thing in moons. They are cumbersome to walk in – as you've probably observed – so Tenuis will have to come and drape me into it outside the gates.'

He nodded. 'Marcus will expect you to bring a slave with you.'

My turn to be surprised. It was so long since I had worn my toga that I'd forgotten that. Social niceties dictate that a togate citizen should be attended at all times, especially when visiting or in the forum. 'It might be dusty with the cooking smoke by now,' I said. 'But I have a clean tunic to change into and I'll do my best to look respectable. So, tell him that I'll come when I've performed the sacrifice. And a little cleansing ritual on myself!'

Callidus gave just the shadow of a grin. 'Then I will report to my master that you are on your way, as soon as the appropriate oblations – and ablutions – are complete.' He gave a little bow.

Despite myself, I found that I was grinning in return. Callidus, when relaxed, was acute and humorous. He might be a useful ally later on. I was sorry that I could not offer him a friendly tip – but I did not have the wherewithal, as he must be aware. So I simply thanked him and sent him on his way, then went inside in search of Tenuis.

I found him assiduously stoking up the fire – so assiduously that I guessed he had been listening at the door. Especially when the broom, which had been propped against the wall, clattered to the floor as I came in – suggesting that it had been left there hastily! 'You heard all that, no doubt?'

He did not deny it. 'You will be wanting your toga, master. It's up there on the shelf. I'll fetch it down for you, and give it a good shake, and your best clean tunic too. And there's a brace of sparrows hanging on the hook, if you want one of them for sacrifice.'

I did not chide him, simply gave him a reproachful look. (Cilla would say I am too lenient.) 'First bring me a pail of water, and a bowl and drying cloth. I must wash before I change. And while you are about it, bring that boxed lararium I use on festal days. If I'm to do a protective ritual, we'll do it properly.'

I served in a Roman household when I was very young, and – though my adoptive father was a Celt, and brought me up in a roundhouse exactly like my own – I am sufficient of a Roman to possess a travelling shrine, for special occasions. And this was one.

Truth to tell, I was actually afraid. Marcus and his new slaves had been in Corinium throughout. But what about infection from the former staff, before he sold them – or from the slave trader, or the magistrates that Marcus had been whispering with in town? I told myself what I'd told Callidus. If there was plague it would have shown itself by now.

I sighed, stripped off my working tunic and permitted Tenuis to pour water over me, then towel me and help me dress again. 'Even the toga,' I told him. 'I'll have to take it off again to walk. But I need to be togate to make proper sacrifice.' I raised my arms as he folded it deftly into place.

Then Tenuis took out the little statuettes (the Lares, the Penates, Vesta and – to be on the safe side – Jupiter and Mars) and placed them carefully around the little shrine. He offered me the sparrows, but I shook my head.

'This is a protective sacrifice,' I said. 'Not just an offering. Dead creatures will not do. Something of value, or we will offend the gods. Bring me a little of that olive oil, and a spoonful of that grain. Put them in the finest drinking vessel that we have. There should be three elements, so you had better pass my hunting knife as well.'

I nicked my finger and permitted a few drops to fall into the bowl, before stirring the contents with the blade. I pulled up some toga folds to make a hood, as respect demanded, then poured a little of the mixture on the shrine, muttered such incantations as I could recall and earnestly prayed to the assembled deities to keep us safe from plague.

Afterwards, to make entirely sure, I took my toga off and went outside again, where I repeated the procedure for the more ancient gods. Water (in the bucket), rock and tree, before scattering the sacrificial remnants in the air. Lastly, something that I learned from my father long ago; I walked three times in silence what he called 'a-gheld' around the pail (what the Romans would call left-wise, and think bad luck, no doubt).

Tenuis clearly thought so. He watched in disbelief.

'Not perfect, but the best that I could do,' I told him cheerfully, when I had finished and could speak again. 'You are supposed to walk around a well, but we don't have one here. And don't look so distressed. This is a Celtic ritual, and the rules are different.'

He gave a shaky smile. 'So we are free to go? Then, master Junio, will you require your cloak? I have got your toga folded so I can carry it. And should we leave a message saying where we've gone?'

I had been wondering the same. It would be possible. Brianus, naturally, could not read at all. Cilla could, a little – she had taught herself by studying inscriptions on gravestones and in town, but could not decipher unfamiliar words. Trovatus was the same, but I had been instructing Carus for a year or two, and even the older of the girls could tell her letters now. I was about to find a slatey stone (and chalk to mark it with) when I was saved from the necessity. Cilla and Brianus were coming with the reeds. I could see them walking down the hill.

I did not want discussion, so I sent Tenuis to tell them where we'd gone, instructed him to follow me and set off down the lane. I did not take Arlina – she'd had the pasture field, but we'd had no oats to spare her until the last few days and she was pitiably thin.

'Next time!' I promised her, and hurried out of sight before my wife could call me back. Tenuis very soon caught up with me. He draped me in my toga, just around the corner before the villa gates.

SIX

The gatekeeper was another slave I'd never seen before – a huge, burly fellow with a ferocious beard and a dark scowl to match. He must have been expecting us – Callidus had returned with the message long ago – but instead of welcoming us in, he came to the inside of the gate and held up one massive hand to halt us where we stood. He did not speak, but when I tentatively announced my name, he opened up and stood back silently to let us pass. Stood so far back, in fact, that you'd suppose we were lepers and should be carrying a bell.

I looked around, nonplussed. There was no slave hurrying towards us down the drive, or anyone visible at the villa door to escort me to His Excellence and whisk my slave away for the usual refreshment in the servants' waiting room. Meanwhile, the bearded giant closed the gates and went on saying nothing – keeping at least six paces distance from us all the while and still frowning like a thunderclap.

I looked at him enquiringly, but all he did was scowl. In the end I was obliged to shout. 'I assume I should attend your master in the atrium?'

He shook his head. 'Uh-uh.' It was more grunt than speech. He raised the massive club he held and gestured towards a little arbour among the flowering bushes beside the outer wall.

I glanced in that direction, in surprise. That nook is generally reserved for womenfolk. Julia and her handmaidens use it on sunny days, as somewhere she can comfortably sit and spin, or have a servant read or play the flute for her. More frequently the latter. She isn't fond of spinning, she confided once to me – though naturally she couldn't tell her husband that. It's a skill expected of a Roman wife. (A waste of time, she said. And she may be right. Her spun thread isn't really needed in the house. If that family don't have the latest fashion sent from

Rome, they purchase fine fabric from the marketplace and maintain a tailor-slave to sew for them. Perhaps Julia's yarn is used to mend tunics for the slaves.)

In any case, there was no Julia today. It was Marcus sitting in the bower, attended – from several paces away – by Callidus, while another younger pageboy with olive skin and lustrous dark-brown hair plucked a lute. Both were dressed in that undistinguished blue, and were squatting down on stools but jumped to their feet at our approach. I might have seen them earlier if I'd looked that way, but Marcus rarely used the garden in the front.

Callidus came to meet us round statues and fountains and across the paving stones. 'Citizen Junio? If you would accompany me, please?' No trace of the earlier informality. 'I have left a stool for you, and my colleague is bringing one over for your slave. In the meantime, perhaps he could wait here? We two will keep him company. The master is hoping to talk to you alone.'

The lutist was already approaching with the stool. 'For your thervant. I'm to thay the matter ith awaiting you.'

He might have been eight or nine years old, perhaps. He was tall for this age, and might have been handsome, but his upper lip was cleft, which obviously accounted for the impediment. A pity, since otherwise he'd be valuable one day. Obviously, I thought, Marcus had purchased in a hurry – and probably from a dealer that he did not know. A lisper and a grunter. Normally his slaves were nothing if not top quality.

I turned to Callidus with some relief. 'Then if you would care to lead the way?'

Marcus also rose to greet me as I approached the bower. This was surprising too. I am not a man whose rank deserves this courtesy.

I was becoming increasingly alarmed. Everything about this meeting was astonishing. Usually Marcus (like any important Roman) makes a point of making callers wait, and the humbler the visitor, the longer the delay – even if, like me, they have been summoned. Sometimes particularly then.

But he was here already and awaiting me. And Callidus was right about the private interview. He was waved imperiously away to join the others by the gate, out of earshot if not out of sight. Another real surprise! Marcus is inclined to think of slaves as furniture, or at best domestic animals, not human beings who have eyes and ears and tongues. I don't know how many times across the years I heard my father gently point that out to him. But His Excellence was very alert to it today. Whatever the problem in his household, it was clearly serious.

However, proper courtesies still had be observed. I bowed politely. 'Excellence, you asked for me, I think?'

'Citizen Junio. It is good of you to come so fast. I was told you were sacrificing to the gods. So since you are newly purified . . .' Marcus extended his ring for me to kiss, but kept his arm at fullest stretch, to keep me well at bay.

I mentally blessed Callidus for his tactfulness, kissed the seal and raised my head to look more fully at my host. He was dressed in a pale green synthesis, that useful (and expensive) combination of tunic and over-mantle, which he often favours while at home. I noted the 'Mars-blessed amulet' around his upper arm, and the bunch of hyssop pinned to his shoulder folds, but he had dispensed with covering his mouth and nose today. I was no longer seen as a potential carrier of plague.

He sat down on the bower bench himself and waved me to the stool, where I could take a seat with my head appropriately lower than his own.

I did so, assuming the distance was as deliberate as the height.

To my surprise, he leaned towards me. 'Junio, my friend . . .'

Alarm trumpets had been sounding in my head since I arrived, but they were blasting now. I've learned the truth of what my father often said – that when Marcus calls you 'friend' there's invariably something that he wants from you. And generally something inconvenient. But, for now, I had no work to interrupt, and I was greatly in his debt.

'How can I be of service to Your Excellence?'

He sat back with folded arms and took a long deep breath. 'Junio, there is a commission I'd like you to undertake.'

Something embarrassing, no doubt, or he'd have spelt it out at once. 'Of course! If there is anything I can do, or advice that I can give about your household here, I should be glad to help – especially after your generosity to my family.'

'Not that sort of commission,' he said impatiently. 'Mosaic work, I mean.' And before I had time to register my gratitude (and astonishment), he leaned forwards and added, in a lower tone, 'I believe you are acquainted with Appius Limpnus Corvinus?'

Another shock! I was, and he was not a man I cared for very much. I had adapted a pavement for him, several years ago, when he first 'retired' here from Londinium and the provincial court. He had bought a country villa which had previously been forfeit to the state. 'To start a vineyard,' he told me at the time, though everyone realised that he'd been sent here as a pair of ears and eyes, reporting back to the provincial governor – and probably to Rome.

Marcus was looking enquiringly at me.

'I did some work for Appius at one time,' I acknowledged doubtfully. I was reluctant to be associated with the man. 'For a few days when he first acquired his country house. Hardly an acquaintance. I barely spoke to him.'

'But you'd be prepared to work for him again? Not at the villa this time. You know that he has bought a residence in town?'

It startled me, like everything else about this interview. 'One hardly needs a townhouse in order to grow grapes.' (I meant it as a joke, to show I knew that this was only a fiction anyway.)

Marcus did not smile. 'But a prerequisite if one wishes to become a councillor. One must have a town-dwelling of a certain size, but this more than meets requirements. It belonged to former member of the curia, in fact. Julius Fortunatus. You may have heard of him?'

'One of the first unhappy victims of the plague. Appius Limpnus seems to have a taste for buying up the houses of the dead.' That villa that I'd worked in was the same. It had been the site of violent butchery – or 'purge', the provincial governor would say. So brutal that the house was abandoned for some years because no one was prepared to live among the ill-omens and the ghosts. Until Appius came along and bought the villa very cheaply as a consequence. No doubt there was similar reluctance, now, to buy a townhouse whose former residents had all died of plague. 'He got another bargain, I suppose?'

'Indeed. Apparently Fortunatus left no living relatives. The public reading of his will was done very quickly, considering the plague. And guess what it provided for, in the event of there being no apparent heir?'

'Everything passes to the Emperor and the public purse?' It wasn't hard to guess. It is not unusual for wealthy Roman citizens to name the Emperor as residual heir – it is a fiction, designed to reach his ears, and win his favour. But, given that most people have many family legatees, they don't expect that clause to actually apply! 'The intended beneficiaries were all dead?'

'They all lived together in the house and died when Fortunatus did – within the self-same day. Buried together, in a hurry, if I remember right.'

I saw where this was leading. 'And with the plague about, no one is going to question in the courts who survived the others by an hour or two?'

'And no one left to benefit, even if they did.'

'So everything reverted to the public purse? Fortunatus! If ever a man was badly named . . .' I said.

Marcus nodded grimly. 'Appius Limpnus has influential friends on high, who saw the house was sold to him at once, and at a pleasing price. It will help him do what he was sent for. You know what that is? And it wasn't to plant vines!'

I glanced around. It's said that walls have ears. 'I have heard it rumoured that he is a spy for the provincial governor.'

Marcus leaned closer. 'Worse. He is a *delator*, paid to seek out so-called "enemies of state" and denounce them secretly.' He sounded venomous. 'Or see that they simply disappear.'

I whistled. 'No wonder that his property purchases went through so fast.'

'Hush!' He held a finger to his lips. 'Junio. I spoke of problems. And they are serious. You know that the Emperor Severus distrusts Britannia because of its support for Clodius in the Succession Wars?'

Of course I did. One could not live or work here and not be aware of it. So, to prevent him from retelling the whole tale, I said, 'You think that Appius has been sent – perhaps by Virius Lupus – to quell the town? I know the governor loathes it, in particular, because of the defeat its former legion inflicted upon his.'

'Not Virius Lupus,' Marcus said. 'A delator reports directly to the Emperor – and is paid by him, as well. By results, which means he wants as many candidates as possible. And I may be a target.'

'Dear gods!' I wished I was anywhere but here, and was reluctant to pursue this any more. I knew that having supported Clodius was still dangerous today, but this was a whole new pail of frogs. Appius might easily have spies in Marcus's household now. Indeed, it suddenly occurred to me that must be why His Excellence had suddenly disposed of all his local slaves, and dressed the newcomers in blue, so they didn't look like his. Everyone knew that famous scarlet uniform.

I didn't say that. It does not flatter a Roman to suggest he is afraid. Besides, there might be someone listening. 'But Severus won,' I said, instead. 'And peace has been restored. The battle's over!'

Marcus looked despairingly at me. 'Over? I don't think so, citizen. There's another disturbing rumour that I had from Rome, in a letter while I was away. The Emperor plans to split Britannia in two, to ensure it is more totally subdued, and prevent any future governor from having too many legions at his command. There's even talk that he may visit us himself, bringing his own army to deal with discontent.'

'Dear gods,' I murmured. 'That is worrying. But, reducing the legions of the governor? I thought our Virius Lupus was his protégé?'

'He is. With a mission to stamp out any remnant of dissent, and he has been merciless in doing so. As I think you are aware. You replaced that villa pavement for Appius, after all.'

I nodded. I'd been paid to make an alteration to a floor – a mosaic in an inner passageway. It was out of public view. But if the house was inauspicious, because of ghosts and evil auguries, this corridor was positively dangerous. It sported a motto saying VIVAT CLODIUS – for which allegiance the former owners had suffered brutal death. I was to remove the offending tiles and rework this wording to VIVAT VIRIUS and replace Albinus's 'crocodile' device with a banal design of bread and fruit which nobody could take exception to.

'And now Appius wants work in his new town residence? Surely not another traitorous pavement?' I exclaimed.

'This is not about a floor. It's about a public shrine. I hear that he's decided that he wants to finance one – a way to gain favour with the voters, probably. I told you he plans to seek election to the curia.'

'But I thought he had officially retired from civic life?'

Marcus treated this with the contempt that it deserved. 'A public shrine,' he went on, as if I hadn't spoken, 'A little niche set in the outside of his new boundary wall. A place where those delivered from the plague can come and make thanksgiving offerings to Mars. He's planning a mosaic wall behind the altar. Depicting a coiled snake around a pole, I understand.'

'The rod of Asclepius?' I said. 'How very Greek of him. Though it's an ancient symbol of healing, I suppose. It came to Rome with Galen, in Marcus Aurelius's time.'

Marcus ignored my efforts to impress. 'I want you to undertake the work.'

SEVEN

I understood, or I thought I did. If Marcus proposed me, and I gained the work, he would expect a 'finder's fee' for recommending me – paid by the one commissioning the work. It was standard practice, and the fee could be a handsome one. Plus, it might ingratiate him with Appius. 'And you wish to act as sponsor?'

I was about to add that I'd be honoured, which I genuinely would. Civic contracts are generally lucrative. But Marcus forestalled me. 'On the contrary. On no account do I want my name involved. Another councillor, a loyal friend of mine, is prepared to sponsor you. And since you are known to Appius I hope you'll get the work.'

I tried to thank him, but he held up a hand.

'What I want from you is to report to me. This shrine is to be right outside his Glevum residence. I want to know who visits him, when he comes and goes – and where, if possible.'

I grinned at him. 'I am to be spying on the spy, you mean?'

'It is no laughing matter, Junio. I fear for my safety, and my family's too.'

I was frowning now, in puzzlement. 'But why should you be under threat? I know you were when Severus first succeeded, because you're related to the old Imperial House and he was eliminating all potential claims. But now?'

No answer.

'Severus is securely on the throne. He must be sure by now that you won't challenge him. What's more, he's made a point of restoring your friend Pertinax to public honour and the Imperial pantheon. You told me so yourself. So as a personal favourite of an ex-Emperor who is now a god, surely you can't be in danger any more?'

Marcus shot me a despairing look. 'Officially, perhaps. But

it would not save me from disgrace and exile, at best, if I could be found guilty of some serious charge.'

I stared at him. Marcus has weaknesses but he is not corrupt. 'What sort of charge? And who would dare to bring one anyway?' Then, putting two and two together on my mental abacus, at last, 'Not Appius Limpnus?'

He held a finger to his lips. 'That's just what I don't know. I hear disturbing rumours, from a friend. I supported Clodius when he was governor, as was my duty then. I am distrusted by the higher powers.'

'But surely you've done nothing to offend? You are on good terms with the commander of the garrison. Of course . . .'

Not wise. Marcus had been very friendly with an earlier commandant who'd been recalled to Rome.

He read my thoughts. 'If there was going to be trouble about that, it would have happened years ago, when he very wisely disappeared in Gaul. And I've had cordial relations with the two that followed him, including the one in office now, though he and his troops were Virius's men. But he's friendly enough to have kept me informed about the plague – he would have warned me discreetly, I believe, if there were official questions being asked.'

'Then who – and what?' I burbled.

He looked ruefully at me. 'You're lucky, Junio. As a humble tradesman you can keep away from politics, and try to make yourself invisible. As the senior magistrate in the colonia, I'm in the public eye. In that position, one makes enemies. The danger is probably not anything I've done, but something I'm accused of. All I know for certain is that there's some sort of plot. An old friend on the curia wrote to warn me of the fact.'

'The one who is to recommend me?' I asked brightly.

Marcus shook his head. 'Unfortunately not. This man died of plague a day or two after he wrote to me. It was the first thing I discovered when I got back to town and tried to contact him. In retrospect, I think when he was writing he knew that he was ill.'

'Because he wouldn't have dared do so otherwise?'

A nod. 'With fewer checkpoints and soldiers on the road

there's much more banditry, and letters have been intercepted and sold to anyone prepared to bid for them. My informant told me to destroy the message, which I did.'

'And that's why you came back from Corinium so soon? Not because you heard the plague was almost past?'

'I wouldn't have come back if that weren't true as well. But that only makes the danger more acute. From what I understand, it put the plot on hold. Before contagion started, Appius had been quietly inviting councillors, in twos and threes, to little banquets at his country house for many moons. Conspicuously, I was never asked. And after the feasting, he'd ask questions about the area, and in particular the people on the curia. Nothing apparently very sinister – he is fairly new to Glevum after all, and lots of other magistrates were variously discussed. But every time, apparently, the talk would turn to me – who were my friends and allies and who didn't like me much. And it was the latter who were invited back. Including, by accident, the friend who wrote to me.'

'How, by accident?'

'Because he was grumbling in the curia one day. It was about another magistrate, but he mentioned he was going to speak to me. He meant that he would tell me, which he did – and I reprimanded the man responsible. But Appius, or one of his cronies, overheard and misconstrued. My friend was soon invited to another feast, this time at the home of Gracchus Elvinus Posthumus . . .'

'That flamboyant man who used to be a councillor?'

'That's right. He's always hated me, because I fined him for a fraud which cost him re-election to the curia. And this time there was a great deal less pretence. The talk was all about me from the start – where I went, and what I did, how I had too much influence, had supported Clodius, and how it would be better if I were removed. My friend said almost nothing, but did not disagree – fortunately for him. Appius warned on parting that it would be "dangerous" to discuss this with anybody else.'

'And he didn't?'

'Not at the time. He knew it was a threat. But he was not invited back. He wrote in his letters that he wished afterwards that he'd pretended to participate – then he might have had something specific to report. But then the plague came, and whatever was being plotted was obviously paused. He wrote when he was dying, as I said before, when Appius could not harm him any more. But he wanted to warn me that there was a plot.'

'And you believe it?'

'Certainly I do. He was old and frail, and easy to intimidate – I can understand that he would hesitate to write. But he was also honest as the day, as even Appius appears to have found out. Though he still believes my old friend had some grievance against me, he was deliberately never disabused of that. He won't suspect that I have heard about his scheming.'

'So there was nothing specific? No details of this plot?'

'I wish there had been. Then I would know what to be careful of. But it is altogether sinister. People have been here, asking questions at the gate about my movements while I was in Corinium. Of course, my slaves were loyal, but they didn't know that there was any danger, and they answered honestly.'

'So you replaced them?' I dared to say the words.

'What slaves don't know they cannot tell to anyone. If Appius Limpnus is collecting information about me, there must be a reason. I know what he is now – and who he's working for. That's why I want you to do this work and keep a watch on him.'

'But he will know that I'm your protégé.'

'Not if you are recommended by another councillor. I was your father's patron, as everybody knows, but you've never done mosaic work for me. I have a letter here, from a previous customer . . .' He reached below the bower seat, produced a little box, and opened it to show a small roll of bark paper. He held it out to me. 'Titus Flavius, you remember him?'

'I did a Cave Canem for him once. A friend of my father's, which is how I got the work.'

'Exactly, so it will not seem strange that he's commending you.'

'It was years ago.' I glanced at what was written. It was a glowing testimonial.

'And I believe that Appius Limpnus came to you before on the suggestion of someone else again?'.

I nodded.

'Then there should be no suspicion that I am involved. And if that doesn't win the contract, I don't know what would. Better in cuttle-ink, and signed, than just in wax, I thought. No question that it might be fraudulent. It might be useful to you in the future too.'

Undoubtedly it would. Another cause for gratitude. I rolled it up again and retied the ribbon holding it. 'Then I can only thank you and tell you I will try.'

He stood up, so I did the same of course. He raised a hand as if to shake my arm and elbow, in customary fashion, but seemed to think better of the act. 'Splendid, citizen. In that case, you can present yourself this very afternoon. He is reportedly at the new townhouse all day, and anyone will direct you if you don't know where it is.'

I stared at hm. 'But I will have to go and change. Even if I keep this tunic on, it will take an hour or more to get there, even with the mule. Then I'll have to kick my heels until he deigns to see me, which might take longer still. Supposing that he's in at all, and I don't have to wait for his return.' I could see him frowning, so I added hastily, 'Of course, daylight hours here are much longer in summer, just as the night-time hours are short, but . . .' (Marcus had told me that this was not the case in Rome. Day and night are still divided into twelve parts each, but for some reason these do not vary with the season, as they do here. It makes Roman water clocks and hour-candles unreliable in Brittania, and there is a saying, 'Useless as an Emperor's sundial,' because the ones Marcus Aurelius gifted round the empire never worked outside the capital.) 'Perhaps tomorrow . . .' I was still thinking of my roofing task.

He pre-empted me. 'I will send a cart for you – better not my gig. It's fastest but it's too conspicuous. But even my cart driver can make sure that you get there and back in half the time. He can drop you a little distance from the gate, and wait till you come back. I suggest you take a few moments to size up the job and you can start tomorrow. The niche is there already, so there's no problem there. Suggest that you will be there at first light. He wants it done, I hear, so he'll be pleased with that. But do not rush the work. Try to make it last as long as possible, and keep your eyes and ears alert while you are there.'

'If he agrees to have me.'

'I'm sure he will. But you will need to change. No toga needed. Shall we say, perhaps, a half an hour or so – before the sun's above that tree?'

So much for my thatching, I thought bitterly. I bowed myself away, picked up Tenuis at the gate, took off my toga when we were out of sight, and went home to break the news to Cilla and the family.

She was anxious, but she accepted it. 'So much for your promise about not going into town. But I see that you could not refuse. Just be sure that you take care. Besides, if you're going to Glevum anyway, perhaps you would visit the forum marketplace and see if any of the shoemakers are back. Carus needs new sandals – he's growing like a tree, and if you get this contract we can afford some more. So go, with my blessing, and impress this Appius!'

But, as it happened, I was not to report to Corvinus that day. Events were about to take a very different turn.

EIGHT

Marcus's ox-cart came for me as arranged. I'd changed into a decent working tunic by that time, and had even found a measuring stick and a piece of chalk, so I looked professional. Titus Flavius's letter was safely in a bag round my neck – together with a sprig of wild hyssop I had found.

I was just gobbling the last of my squirrel stew (ah, the delight of turnip and fresh bread!) when Brianus came to say the cart was at the gate. I grabbed my cloak and hurried out to it.

It was carrying a load of turnips. Marcus was using the opportunity to sell some in the town – and he'd get a handsome price for them. The driver was not the usual gig-man, but a shaggy land-slave whom I did not know. I was not familiar with any of the outdoor labourers, so I could not guess if he was new or not. I smiled a greeting, but he simply gestured brusquely that I should get aboard. No question of any gift of turnips to my house today!

I thought of asking him to let me have some anyway, on the basis that I was likely to get paid a small deposit before the day was out, but his scowl deterred me. So, I clambered up (without assistance, although the step was high) and sat down beside him. He didn't speak. Because he couldn't?

I was just wondering how he'd fare at market, in that case, when suddenly, a voice! 'Raise your hood, please. Master's orders.'

A precaution against being recognised? Marcus was seriously nervous. I complied, and Shaggy used his switch to urge the animal to walk again. We trundled off – so slowly that I thought it might have been quicker if I'd walked.

The main lane is better – flatter and wider than the ancient track – but there are still rocks and muddy patches, so even at that pace it was a jolting ride. I held on grimly to the seat – there was no side to cling to – and did not attempt to speak. My companion did not look as if he'd welcome it, in any case. He did not glance towards me once, but simply kept on frowning fiercely at the road.

At last, we reached the military road where the going was easier, and at once the ox increased his pace, as if it knew the load was safer now. Roman paving is kinder to passengers as well, and I ventured into speech.

'Are you among the new slaves at the villa?' I enquired. 'I know that Marcus had replaced a lot of staff.'

He turned to look at me. The dark eyes were suspicious under his bushy brows. 'I've served him many years – that's why he trusted me today. But I'm under orders not to talk to anyone – except about the turnips.'

'Not even me?'

'Especially not to you – in case we are observed, and someone wants to question me about it afterwards. Those are my instructions. Don't be offended, citizen. It isn't personal. All the land-slaves have been told the same. Our only conversation with outsiders is to be about our work. And already, I have said too much.'

So, Marcus was really worried about people talking to his slaves. Even the land-slaves – who rarely saw their owner anyway, so they'd have little they could tell which would help his enemies. Unlike the gatekeeper. Did that explain the grunting? There were slaves who'd survived the slitting of their tongues. They could not betray their owners, even under torture – especially if they'd never learned to write. Had Marcus deliberately chosen a gatekeeper like that?

I asked the shaggy driver but he did not answer me, simply went on grimly staring at the road. I said, 'The turnips, then. That's a permitted topic of discussion, I believe. You're going to sell them in the marketplace? Surely people there will want to talk to you?'

He shook his head. 'I'm not to go into the town at all. I'm to choose a spot and moment when there's nobody about, then use the cart to make a kind of stall and sell them by the roadside, before we reach the gate. I'll let you down, and you'll know where to find me when you return. Selling turnips is only a pretence. If anyone goes past when you're getting up and down, act as if you've come to buy until they're out of sight. I'm sorry citizen, but that is all that I'm permitted to communicate.' He turned his gaze onto the road again.

Marcus was being very careful. And he'd chosen quite a clever ploy. There used to be dozens of impromptu stalls beside the road, before contagion struck, though I realised that we'd seen none so far today. If the cart was noticed, it would be supposed that it was coming to sell turnips, not conveying me. Anyway, there was nothing to link it with His Excellence. He does not generally sell his surplus in that haphazard way, and Shaggy wasn't wearing distinctive uniform. (Marcus's land-slaves don't – they have anonymous ochre tunics and, in this case, an equally anonymous brown cloak against the cold.) My own working cape wouldn't draw a second glance. Anyone would take this for a farmer's cart.

I shrugged my shoulders and sat back on the seat, prepared for a silent journey until he chose to stop, but we had not gone above another half a mile before I had a shock.

'Stop the cart. There's something back there, in the ditch beside the road. Looks like a body. I thought I saw the feet. Another victim of the plague, no doubt. We'll have to report it to the garrison, if so.'

He looked at me, reluctant. 'The garrison? They say it was the troops that brought the plague.'

'Stop the cart!' I said. 'That is an order. If someone has dropped dead, we're legally obliged to tell the fort, so they can send the death-cart out and stop infection spreading. I'll report it. You don't have to come – though I may want a witness, if there are questions later on.'

Shaggy looked doubtful, but he stopped the cart. We were some distance down the road by now. To my surprise, he actually spoke. 'You're not going to approach the body, surely, citizen? There might be miasma . . . who knows what?'

'The briefest glance, that's all. And you are coming with me; I might need your testimony, as I said before. We'll keep our distance, I can promise you. I have no wish to join him – or her – by falling ill myself. Most probably a male, from the feet. But we'll need a clear description for the fort, so they know what they're looking for, and where.' I climbed down from the cart. 'Come on, man, tie the ox up to that tree and do as you are told. Forget what Marcus told you – this must take precedence. Don't worry – I will take responsibility.'

He gave me an unhappy look, but obeyed – he was, after all, assigned to me today. I started to walk back to where I'd seen the foot, and he trailed unwillingly behind.

'Over there, beside that upturned tree! Some unlucky peasant, judging by that boot.' I paused, so he was obliged to catch me up. I pointed to the foot which was just visible again 'That looks like the home-made kind the poorest people make.'

He looked quizzically at me, and I realised he may never have encountered them. Land-slaves rarely leave their master's land, and – unlike some owners – Marcus gives his workers proper sandal-boots. 'You must have seen them, surely? Like big clumpy bags. They wrap raw cowhide around their feet, and leave it there until it dries to fit.' I had drawn him nearer now. 'Or this might be a beggar. It's hard to see from here. What's your opinion?'

I asked the question to give him the cue to speak, but he did not directly answer. He might be a big fellow, but he was genuinely afraid. 'So, it's unlikely the army will be able to identify the man . . . supposing that it is a man?' He was hanging back again. Clearly he wanted no part in this at all.

'They wouldn't try. They'll simply pick the body up and tip it in the pit. If this was a person of high quality they might take an interest – or if a slave had been reported as having run away, and the owner had asked for an official search. But this is clearly neither of those things.'

'But supposing there are living relatives? Won't they have asked the fort?'

'Only rich households, like your master's,' I replied. 'The army isn't going to look for anybody else. Of course, the family might be doing so themselves, though it's unlikely that there is one, if this person died of plague. When somebody is sick, you'd expect them be tended in their home.'

'Unless they'd deliberately come out here to die.'

That was intelligent. I hadn't thought of it. A man who is desperately ill might stumble off alone, to protect the rest of his household from the plague.

'Possible.' I nodded. 'Though this contagion seems to spread too fast for that – a whole family can die within a day. And, of course, this person may have simply fallen among thieves – I imagine bandits will be busier than ever while the army is occupied with other things. All the more reason for reporting it.'

'But the corpse won't get a proper funeral? What about . . .' He gestured to the air. 'The spirits of the unburied are forced to walk the earth.' So that's what Shaggy was so frightened of. He was terrified we might encounter one.

'The death-cart will see that he is buried,' I replied. 'Unless this was a robbery, I shouldn't think that relatives would dare collect the corpse . . .' I broke off as I realised he was no longer at my side, but had come to a sudden halt a pace or two behind.

He had clearly seen what I could see protruding from the ditch. He'd turned whiter than a curial candidate's toga under his facial hair, and was staring in dismay. I swallowed hard myself – it did look quite grotesque, one foot huge and bulky in its crude, enormous boot, and the other white and bloodless as my companion's face.

But I asked, 'What's the matter?'

'Surely, citizen,' he stammered, 'we've gone close enough? Even the death-cart must be cautious with victims of the plague, though I hear the army are not catching it themselves. But if they put it in the common pit, won't that pose a risk for everybody else? I know what happens with beggars and common criminals. It can be days before they cover them.'

'Not during times of plague. I speak from personal experience,' I said. 'My own adoptive mother died when there was merely a rumour of pestilence about. They didn't even touch the corpse themselves – just found something they could move it with, rolled it in a blanket and slung it on the cart. They'll do the same with this. They'll bring the body to the pit as fast as possible, sprinkle it with lime and cover it immediately with earth. They'll even keep a guard on it, in case some grieving person tries to dig it up and give it a decent funeral. Though it's unlikely the family will even hear of it, however quickly news travels in this town.'

Shaggy had turned even whiter now. I'd meant to reassure him and done the opposite.

'But it will be properly disposed of, in a fashion anyway,' I said. 'The Romans are no fonder of vengeful ghosts than you and I. And that's exactly why something should be done. Besides, it could be a public danger where it is. So do what I am doing, pull your cloak around your nose and mouth, and come with me and see if this is what we think it is.'

'You really think there's danger if we don't report?' But he'd done as I suggested and his voice was muffled now.

'Not from ghosts.' I tried to adopt a casual certainty, though I was far from feeling it. 'But who knows what dogs or . . . goats might chance on it, and take infection to their masters afterwards?' I spoke of goats, but I was thinking more of bears and wolves that roamed the woods at night.

'It will take some time before the death-cart comes. Perhaps we can find something to cover it, meanwhile?'

It would make no difference to wolves, but I encouraged him. 'It would give him dignity, at least, if one could find anything . . .' I looked around but nothing suitable occurred to me – beyond my cloak which I certainly did not wish to sacrifice.

'There is a piece of sacking on the cart, tied over the top turnips to stop them shaking loose. Should I fetch that, perhaps?'

'Very well. You go and get it, and I'll take a closer look.' But I was already talking to myself. He'd shot off like a *ballista*, and I wondered for a moment if he'd simply drive away. But I saw him picking at the knots. Relieved, I edged a little nearer to the ditch so I could see more clearly what was lying there – without getting close to it – and tried to draw such conclusions as I could.

It was indeed the body of a man, who had fallen on his face. Of middle years, by the look of it. And not dead for very long – the corpse had not decayed – though I was right about the wolves. Something had obviously gripped him by the leg – one could see tooth or claw marks in the flesh – and presumably tried to drag him from the ditch, which was why he was now lying partly out of it. Otherwise he might have lain there, unobserved, for days.

But the hole was deep, the body was well built, and the creature had clearly given up. It had made a meal by simply gnawing at the thigh. The grubby tunic had bunched up round the hips, exposing part of the hairy buttocks, and pair of equally hairy, strong-muscled legs.

The upper body was partly wrapped already in a cape – although not a long one, and very tattered too. There even seemed to be a slender purse-bag lying under him – the plaited belt around his waist was what had caused the clothes to ruck. Not robbers, then (not that a man like that was likely to have much to steal)!

So, was this a victim of the plague or had he simply tripped? Or both, perhaps? There was a cluster of small purple lumps, high on one thigh – which made me swallow hard – though if it were a fever rash it had not spread far yet. Hardly enough to cause a death, I thought.

Nor did it seem the fall had killed him of itself. There was no sign that blood had seeped onto the hood that was pulled up around the head, and no other injury that I could see. He seemed to have stumbled somehow into a huge hole beside the verge, where that tree had clearly blown over in a gale. It had taken with it both its roots and part of the sidewall of the ditch.

It was not the only accident to have happened here, it seemed – someone had lost a quantity of stones as well, presumably when a cart had pulled over to the side and dropped a wheel into the space. Most likely in the dark. One could still see tracks and footprints in the mud where people had been struggling to shift the vehicle, and a baulk of wood they'd used to make a ramp for it.

It may even have been that which tripped the man, I mused. It was where a traveller might have been walking on the verge. Perhaps he had not seen it in the failing light? Simply fallen face down in the mud and lacked the strength to gain his feet again? He had clearly been here overnight – the wolves were proof of that – but not much longer, from the state of him.

'Look for what's missing that you'd expect to see.' I could almost hear my father's voice instructing me.

Of course! There was no sign that the dead man had been carrying a lantern or a torch – or any kind of walking staff. So probably he had not been walking late, or been intending to travel very far. And what had happened to that missing boot?

I looked around and saw it lying off towards the woods. The undergrowth was trampled in that direction too – almost as if he might have come that way, and not along the road. And further off again, beneath the trees . . . I crossed the ditch at a safe distance, where it was narrower, and took a few steps to investigate.

'Dear Jupiter!' I called to Shaggy, who was still undoing knots. 'I do believe he had his father with him. There's a second body – a much older man.'

NINE

Another, skinnier, peasant, dressed exactly like the first. The neck was at a peculiar angle, and the fluffy wisps of greying hair I'd seen – visible because the hood had fallen back – were speckled in dried blood. Scuff marks – both on the body and the ground – suggested that it had been dragged here from the ditch. Obviously this one had been easier to move.

Probably been turned over in the process too, because although the corpse was now lying on its side, the whole face was abraded. Quite appallingly. Perhaps – apart from damage caused from being hauled over stones and undergrowth – the wolf had also been gnawing and clawing at the flesh.

I tried my father's trick for overcoming shock and nausea – noting detail and seeing what you could deduce. I even edged closer to get a better look.

Not much of the half-flayed face remained, beyond a hooked nose and a pair of high-set eyes. What was left, especially the area round the lips and chin, was so discoloured I thought it must be bruised. (It was not the purpling blood that pools downwards after death – that was visible on the lower legs, showing that the corpse had once been lying on its back. This skin was greyish-blue and yellowing.)

But, sickeningly, the wolf – or whatever creature was responsible – had not confined its interest to the face. One of the tapering, pale hands had lost several fingers and a portion of the palm, though there was not a lot of blood. And the way that mangled limb was lying – or not exactly lying – was distinctly odd. It hadn't fallen limply to the ground, as you'd expect, but was sticking slightly sideways, unsupported, like a rod. And at an unnatural angle, like the head. It made the whole appalling scene yet more disquieting.

I tried to drag my eyes away and think. What did this tell

me? Well – obviously – the body must be stiff, as bodies are a few hours after death. But after a little while that stiffness goes again. By my calculations (or my father's, I should say), the man had therefore been dead for several hours, but certainly no longer than a day. Good. That was something helpful that I could tell the fort.

Also, it had originally been lying on its back, which didn't help at all. But then an interesting thought occurred to me. It must have already been rigid when it was dragged across, otherwise it would not have held position in that way. So it had been dead before the wolf arrived – which also explained the lack of blood around the wound. I was proud of having worked this out – and trying to be logical had settled me, besides.

'Do you want this over the old man or the son?' The voice of Shaggy cut across my thoughts. He was standing safely on the far side of the ditch, waving the piece of sacking from the cart.

'This one, I think. I don't know which is worse.' I gestured him across to where I was. The driver held his cloak around his bearded face again, but I saw him pale as he glimpsed the bloodied sight.

'Oh, dear gods.' He dropped both sack and cape and clapped both hands across his face. The cloth fell in a heap across the corpse's feet and he backed away, clearly reluctant to pick it up again. 'I'm sorry, citizen. But I see it is already too late. The wolves have been at him. And at the other one, by the look of it.'

'One wolf, in any case,' I said, still struggling to make sense of what we saw. 'A single individual out scavenging, I'd guess. Disturbed by something passing on the road, perhaps, before it had time to signal to the pack that it had found a meal. If the whole pack had come here they would have dragged the bodies off and they would never have been found. Or disposed of – even in the pit.'

'Merciful Jupiter!' He glanced towards the forest nervously. 'Supposing the creature's found the pack by now and is leading it back here?'

I said, with a confidence I didn't feel, 'Unlikely in the daylight. And the wolf did not kill these men, in any case. They were dead already.'

He came no nearer. 'But how can you be sure?'

I explained my reasoning. 'That hand was never bitten off in life – there would have been more blood. And the same with the wound on the other fellow's thigh. So very probably they perished from the plague, as we first supposed. It's clear that they were ill. The younger man did not even put out a hand to save himself. They must have been dead, or dying, before they hit the ground. Wouldn't you agree?'

Again, I'd asked directly for his thoughts. He surprised me. 'Both at the same moment?'

From a slave this was impertinent – questioning the judgement of a citizen. But I'd sought his opinion, and it served me right. Besides, it was an interesting idea. 'You don't think so?'

He turned bright scarlet this time, sensing a rebuke. But he was more frightened of plague and wolves and corpses than of me. 'Forgive me, citizen, if I'm speaking out of turn, but is it likely that they both dropped dead at once? Even if they were ill and staggering? Doesn't it seem more probable that they were set upon? By thieves, if not by wolves at first?'

I made no answer because I could see that he was right and was considering the implications. He interpreted my silence as a demand to justify himself.

'Perhaps robbers killed them, and the wolf came afterwards,' he burbled anxiously. 'There are many thieves about. My master will not travel without a bodyguard, even on the busy high road to Corinium. He says that even law-abiding folk will stoop to anything when they are desperate.'

I had my own ideas about why Marcus had that guard, but there was truth in this as well. Shaggy was worth discussing matters with, though at the moment he was totally preoccupied with our being in danger here ourselves.

I tried to reassure him. 'There's no sign of robbery. The younger man still seems to have a purse – though a very slim one – fastened round his waist. And what else would these men have that anyone would want? Apart from clothes and boots, perhaps, but they're still wearing those. Besides, highway thieves don't leave their victims living, as a rule – the punishment for robbery on the public road is crucifixion. They don't want witnesses to describe them to the authorities.'

'But these men aren't living. They are very dead. And someone might have chopped that hand half-off to remove a ring if they couldn't pull it free.'

'Why would a robber do that, then leave the purse untouched? And does this look the sort of fellow to have a costly ring?'

Shaggy looked abashed.

I tried to undo my tactlessness. 'Besides, as I was saying earlier, all those wounds must be post-mortem or there'd be a lot more blood. And there are no signs of a fight. Or self-protection, even. Not a scratch, elsewhere, except where they've been dragged. And none of their injuries – nasty as they are – would be enough to kill. More likely send them crawling, which would leave a trail of blood. And you can see for yourself there is no sign of that.'

He looked at the corpse unwillingly, and gave a doubtful nod. 'This one has lost his ring finger . . .'

I was warming to my argument. 'I don't think this was done by thieves – there is no bludgeoning, or sign of broken bones. None of the injuries look like knife wounds – they are not clean enough. They weren't throttled, either. There'd be marks around their necks, and they wouldn't look like that. Their eyes would be bulging and—'

The list of horrors was too much. Shaggy interrupted, despite our different ranks. 'Citizen, I see that you are right. They must have died of plague, together, as they walked along. Perhaps it's what they planned, poor creatures. Only a wolf disturbed them after they were dead. As you say, we'll have to report this to the fort, so they can collect the bodies.' He gestured to the sack. 'Meanwhile, should I fetch a stick, perhaps, and retrieve that cloth? We can cover one of them at least, and give the corpse a bit of decency?'

But suddenly, I was beginning to develop doubts myself. Two men dying of contagion at exactly the same time? It did seem unlikely. 'It might have been exhaustion that killed the older man,' I ventured doubtfully. 'Perhaps he staggered on a little when his son fell in the hole, and then collapsed himself . . .' I trailed off. This was not convincing even to myself. It was clear from those drag marks he'd been hauled from very near the ditch.

There was something very peculiar about this, after all. Think, Junio!

It was, of course, entirely plausible that these two men had both contracted plague from the same source at the same time – especially if they lived together, as a working son and father often do. Maybe they'd attempted to escape the town to dodge contagion, but left it far too late. Or, most probably, Shaggy's guess was right – they were already ill and wanted to avoid contaminating anybody else.

But, whatever brought them here, wasn't it highly doubtful (given the evident differences in their age and strength) that they'd expire simultaneously a pace or two apart?

Indeed, were these men victims of the plague at all? Wasn't that supposed to cause a raging fever and suppurating rash – so disfiguring that even wealthy Rufus had no public funeral? The only rash here was on the younger one – and that was merely a few small purple lumps, like a bedbug might have left.

And probably had done, I realised suddenly. The older man had no such spots on him. Apart from the abrasions and the wounds inflicted by the wolf, his flesh was unblemished and almost greyish white. What's more, the corpses had not really yet begun to smell. What happened here had not been long ago.

I dropped the cloak from round my face and looked down at the older man again. More closely this time, and with more attentive curiosity. And saw what my wise old father would have seen at once.

If this was the sire, he was not much like his son. The younger man was stocky and no more than average height, while this one must have been – in life – both slim and very tall. And lacking muscle too. The long legs stuffed into the bag-like shoes were white, so white – where the purpling of pooled blood had not disfigured them – that they were almost blue. And so thin it seemed a wonder he had kept them in those clumsy boots.

I said as much to Shaggy, who agreed. 'I noticed that. I wondered if they were really his.'

I stared at him. 'You're right! Or, now you make me question it . . . his other clothes? Even that skimpy tunic. It's torn and tattered where it's been hauled along, but it doesn't look as if it ever reached his bony knees!' Then inspiration struck. 'And look at those pallid lower legs. No sign of tanning. None at all, as there surely should be if he'd been a peasant all his life. Those legs have never been exposed to sunlight very much.'

'No real muscles, either,' Shaggy said. 'Which tells us what? That he more normally wore something else . . . like Celtic trews?'

I shook my head. 'That hawk-like nose shows Roman heritage. That's not uncommon in a slave, of course, but that slim hand has never seen hard work. So, some sort of senior slave? An amanuensis possibly? They often wear long Grecian robes to mark them out. But why, in that case, is he lying here?'

'And why in company with that younger man, who looks every inch a labourer?' That was Shaggy, who was still goggling at the scene.

'A good idea of yours to fetch a stick,' I said. 'Bring me the longest one that you can find. A good, stout, thick one, but not that baulk of wood! Just something long and strong enough to move the sacking with.'

He hunted round for a bit, and then I saw him stoop. 'This one, master?' (I had been promoted now.) He held what had clearly been a side-plank of a cart – perhaps the one that had bogged down in the ditch. 'It's not too heavy, and it's broken at the end, which makes a point.'

'Excellent,' I told him. 'Bring it over here. I want to see if this man has a slave chain round his neck, or a brand on his shoulder, but I don't want to get too near. Though I'm beginning to doubt they died of plague at all. I'm starting to think they might be runaways, in which case the authorities will really want to know.'

He had paused beside the younger corpse. 'Pardon my

presumption, citizen. The same thing occurred to me. This does not look like what I've heard of the disease. So, if there's no risk of catching anything, do you want me to look for the same thing on him, while I am standing here?' Now that he was no longer frightened for his life, he was a useful aide.

'Good idea,' I told him. 'I haven't asked your name.'

He gave a wry smile. 'They call me Hirsutis, citizen.'

Shaggy! So I was right to call him that! Though if he were mine I might have named him for his intelligence. That was why Marcus had entrusted him with this trip, no doubt. 'Well then, Hirsutis,' I said, 'any sign of a slave disc or a brand?'

He shook his head. 'Nothing of the kind. But there is something that perhaps you ought to see. This one is missing half a hand as well. I didn't see it until I moved the cloak.' He stood back as I approached to let me look. 'Surely that can't be coincidence? Unless that wolf has somehow got a taste for hands! Though, with your permission, citizen, I don't think this one is a recent wound.'

I stepped past him to see. And got another shock. It was a mutilation that I recognised. The two outer fingers, with a portion of the palm. And Hirsutis was right again – the injury had healed. I took the stick from him and used it to reveal the upper arm. A jagged scar ran almost to the elbow joint. Almost reluctantly, I pushed the hood back to reveal the face. And knew that I was right.

I turned to Hirsutis. 'I know this man,' I told him. 'He is – or was – a miller in the town. I've even bought a sack or two of flour from him myself, although he was expensive and not my normal source. Name of Craithaw, if I remember right. He's no peasant, and he wasn't poor.'

'So, it's not that he was starving?' Shaggy was frowning at him in dismay.

'Not him,' I said. 'He had a donkey mill. And he must have earned good money – at least before the plague – because he had enough to take a man to court.'

'What for? Failure to pay?'

'Personal reasons, but a trumped-up charge of contaminating flour, I'm told. He was thriving then. He might have had problems with supplies since the contagion struck – though obviously some folk bring their own grain for him to mill – but if he did find anything to grind he could be selling every scrap. Even in plague times people have to eat. And I understand that prices have been soaring to the skies. So, if he avoided catching pestilence – and it looks that way – he might have been doing particularly well. Whatever else, he does not look ill-fed.'

'So what's he doing dressed like that, and lying dead out here?'

'I can't imagine.'

'And who's the other man?'

'I'm beginning to wonder if I might know him as well. It's very likely to be someone from the town. He's not a peasant either, of that I am quite sure.'

'Dear gods!' Hirsutis spat into his hand and rubbed behind his ear, as people do to protect themselves from curse. 'What have we stumbled on? But at least you will have something certain to report. The miller anyway. Did he have family?'

'He had a wife but no children, I believe. I suppose we ought to tell her as soon as possible, so she can see he has a proper funeral. Though I don't know how she could collect the corpse – even supposing that she has escaped the plague.'

Shaggy looked at me and took a risk. 'Forgive me, citizen, but would it not be better to leave that to the authorities? Of course, this must be reported to the fort, and they can contact her. But shouldn't we make haste? You have an appointment with Appius Limpnus, I believe.'

And then of course, I realised what I'd seen. I went back to look at the older man again. A bald face with an eagle nose, high-set eyes and tufty hair. A tall, thin individual who used to wear a Grecian gown when he was not in the toga with the purple stripe he was entitled to. No wonder those peasant garments did not fit! A man whose slim, white hands had worn a heavy golden ring the last time I saw him, when I went to mend his floor. Not just a Roman citizen, but a patrician delator with links to the provincial governor, and the Emperor himself. I went back to Shaggy, shaken to my bones.

'Appius Limpnus won't be needing me,' I said. 'That's him,

lying over there. I'm almost sure of that. And I'm starting to think you were right about the ring, and his missing fingers were not eaten by a wolf. But what's he doing in the miller's company? Especially dressed like that? And most of all, what are they doing here and why are they both dead?' I took a swift decision. 'Forget about the turnips. This must be reported instantly. This was murder. And it happened somewhere else. I think someone simply came and dumped them here.'

Hirsutis rubbed spit behind his ear again. 'But who?' he murmured, ashen.

'I've no idea,' I answered. 'Or why they'd take the risk of carrying two corpses down a public road, simply to leave them by the forest verge. Probably hoping that they'd be left to rot, or wolves would get to them – as it seems they might have done.'

'Or simply that the army would send the death-cart out and stuff them in the plague-pit where'd they'd not be seen again.' Shaggy was gracious enough to add, 'Thinking them peasants, as you said earlier.'

I tried to take control. 'Of course, the fort will take a lively interest now, and so will everyone from the Emperor down. But if I'm right that it's Appius, and I suspect I am, your master ought to hear about it first. Turn the cart around and I'll go and tell him now.'

And Shaggy was only too happy to comply.

TEN

Hirsutis deposited me at the gate then went off to deal with the cart. Grunter immediately let me in and gestured to the bower. He gave a piercing whistle, and the lisping page came out to set a (rather draughty) stool for me. Then I was left to wait.

It seemed an age before Marcus appeared, but it was clear why he had been so long. He was in the process of being attended by his barber-slave; one leg was just half-shaved and he was in a state of partial dress – merely an under-tunic and a shoulder cape – though naturally it was all of finest wool, and would have been smart clothing in itself to most of us.

I was astonished that he'd let himself be seen in such a state. It was an indication of how anxious he must be. And he remained very careful with his slaves. Callidus had emerged, attending him, but Marcus waved him off to squat beside the wall, before hurrying to join me in the bower.

Hurrying was not His Excellence's usual style. I've never known him move so fast (though, of course, in his customary toga that would be impossible!). But he was at my side, extending a ringed hand, almost before I had time to rise and bow. (I had the wit to merely feign the kiss. If Marcus caught the contagion I didn't wish to take the blame.)

'Citizen Junio!' he said, as I straightened up again. 'You were extremely quick. Did Appius not receive you? Or did something turn you back?'

'Both, after a fashion, Excellence,' I said, carefully.

He frowned. 'Don't prevaricate. You saw him?'

'I think so. But if I'm right – and I am almost sure I am – he won't be wanting mosaics any more. We've just found him lying by the road, together with a tradesman I recognise from town. Both dressed in clothes that were clearly not their own, and both extremely dead.'

His Excellency turned deathly pale. 'Dead?' He sat down heavily on the seat inside the bower. 'How? Plague or robbers?' He was breathing hard, and did not speak again, simply gestured weakly that I should tell him more.

'Neither, Excellence, if I am any judge. Though there might have been a wolf, which has not improved the state of them.'

'A wolf?' Marcus looked, if possible, even more appalled. 'The Emperor's appointee has been mauled by beasts?'

'There seem to be claw marks, and possibly a bite, on both. But not inflicted while they were still alive. There's scarcely any blood. I think the creature may have found the bodies, dead, and tried to drag them off towards his lair. Or Appius at least, because the two were discovered a little way apart. But I'm certain they were together at the start.'

'What makes you imagine that?' There was something disdainful in the tone. 'Two men of such completely different rank?'

'The fact that they were identically dressed, and as poorest peasants too. Wholly inappropriate – even for the tradesman! On closer inspection the garments did not even seem to fit.'

'But why, by all the deities . . .' Marcus was more and more appalled, '. . . had they dressed in such rags?'

I shook my head. 'Or were put into them? I can't begin to guess. Nor how they came to die together, and what they were doing out there, miles along the road? I don't understand it. But I thought you ought to know. And as soon as possible, judging by what you told me earlier.'

There was a pause while he considered this. Then, 'Have you reported this to the authorities?'

'I am doing so, this moment, Excellence!' I said. 'You are the senior regional magistrate, after all. That should cover the requirement, I think?'

He did not smile. He snapped at me, in fact. 'This is no time for jest. You realise, Junio, how serious this is? The paid informant of the Emperor? Virius Lupus's personal appointee?'

I gulped. 'Apologies, Excellence, for any flippancy. I do realise how serious this is – that's why I came to tell you first.'

Marcus buried his head in both his hands. 'The whole of

Glevum will be under even more scrutiny than it was – I shouldn't be surprised to find additional troops sent to reinforce the garrison. And yet more spies, no doubt.'

Which would be a problem, I could see. 'Better an informant that you know about, than one that you do not?'

Marcus held his brows as if his head might burst. 'True enough, but it could be far worse than that!'

'Oh Mars! You think they might start forbidding people going out after dark?' It had happened elsewhere in the Empire recently, when there was fear of treasonable plots. 'What would happen to our traders then – supposing that there's trade at present, anyway?' My voice was rising to a squeak as I began to envisage the problems it would cause. Everything would have to be physically carried in on animals, or on people's backs – or pushed on handcarts at the very best – if no one could bring wheeled transport into the town at all. (It is already forbidden here in daylight hours.) 'It would make life very difficult.'

Marcus looked at me as though I were an idiot. 'More difficult for me is what I meant,' he said despairingly. 'Listen, Junio. If Titus Flavius knows that Appius was plotting against me – a fact he personally confirmed when I first returned to town – then the rest of the curia will know about it too. What's worse, he's been discreetly sounding out – at my request – those who might have loyalty to me. So I clearly knew about the dangers Appius posed for me. Hence, if his body is discovered on a verge beside the road – on a route which I take every time I go to town – whom do you suppose that they are going to blame?'

I stared at him. Such a possibility had not occurred to me. 'You think they might imagine that you murdered him?'

'Not directly, obviously. But arranged for him to die? I think they'll consider it very probable.'

'But you've not been here!' I said, sounding like an advocate pleading in the court. 'You've been away in Corinium for moons. How could you have plotted anything? You've only just returned.'

Marcus flashed me that scornful look again. 'Junio, you must have heard of messengers? Of course it was possible for me to be in touch. I have corresponded with several councillors, in fact. Titus Flavius, in particular, asking for his help. And, unfortunately, also with the fort – asking whether the plague was passing or still spreading death.'

'Exchanging messages with the commandant himself?'

'Exactly. By a courier who, at the time, was wearing my distinctive uniform, which was no doubt noticed. It was designed to be. As to my returning only recently, can't you see that makes it worse? I come back and a few days later, Appius is dead.'

'Do people know that you are here again?'

'Of course. I told you I was at that special curia meeting that was held about the tax. And afterwards I stopped to speak to several magistrates. Men whose loyalty Titus had assured me of – just a word or two, but mostly about fearing Appius Limpnus Corvinus.'

'Were you seen to do that by anybody else? Even your distinguished presence might go unobserved, except among your friends. And they would not betray you readily. You waited till the rest of curia had dispersed, and I understand there are not many people on the forum nowadays, for fear of catching plague.'

'And – because of plague – we did not stay inside. We stood right in public view, on the steps of the basilica. We certainly were seen. And not only by the market traders at the few forum stalls. There were other councillors lingering who are no friends of mine.' He shook his head. 'And that's another thing. Titus Flavius himself. He made it clear to Appius Limpnus that he refused to be involved in any plot. No doubt Appius warned his co-conspirators, so Titus is in danger of suspicion too.'

'You really think there was a plot against you?'

'From what I hear from everyone, I am quite sure of it. Appius thinks – or thought – that I have too much dangerous influence and am not a devotee of Governor Virius. And I confess I'm not, though I don't say so publicly. Appius was looking for some way to bring me down – have me accused of some imaginary crime.'

'Have you exiled from the Empire?' It seemed unbelievable.

'At least! What court would find against him if he brought a case? With his connections? He could doubtless produce witnesses that he'd suborned. I'd be banished and sent to perish on a barren rock somewhere. Supposing that he wasn't planning to take the easy way – have someone meet me in an alley and run a sword through me.'

'They wouldn't dare!' It was my turn to look appalled. But, of course, they would! 'And you think Titus Flavius may be in danger too? But he's done nothing!'

'Except speak to me in public,' Marcus said. 'And make it clear to others that he's supporting me. After rebuffing Appius. And now the delator is dead. If you were one of the plotters, what would you suppose? Besides, the way things are in Glevum nowadays, doing nothing wrong is no defence. May I remind you that the same applies to me? I have done nothing unlawful. Indeed, I've been extremely careful to comply with every new edict as it comes along.' He gave me a piercing look. 'You're doubtful! Surely, you can't suppose that I had any hand in *this*?'

'Not for a moment,' I told him truthfully. 'And I can see your point. Appius Limpnus had connections of the highest kind. There will have to be a trial, and someone must be found responsible, but surely that could not conceivably be you? It's so absurd that no one could believe the claim. And even if an allegation should be made, surely it is easy to deny?'

He leaned back in the bower with folded arms. 'But very difficult to disprove,' he said. 'Especially to a court. And when it is stacked against you, doubly so. There is often proof of what one's actions were, but no concrete evidence of one didn't do, unless you have witnesses to prove an alibi. Any serving magistrate will tell you that. With this infection raging I have scarcely left the house, but who but my servants can attest to that? They would be subjected to the torturers, of course, when the death of a man like Appius is involved. And who knows what information might be forced from them? Those of them who can say anything at all.'

'You deliberately selected slaves who could not talk? I thought you might have done. As a defence against Appius Corvinus and his spies, I suppose?'

He nodded sadly. 'I sincerely wish I hadn't, after this. My old slaves might be sometimes careless with their tongues, but I could have depended on their loyalty – to death. They knew too much about my habits and my friends, that is why I let them go – to save them from this kind of questioning. This group have not been with me very long. There must be a temptation to make the beatings stop by telling people what they want to hear.' He gave me a wan smile. 'Your father used to warn me that such evidence was unreliable. I never thought I'd suffer from that truth. Especially when I tried to circumvent the possibility.' He shook his head and buried it in both his hands. 'Citizen, how I wish Libertus was here now. I need his counsel. I don't know what to do.'

His despairing manner made me bold. 'With permission, Excellence, I know what I'd advise.'

He raised his head and frowned at me. 'What's that?'

'I think it would be wise for you to come to town – with me, for preference. Check if you think that I am right about the corpse – it's always possible it isn't Appius – and report it to the garrison yourself. That's not the action of a guilty man. You could even offer a reward for information leading to the killer being caught.'

'The town? The fort? But what about the plague? It's said the soldiers were the ones who brought the pestilence.'

'And are the ones who have not suffered with it since. They're under the protection of Jupiter, no doubt. But you have your special amulet, I think. Blessed by the priest of Mars himself. It seems to have protected you so far. You attended that meeting of the curia. Besides, you say yourself the contagion is very largely past. The other risk is greater, if you do not go.'

He gazed at me in silence for so long that I thought I had offended him. I was just considering how I might apologise for daring to advise him – uninvited – when he said suddenly, 'Junio, I think I underestimated you. You are quite right, of course. I'll have my gig prepared and you can ride with me – and bear witness to the fact that I was here and you led me to the corpse. Do you wish to go and put a toga on?'

It was expected of a citizen, of course. The law requiring a Roman citizen to be togate in the forum at all times is not much enforced. But one is expected to wear the wretched thing – which is always an uncomfortable encumbrance – on formal occasions, like calling on the commander of the fort. But today, I thought, was different.

'Rather better if I don't, perhaps.' I was emboldened now. 'If I appear like this, it shows we hurried to the fort. I was due to see Appius as a tradesman, and I can tell them that – and I was hoping for a handsome commission from that shrine, so I stood to lose from Appius being dead. I don't want them supposing that I had a hand in this myself. I am a known associate of Your Excellence.'

'But that recommendation letter came from Titus Flavius,' he said wearily. 'Tying us together in the public mind. Perhaps it would be better to destroy it after all.'

'On the contrary, Excellence. It proves that he too, stood to gain from keeping Appius alive. He would have been paid an introduction fee if I got the contract.' I spoke quite forcefully. That letter was more than just important evidence for me.

His Excellence rose heavily to his feet. He looked much older very suddenly. 'I will take your counsel, Junio. I'll let my barber finish shaving me, and pick you up at your enclosure gate as soon as possible. I presume that you will wish to tell your family where you've gone – and that you won't be getting that commission after all.'

I nodded. 'I'll send my slave-boy to the workshop with the mule. If I travel with you in the gig there won't be room for him. Depending on what happens you may wish to stay in town – and the way things are at present I'd rather not be walking miles along deserted paths alone. This way I'll have an escort – or a messenger, if one should be required.'

'Then I will see you shortly, citizen.' And I was dismissed.

It was not all that shortly. Finishing a shave to Marcus's standards takes a little time, so I was able to get home and talk to Cilla before the gig arrived.

She was not delighted. 'Oh, husband, whyever did you get yourself involved? Why didn't you ignore the bodies and go on into town – leave them there for someone else to find? Most people would have done.'

'It's a requirement to report them in a time of plague,' I said, not at all pleased to be chided by my wife.

'Reporting them is one thing. If that was all you'd done, they would probably just have been tipped into the pit. And that would have been the end of it. No further questions asked. But you had to go over and investigate. And now see what you've done.'

'You think it's better to ignore the fact that two men have been murdered and dumped beside the road? Appius Limpnus Corvinus may have been a spy, and won't be greatly missed, but the other one, at least, has a thriving business and a wife who must be wondering where he is. How would you feel if the body had been mine, and it had simply vanished – as you say – into the pit? As whoever put it there was clearly hoping that it would.'

I had spoken with some feeling and she hung her head at that. 'Put like that, husband, I can see that you are right. I only spoke because I fear for you. The authorities won't care a quadrans that a miller is found dead, but the governor's pet spy? They will not rest till somebody is found to blame, and there is too much connection with Marcus – and now with you. You know how information travels in the town. Everyone will know that Appius expected you today.'

'With a view to employing me to decorate a shrine. A handsome commission, and a reason why I wanted him alive,' I said. 'Which works in my favour, more than otherwise.'

'When you're known to have had the opportunity to be alone with him?'

'By the time that we were due to meet, Appius was long dead. Any undertaker could testify to that from the condition of the corpse. He had been dead for hours by the time I chanced on him.'

'But can you prove you didn't meet him yesterday? You were to call on him today, at Marcus's express request, but you've been out foraging and setting traps, and not even I could not absolutely swear you'd not already had a secret interview. You have that letter. And the authorities won't take the household's word for it.'

It was exactly what Marcus had been saying earlier. It's very hard to prove a negative. But, hoping to reassure her, I waved a lofty hand. 'There may be no one to witness what I did myself, but I'm sure there'll be people who saw Appius elsewhere. He's known to be a spy. People have learned to be aware of where he goes and who he sees. When I get to Glevum I'll find a few of them.' I gave her arm a squeeze. 'But thank you, wife, for reminding me that such a thing is wise. And remember that I did not realise who the corpses were when I went over to investigate. I didn't involve myself on purpose.'

She stood on tiptoe to give my nose a kiss. 'Of course not, husband. I am anxious, that is all. And here's the gig now, stopping at the gate. You'd best not keep him waiting. I'll send Tenuis to Glevum with the mule and you can meet him at the shop and ride back home. And bring provisions with you, if there are any to be had – oh, though you won't have that commission now. You won't be able to.'

'I might find something in the shop that I can sell or trade. I've got to call at the miller's anyway. I might find a way to bargain for some flour. I'll see what I can do.'

And I went out and climbed up on the gig.

ELEVEN

I was expecting Marcus to discuss his anxieties again, and rather dreading it. I'd driven with him once or twice before – he is always keen to talk and it's always problematic to reply. My teeth rattle as we bounce along, and my bones jar with every imperfection in the road, all of which makes thinking difficult. But I needn't have worried. This ride to Glevum was as silent as the earlier one had been.

Marcus (who was much more accustomed to travelling by gig, and handled the motion with patrician ease), sat sunk in gloomy thought. And if he did not speak, I was not expected to, any more than the blue-clad Callidus squatting at our feet. Marcus never travels anywhere without a slave, and for a togate magistrate in town it is formally required. But I'd rather expected it to be one who could not speak. (Perhaps with Appius dead, the risk was not so great, as the gig driver could talk, in any case – though he'd been with His Excellence for years, and was doubtless loyal as the sun.)

So, thank Mars, I could simply concentrate on clinging to the side-strut for support, and keeping a lookout for where the bodies were. Though, remembering the condition they were in, Appius in particular, I wondered how Marcus would react on seeing them. His rank had largely preserved him from such horrors up to now.

But I had other things to think about. The gig was moving at a considerable clip – a good deal faster than the cart had done – and I began to fear that I might miss the spot. So much so, I eventually judged it prudent not to wait till I was spoken to.

'Your pardon, Excellence,' I managed between jolts. 'We must . . . be getting close.' Even as I spoke, I recognised the fallen tree. 'Just up ahead . . . where you see that broken oak.'

Marcus roused himself and leaned forwards to touch the

driver's arm. 'A little slower. This citizen will tell us where to stop.'

I was already looking for the hole and the telltale booted leg. But I almost missed the place because there was another vehicle drawn up on the verge.

That was surprising. We had passed almost no one on the road. Presumably the plague had seen to that – it would be unimaginable in ordinary times. But today there'd been nobody to cause delays, or needing to be forced onto the mud to let the gig go by. No loaded wagons creaking on their way, no laden mules and donkeys ambling along, or people driving flocks of geese or goats to town. We'd only seen one horseman – a courier for the Imperial post – who scarcely slowed to sketch Marcus a salute, before galloping onwards at undiminished speed. No one else.

But here was this big cart, stopped beside the road. Transport for a travelling family from the looks of it, with a leather cover stretched across a wicker frame. A large-framed peasant woman was standing at the front, feeding something to a skinny ox still chained uncomfortably between a pair of makeshift shafts (it seemed the usual central one had been inexpertly removed).

The woman looked up and glowered as we rolled slowly past, and I recognised the haggard pinch of want etched in her face. She must have been an enormous person once, and even now she was a formidable sight, although – like her animal – she had shrunk to skin and bone. From hunger, almost certainly. The voluminous ochre tunic was slipping down across her scrawny shoulders, and only prevented from falling all the way by being tied tightly with string around the waist, with a piece of sacking tucked above her breasts for decency.

She was in charge not only of the ox, but of a squabble of small children, rolling in the dust. As we passed, I saw that she was busy with a knife, doling out, to her noisy little brood, slices of something greyish-white – it might have been raw turnip or a lump of bread – from a basket on her arm. It didn't look appealing in the least, but they screamed and snatched it, wolfed it down and went back to their skirmishing again.

Almost all of them. One of the smaller ones went toddling

away, holding his prize out for somebody to see, and it was then that I realised there were menfolk here as well – of an age to be the husband and perhaps the grandfather. I hadn't noticed them at first because they were squatting on the ground behind the cart and had been obscured as we went jolting past.

The pair of them were as brown as their tattered tunics were, sun-baked and every bit as bony as the ox. They had a cloth spread out between them, on which they were apparently engrossed in playing dice. The woman had not offered anything to them, but each had his own large basket at his side, so I presumed that they were catered for. Neither even glanced towards the gig, though two of the older children stood up to stare at us, before the woman chided them and they turned back to their play.

I murmured to Marcus that we ought to stop.

He shook his head. 'Best ignored, in my opinion, citizen. They may be gambling in public, but it seems a family matter, with no coins involved. We have more important things to think about today.'

There spoke the magistrate. Gambling for money is not permitted in a public place (except at Saturnalia), but that law is not very much enforced. Romans are fond of gambling (I'm not averse myself). Everyone bets quietly on almost anything – chariot races, the fall of dice or even two raindrops running down a door. Sometimes for quite enormous sums.

But these poor souls appeared to be using merely stones as stakes. Unless there was something in their baskets fit to eat. There's no law to stop you hazarding for food, and it was hard to imagine what else they could be playing for – they clearly did not have a single *as* to spare.

And then it struck me. Stones? Surely the same stones that I had noticed earlier? We had moved some distance past the place by now, but I looked back and noticed what I should have seen before. It was the right tree, after all. Over towards the forest there was a sacking mound, just visible among the undergrowth. Unless I was mistaken it was Appius's corpse!

That wagon had stopped precisely where I'd seen that 'country boot'. And that spread cloth was surely covering the hole! The dead miller must be under it, and that scene of seeming innocence was nothing of the kind. And every moment took us further from the spot.

'Stop the cart,' I told the driver – for the second time that day. Startled, the gig slave did so instantly. I turned to Marcus, who was furious at my presuming to give orders to his man.

'You pardon, Excellence,' I hastened to explain. 'Those peasants are not really playing dice at all. I thought I recognised that broken tree! And now I'm sure of it. That cart is parked exactly where the . . .' I stopped and glanced meaningfully at little Callidus.

Marcus shook his head. 'You can speak freely. If those peasants know what's there, the news will be round Glevum in a flash. And we mean to report it to the fort in any case. You are telling me this is where the bodies are?'

'Exactly.' I tried to ignore the slave-boy's stricken face. 'That family's found the corpses, and I fear they're stripping them. Or would have done if we had not come by.' I felt sympathy for the peasants, though. These folk had nothing. Even those crude boots would seem a Jove-sent miracle. And as for that slim purse . . .

Marcus was looking at me in alarm. 'You think those people are the murderers? That might be, I suppose. Met their victims on the highway yesterday, killed them for what they had, and have come back for more?' He was excited by this theory, I could see.

'I think it most unlikely, Excellence.' I answered carefully. 'You have not seen the bodies. But you'll shortly be able to witness what I told you earlier: there are no injuries, except those that have clearly been inflicted after death. And anyway, surely they'd have stripped them at the time, not carefully left them dressed in clothes which are smarter than their own?'

Marcus gave me a sharp, doubtful glance. 'I suppose you may be right.'

'I think so, Excellence.' One must be careful when arguing with a man of rank. 'Whoever did this intended to disguise the dead by dressing them in clothes which do not fit their real identity and rank. It was done on purpose to mislead. These poor souls have barely enough garments for themselves, and what they have are scarcely more than rags. They'd hardly waste better ones upon the dead.'

'I suppose that's true,' he muttered grudgingly, clearly unwilling to let his theory go. 'Though the dead men's proper garments would have value, wouldn't they? Even those the miller wore? They might be worth stealing, for a family such as that?'

'But, Excellence.' I tried not to let exasperation show. 'How could they sell them – Appius's in particular – without bringing suspicion on themselves? But the clothes on the corpses would be of considerable value to this family – things those men would gladly wear.'

He sighed. 'Let me get this right. You think whoever left Appius here, stripped him and dressed him like a peasant? But why bother doing that? If the bodies were naked when the death-cart came, they would scarcely have earned a second glance.'

'Forgive me, Excellence, but that may not be the case.' I glanced at the page who looked away and tried to pretend that he wasn't listening. 'It can't be long before Appius is missed – by his household, anyway. The garrison may already have been alerted to the fact that the governor's favourite has failed to come home overnight. And the miller too, if he is already being searched for by his wife.'

'They would not be actively looking for *him*, though. A man of no especial rank, who's just been gone a day? With nothing to show he did not leave home of his own accord?'

'Of course, the miller's fate would hardly interest them, unless there was some promise of reward. But Appius would be sought for actively. Don't you think that – far from being more or less ignored – naked corpses might have been scrupulously scrutinised when the death-cart came, to see if either could be the missing man? Whereas if they were merely paupers . . . peasant folk . . .'

'They would be tipped into the plague-pit without a second thought, and not be seen again?'

I nodded. 'And the army would only be looking for one man.

No slaves are missing, so far as we're aware. So, the fact of two bodies would divert their thoughts away from Appius, if anything. Especially since the other man is clearly not a slave – no brands or collar disc. Simple peasants from all appearances.'

'While, if no trace of the delator was found, it would be assumed that he had simply disappeared on some secret purpose of his own?' Marcus was thoughtful. 'What would connect him with the miller, anyway? You'd not expect their paths to meet.'

'A question which we'll have to answer, if we are ever to understand this. Of course, out here, there was always a good chance the wolves would find the bodies before the death-cart came – which, from the killer's point of view, would be just as satisfactory.' (I saw Callidus flinch.) 'But given Appius's rank, there was bound to be a search. So, dressing both bodies that way was a clever move, which I think this family was unwittingly planning to undo.'

Marcus thought about this for a moment. 'So, what I am I do? Confront those travelling peasants on the cart?' He made a gesture of disgust. 'But they might be carrying the plague!'

'I think it's all you can do, Excellence. No need to get too close. They may be starving, but they are on their feet – and there's no sign of fever or convulsions or a rash, which are the symptoms of the contagion, so I understand.'

Marcus was still looking unconvinced, but I had another point to urge.

'Besides, if you choose to be magnanimous . . .'

'About the gambling?'

'About attempted theft, since after all they haven't taken anything away. Indeed, their presence may even be useful to your cause. They are witnesses to your arrival here – and might be induced to testify as much. They won't willingly get involved with authority, of course, but they might be persuaded.'

'With a bribe, you mean?'

'Well, clearly a small reward would be of help to them, but so is the promise that they will not be accused. Robbery on the highway is a crucifying offence. They clearly aren't Roman citizens, so that could be the punishment. Yet, from their garments, they're obviously not Celts. So they are either freemen or freedmen of some kind. Either way, their testimony has more value than your slave's. Or even mine, since I m a known associate of yours. If you are worried that you might be blamed, they can attest that you weren't here till after they arrived.'

'That Imperial courier could also testify that he had seen us further down the road, after he'd passed them. He must have noticed them; there are so few carts about.'

'But it might take some time to find him. He was going the other way. I think you should suggest that they cooperate,' I urged.

Marcus looked at me. 'You have my authority. Ask them what you please. My page will help you down.'

If anyone was going to catch the plague, evidently he intended it should be me!

TWELVE

I wasn't keen. If the Greeks were right about invisible miasma rising from the cursed, I could think of no one more likely to attract it than Appius Corvinus.

But I got down from the gig and walked back to where the woman was still standing by the cart. She shooed the children off and looked sullenly at me. 'You want something, freedman? I think that's what you are? Though I'm freeborn myself.'

I was suddenly aware of my own plebian clothes, and wondered if she'd seen the scar where my brand had been removed by my adopted father. But my shoulder was covered by my cloak. She was guessing – from the fact that I was travelling in the gig, dressed like this but assisted by a slave – that her social rank was higher than my own.

I assumed my most officious tone. 'I am a Roman citizen,' I said, and saw her blanch. 'Although a tradesman too. But my companion is a magistrate. The most important man in half Britannia.' I was about to mention his connection to the Imperial family but – remembering how Severus dealt with potential rivals – I decided I'd better not.

She was shaken but unbowed. 'So?' She'd put the basket down, but she was still carrying the knife, which she held before her like a weapon. 'We are freeborn traders, and we have a perfect right to use the highway, and to stop beside the verge. We are not harming anyone. What's it to do with him?'

She was defiant, but I saw the fear behind her eyes. I chose my words with care. 'It is not your presence on the road which interests him, but the place you chose to stop. I brought him here on purpose because earlier today I chanced to come this way and spotted two bodies lying by the road. One of them was a tradesman – despite the peasant clothes – but the other is patrician and a personal favourite of the Emperor.'

Her face turned the colour of that lump of food and – to my relief – she dropped the knife, which clattered to the ground.

I pressed my advantage. 'You have found at least one corpse, I think? He is underneath that cloth – where you must have moved him slightly, so you could cover him. When I came by before, his booted foot was sticking from the ditch. My guess is that you noticed it and stopped.'

She reddened but made no reply.

'And the other body?' I gestured to where Appius lay.

'Never touched it!' the woman said. 'We didn't notice it until we stopped. It was only this man's boots and cloak that we were after. Thought we might sell them or swap them for some food before we died ourselves. We have already had to kill our other ox to eat – though Jove knows there was little enough meat on the poor thing. Losing it has made it very hard to use the cart, and if we had to do the same with this one . . .' She broke off in despair.

I said gravely, 'And then you found the purse?'

'We meant no disrespect,' her voice was sharp with fear. 'The man was clearly dead – and no one seemed to care that he was here. We didn't know . . .'

'Be silent, wife.' The younger man was on his feet. 'You make more trouble for us with every word you speak.' He came and seized her arm to pull her back.

'No trouble, freeman,' I assured him peaceably. 'His Excellence accepts that it was only desperate want that made you stop. Of course, that's no excuse before the law, but I don't believe you've actually stolen anything? Not in the sense of taking it away? So, he's prepared to overlook it – this time – on one condition.'

'Anything!' The husband was eager to appease.

'Then you will agree to testify before the garrison, or possibly a court, that you were here and saw the corpses before he came along. And describe exactly what you saw. As I say, those peasant clothes don't belong to the people wearing them.'

The two of them exchanged a glance. The man said, 'Go before the authorities? Perhaps even in a court?'

'Only if required,' I soothed. 'Which I don't expect. Our

word should be enough. But these are troubled times. You must agree to stay near Glevum for a day or two, in case we do need you to testify. You can stay right here, for now – the verge is wide enough – and it will help the death-cart find the place. Then you'd be doing exactly what the law requires, reporting corpses on the public road.'

'But citizen, we need to earn or we shall starve,' the woman said. 'Especially now we have no boots or cloaks to swap or sell. We just ate our last turnip, thinking we'd found something we could trade. If we don't attract at least one customer – which we won't, out here – we'll have to kill the ox . . .' She made a gesture of despair.

I had an inspiration. 'If you guard the place for us, so others cannot do what you'd planned to do yourselves, I'm sure His Excellence would feel it deserved a small reward.' (I wasn't sure at all, in fact, in which case I'd be forced to offer it myself, as soon as I had earned a little from my trade! But I'd been told to speak for Marcus and I was doing it.) 'You'll be acting for His Excellence, Marcus Septimus. You can tell people so. And tell the death-cart too. They're not to move the bodies till instructions come – they would not question his authority.'

The man still looked as if I'd forced him to eat bitter herbs. 'I knew there'd be trouble, but when we saw that boot . . . My own are worn to tatters. They let in the rain. I could have used them, if we'd sold the cloak.'

I was on uncertain ground now, but I took a risk. 'You may be permitted to keep them afterwards,' I said. 'They don't belong to the miller anyway. His widow will want him in his own clothes before he goes onto the pyre. I cannot promise, but I think it's possible – if you are not afraid of catching the plague.'

It was his wife who answered, rather scornfully. 'That man was never a victim of the plague,' she replied. 'You've never seen one, clearly, or you'd be sure of that. We thought he'd died – as we're like to do ourselves – from fatigue and cold.' She glanced at me, seeing something in my face. 'Or do you know something different?'

'How they died, I am not sure at all – but I don't think it was here. Someone brought them here and dumped them.'

Fear – and what might have been excitement – flashed across her face. 'Are you saying they were murdered?'

'It's possible. Though I can't imagine why. Or who might have done it. I can think of people who might want either dead, but nobody who might conceivably kill both.' I rather wished I hadn't said that. It was ill-advised. 'They're such an ill-assorted pair,' I added hastily.

The woman was looking self-important now. 'In that case, citizen, we'll willingly keep guard. Don't argue, husband. Forgive him, citizen. We've been struggling now for moons. Generally, we move from town to town, and he sells and sharpens knives. Makes us a good living, on the whole. But we were in Glevum when contagion struck, and since then we have been welcome nowhere else. We've had to trade our stock for food, and there's no money to replace it with. Then we heard the plague was waning, and were going to try again, though it's not easy with a single ox. If we're forced to eat that, we shall have to sell the cart, which means we lose our home. We've got so desperate we're thinking that one of the children might make a slave, perhaps – and we could use the price to feed the rest of us.' She broke off suddenly. 'I'm sorry, citizen. You don't want to hear all this . . .'

'On the contrary,' I said. 'You confirm my view of you. I believe you can be trusted, and I will leave you here. But whatever you have hidden in those baskets, gentlemen, you will replace them now.'

The husband nodded sullenly. 'I suppose we have no choice. I knew there'd be trouble, wife. I told you so . . .'

He was still muttering as I walked back to the gig.

THIRTEEN

Marcus was waiting, looking rather sour. 'What took you such a time?' He gestured me to join him on the seat again.

The page scrambled down to help me, but I stood my ground. 'Excellence, I was persuading them to testify for you,' I replied. 'I think you need to speak to them yourself.'

'What for? They have agreed, I hope! Even if they're travellers, not from this area, they must realise I'm a man of rank.'

'Of course. Though they needed persuasion. They're wary of dealing with the authorities. But not only have they agreed to speak for you, they've promised to guard the bodies until someone comes for them. For a small consideration, naturally.' I saw his disapproving look. 'You wouldn't wish to have it said that Appius Limpnus was slung into the plague-pit when you might have prevented it.'

'There'll have to be a proper funeral for him,' Marcus fretted. 'At the curia's expense. He has no living relatives, as far as I'm aware, but – given who he is, or was – it can't be left to household slaves, or to a funeral guild, supposing he belonged to one.'

'The vine-growers, perhaps?'

He was in no mood for levity. 'We must ensure he has everything the Emperor could wish – speeches and musicians and paid mourners to lament – and possibly a lying-in where folk can pay respects, even in these inauspicious times. The whole town council will agree, I'm sure.'

'And even Craithaw's wife would like to see her husband given whatever rites she can afford.'

For a moment Marcus looked abashed. But he rallied quickly. 'From what you tell me, citizen, I gather you've told those peasants who the dead men are. Do you think that's wise? You know how quickly gossip spreads.'

'Your pardon, Excellence, but if they're staying here, they'll be in no position to spread the news until long after you have notified the fort. There's little passing traffic, as we have seen, so it's unlikely they'll have the chance of telling anyone.'

'Except the death-cart,' he said sourly.

'And that was why they had to know the names. Otherwise, how could they dissuade the soldiers from collecting the bodies and hurling them into the pit?'

He muttered grudgingly, 'I suppose you're right.'

I heard a little noise and glanced at Callidus. He was clearly aghast that a person of my rank should dare to argue with his master in this way. I'd been so concerned about my message that I hadn't thought about the impropriety. But I hadn't finished, and I was obliged to burble on. 'And that's exactly why I think you ought to come. I've promised that, if they do as we request, you'll see they face no charge of highway theft, and if they stay on watch there might be a small reward. But they'd be more convinced if they heard that from you.'

'Give them money? For simply standing guard? When they were here in any case?' Marcus was scornful. (He is famously careful with his cash – doubtless a reason why he has so much of it.) 'What need is there for that? Surely a simple command from me would be enough.'

'Excellence, I fear their instinct, otherwise, might be to run away. And then there would be no one to talk to the patrol, or prevent others from stealing from the dead. Remember, we might need their testimony too, about the clothes. It's all the evidence we have that someone brought the bodies here and wanted to disguise their true identities.'

That earned a grudging nod.

'Speaking of which, Excellence, I think – in any case – that you should come and look. Make quite certain that it's truly Appius.'

He could not have looked less willing. 'You really think it's unavoidable?' he harrumphed. 'I am perfectly prepared to take your word for that.'

I took a deep breath. 'Excellence, you said yourself the man was known to be your enemy. If you propose to report this to the fort, you cannot simply give the news at second-hand – you must see the corpse yourself. Firstly, to be sure it's really his. But also to give authenticity to your report.' (Because you cannot feign the shock the sight will cause, I thought, but did not say.) 'To deflect suspicion, you must give a full account. There may be questions you can't answer if you only have my description of events.'

He heaved a heavy sigh. 'Oh, very well.' He gestured to his slave to assist him to the ground. 'Great Jupiter! I don't like corpses at the best of times – ill-omened things, even when they are properly prepared for funeral. Unburied murdered ones are said to be especially accursed,' he grumbled as he straightened his patrician toga folds. 'I only consent to look at Appius, though. I would not know the miller from Romulus, anyway.'

I began to lead the way towards the cart. 'And that, Excellence, is a point in your defence. The victims are two such different men – one of whom, as you can doubtless prove – you've had no dealings with. That may . . .' I tailed off. He wasn't following. He was standing frowning by the gig. I knew when not to pursue an argument. 'But, as you command, of course. Now, those peasants are waiting by the cart.' I saw his little shudder of disgust. 'They'll keep a respectful distance, I'm sure,' I added. 'And you need not fear. They're not carrying the plague.'

Another humph. 'So you declare!' he muttered. 'But I suppose there's no escape. Callidus can stay here – no need to inflict these things on him. You can act as my attendant. Approach them and announce me when I give the sign.'

That sign – a slight declension of the head – came much further from the peasants than I would have wished, but I did my best. I stepped forward with a formal bow and declared in my most ringing tones, 'His Excellence, Marcus Aurelius Septimus, has come and graciously wishes to see what you have found.' (That should give him no way of backing out with dignity.)

The family were standing in a huddle by this time, the adults with their arms about the children, as though to shelter them. But Marcus's titles and patrician purple stripe had the desired effect. On the adults, anyway. Both men made a hasty bow, and the woman politely bobbed her straggling curls. The children simply stood and stared, except for the youngest, who stuck a thumb into its mouth and hid its face against its mother's filthy skirt.

I expected one of the menfolk to respond, but Marcus's resplendence seemed to cow them utterly. It is unusual for a female to take the lead in things, but this one was clearly a forceful character, and – after a short pause – the old man nudged her and it was she who spoke. 'You are welcome to inspect the corpses, Excellence. I hope you'll find things are in order.' She gestured to the ditch.

I had come to a stop so far away (thanks to Marcus) that I had to crane to see, but the party had been busy since I went back to the gig. Their cloth across the cavity had been removed, and Craithaw's leg was no longer sticking out of it. He had been pushed entirely into the hole, wrapped discreetly in his cloak. He was presumably naked otherwise, since his tunic lay neatly folded on the verge, with both his clumsy 'country boots' beside it.

The woman saw me looking and said defiantly, 'It's not quite as he was. We tried to put the clothing on again, but he's getting stiff and we were afraid of breaking bones. But everything is there.'

I raised an eyebrow. 'Not quite everything, perhaps? There was a purse, I think?'

She flushed. 'You are right, of course. I took it for safekeeping and put it in the cart. I will fetch it for you straight away.' But she moved off no faster than a snail.

I glanced at Marcus, who was still standing back. 'Safekeeping?' That was scarcely an excuse. If they were standing guard till someone came to claim the dead, from what – exactly – were they safeguarding the purse?

But he simply gave me a little knowing look, and approached from behind to murmur in my ear. 'I understand that it is pretty thin, in any case?'

I nodded and he turned to the men with his most gracious smile. 'I think you might reasonably keep the purse – as my companion has suggested – for agreeing to be both a temporary guard and, if necessary, witnesses on my behalf.'

I had, of course, suggested nothing of the kind. Marcus had seen an opportunity to give them a reward without it costing him a quadrans of his own.

I murmured a demurral but it was waved aside. He dropped his voice again. 'No matter, citizen,' he murmured. 'Not quite what you proposed, but this is sensible. The death-cart soldiers would have had it, otherwise.'

He had a point, of course. I nodded, doubtfully, but there was no time for reply. The woman had understood his offer.

Relief – and pleasure – were etched on her haggard face. She dropped a clumsy curtsey. 'Thank you, Excellence. And you, too, citizen. You can't imagine—'

I had to interrupt. 'Have the value of the contents, by all means,' I said. 'But we'll need to see the actual purse in any case.' I turned to Marcus, who was looking vexed that I had interposed. 'I don't wish to deprive these good people, naturally, but we should check if the miller was carrying enough to suggest that he intended to leave town. In fact, I think that we should take it to show the commandant.'

'And bring it back to them as their reward? I suppose there's sense in that. Who knows if we should find them still here otherwise?' Marcus spoke as if they could not hear.

'Better that you promise them the same amount, perhaps?' I ventured. 'It occurs to me that – since we know the man's identity – the money should go to his widow, shouldn't it? It may help her provide him with a decent funeral.'

Marcus looked furious. But he'd dug his own trap, and he crossly nodded his assent. 'Oh, very well. I'll match it,' he agreed. 'When they've proved they've earned it.' He saw the woman's dubious face, and sighed. 'I swear it by the gods. So, if you would be good enough to fetch it?'

With a doubtful glance towards her menfolk, she climbed up on the cart and appeared a moment later, carrying the purse. And, I noticed with dismay, she had the knife again.

'Let's hope she's brought us everything.' Marcus was at my ear again. 'I would not put it past her to have taken a few coins. Even now she's unwilling to hand the purse to us. You don't think she means to threaten us?'

Her demeanour told me otherwise. I said, 'Reluctant, Excellence, to encroach upon the space which you have left so markedly between ourselves and them.'

He gestured me to go and get the purse. He clearly did not want to venture near, so I stepped forward and took it from her hand. It looked exactly as I'd seen it earlier, except that somebody had cut the cord to remove it from the corpse.

And it was immediately clear why she had brought the knife. There was no question of money having been removed, because of the knot which held the drawstring tight. It was intricate and wet, and had been dragged across the mud into a tangled mess. There had clearly been no time to pick it loose.

Wordlessly, she handed me the blade, and I sawed through the leather thong. It took some moments before suddenly it gave, but then it was easy to pull the drawstring free. I opened the purse-folds and shook the contents out – and frowned in some surprise. In my palm lay two bronze quadrans and three *denarii*.

I was perplexed. The quadrans were no problem. Just what I'd expect – small change for a man whose services were paid for in low-value coins. But the rest? Not a *sestertius*, or even half a one. Just denarii?

It was no enormous sum, of course. Roughly what a legionary earns for two days' service, now, since Severus increased their pay. More than I'd hoped to earn myself today as a deposit on a flashy small commission like Appius's niche. Not what one would expect a miller to carry in his purse. Unless he was proposing to buy grain himself, perhaps? In what had clearly been the middle of the night or the small hours of morning – since his corpse had not been rigid when I'd first found it here?

I stood and stared at the money in my hand.

FOURTEEN

The woman was as startled as I was by the contents of the purse. Her face lit with delight, and a surprise which couldn't have been feigned. Marcus noticed too, and was quickly at my side. 'How much have you cost me . . .?'

I showed him the coins, and he turned to her, all sudden graciousness. 'You shall have the whole amount, and I will see the widow has this sent to her today.'

The woman flung herself upon her knees. 'Excellence, you are more than generous.'

He almost held out his ringed hand for her to kiss, but thought better of it and turned it into a gesture inviting her to rise. 'Stand up, woman. You have a name, I suppose?'

She was flustered at the condescension. 'They call me Decima, Mightiness, and this is my husband. And my father, over there . . .' She had not risen but was motioning at the members of her family as spoke.

He cut her short. 'Thank you, that will be enough. I shan't remember more.' He raised his eyebrows at me, murmuring over her emaciated form as she scrambled to her feet. 'You're satisfied, I hope?' There was no mistaking the self-congratulation in his tone.

I sighed. It wasn't really very generous. Three denarii. Nothing to Marcus, though it would be a fortune to this small family. I bowed. 'It's a great deal more than I possess myself at this moment, Excellence,' I said. Pointedly, since I'd failed to earn the contract with Appius today, but I took care to speak with courtesy. 'And I'm sure you're wise – and most magnanimous – to agree to reward these people from your private means. It's more obvious than ever that this purse is useful evidence.'

Marcus is susceptible to flattery, and I was rewarded for 'magnanimous' with a patronising smile. 'Because it's proof – at least – that bandits and rebels weren't involved?' He was clearly pleased with his own cleverness.

'And even more than that. The contents are quite enough for anyone to steal – but not enough to finance travel very far.'

He frowned. 'You mean, it looks as if this miller did not plan to leave town?' He flapped a disgusted hand towards the ditch. 'Is that him, lying there?' He took a step forward and a fleeting glance, then turned away, obviously disinclined to look. 'Disgusting.' He shuddered. 'And there are spots on him, I see. You're quite sure that this was not the plague?'

He was addressing me, but it was the woman who replied. She dipped a smiling curtsey – evidently encouraged by his promise of reward. 'Your pardon, mighty one, but it is clear you've never seen a victim of this pestilence.'

Marcus was affronted by her impudence, and showed it in his face, though she seemed unaware of anything inappropriate. Though no low-born person – especially a woman – should be interrupting a man of Marcus's rank.

She misinterpreted his flinch. She went on eagerly. 'I can reassure you, Mightiness. We know it all too well. We've passed victims lying dead beside the roads. Mostly swollen and disfigured, with suppurating blisters everywhere. Believe me, citizens, if this had been the plague we'd never have gone near this wretched corpse ourselves.'

'Not even for the money?' Marcus said, by way of a rebuke. 'It would feed your starving family for some time, I think?' He had adopted his most magisterial tone by now, as though questioning in court.

It did not cow her. 'If we'd known there was silver in the purse, I might have risked it – covering my face to cut it from his belt. But he doesn't look the sort of man to carry much, and we didn't know there was any more than bronze. Even if we had, I doubt I would have dared if there was the slightest suspicion of the plague. Not as long as we had a lump of turnip on the cart and our children would not actually starve.'

Marcus was still frowning. 'I wish I could believe you.'

'Mightiness, even silver coins are no use when you are dead. Not even to that corpse. That's why we took the purse – before the death-cart came and helped themselves to it. From the look of him, we thought he'd simply died of cold or weariness – or a mix of both – as we have often feared that we would do ourselves.'

'Exposure and fatigue? Not hunger?' Marcus was surprised.

Decima shot him a pitying glance. 'Hardly likely, Mightiness. He's far too well-nourished to have died of want. That's what we concluded. And it seems that we were right.' She turned to me, looking boldly in my eyes – in a way no well-bred Roman woman ever would. 'You say he was a miller, so his household would have bread.'

'And the other corpse?' I asked.

She shrugged. 'We didn't know it was one – for certain – until you told us so. We didn't even notice it when we first arrived – we stopped because we saw the body in the ditch. We did spot something in the undergrowth but we thought it was just a bundle lying there – something fallen off a wagon possibly, and dragged away by wolves or bears.'

'But you did not investigate?' I was sceptical.

'We were planning to. We thought to take that cloth, if nothing else. It is large enough to be of use. And we were hopeful about what else it might contain. If wolves were interested, it might be edible, or something we could take to town and sell. Then one of the children went to look and said he thought there was another body underneath the sack, so there might be other clothes. But we had not managed to go and look before you came along. And now you say it is a man of rank. We would not have dared to interfere with that.'

Marcus ignored her and turned excitedly to me. 'Junio, perhaps there is no mystery at all? Perhaps these men did simply perish from the cold. The nights are chilly at this time of year.' He gave a scathing glance at Craithaw. 'Well, this man is clearly dead and you can verify his identity, you say. So let us waste no further time on him. If it's certain there's no fear of plague, I'd better ascertain that the other man is truly Appius. Stand aside!' He waved the woman from his path and strode towards the place, fastidiously holding up his toga hems so they did not touch the mud.

The corpse was exactly as Shaggy and I had left it earlier – still covered by the piece of sacking cloth. I could see why Decima and her family had thought it was something fallen from a cart.

Marcus looked at it for a moment, then turned uncertainly at me. I found the pointed stick that we'd used earlier, and proffered it to him.

He scowled and shook his head, then turned and clicked his fingers to the men. 'Uncover that for me.' He tried to sound like his imperious self, but he looked and sounded about as eager to begin, as a whipping boy awaiting punishment for his master's schoolboy faults.

I was almost reluctant to approach the corpse again. I'm not a great believer in curses as a rule, but it's foolish to ignore the possibility. Appius had been a delator, responsible for many executions and deaths in exile. If his demise was due to vengeance by the gods, invisible miasma might be rising as we watched.

So while the peasants knelt and pulled the sacking back, I took good care to finger my lucky amulet and use my cloak to cover up my nose and mouth.

Appius looked even worse than I'd remembered him. The hand was sticking up less stiffly now, and the remains of the undamaged skin seemed more blue and bloodless than before, in dreadful contrast to the mangled face. I looked at Marcus. He had turned almost as pale and ghastly as the corpse. I thought for a moment he was going to lose his Roman dignity by vomiting in public, but he contained himself.

'That's a patrician?' the older man exclaimed. 'It doesn't look like one!'

'It certainly does not!' Marcus was emphatic. 'What makes you think,' he added, in an uncertain voice, 'that this . . . thing . . . is Appius?'

I told him. Pointed out the hair, the height, the pale legs and the remains of what had been an eagle nose. 'And the hands,' I added. 'The ring finger is conveniently missing, as you see. And they have never seen a day of peasant work. Look at the manicure!'

Marcus looked a moment, then closed his eyes and shook his head. He ran a tongue around his lips before compressing them. He didn't speak.

I waited, half-expecting a torrent of reproof for daring to bring him to such a scene. He seemed not to believe that this was Appius. His silence almost made me doubt myself.

Marcus gestured brusquely to the two men from the cart. 'Cover it again.' He turned to me. 'I fear you might be right. There is a wart on that undamaged wrist which I have seen before. One of the councillors composed a verse about it when Appius was not there to hear.'

'Dangerous,' I said. Such warts are caused by sexual excess, the whisper is.

Marcus nodded. 'A joke around the curia, that's all. Funny, but almost certainly untrue – no one's ever seen him in female company, except perhaps a slave. But there's no doubt about the wart. You did well to realise who it was – I never would have done. Dressed like that, and in that mutilated state . . .'

'Excellence,' I put in gently, 'I think that was the plan. The killer meant that he should not be recognised. It is the purest chance that I should find him and work out who it was – and only then because I recognised the miller first. And, of course, I'd worked for Appius before . . .'

He held up his hand to interrupt, more in control of his emotions now. 'Very well. It shall be as you suggest.' He strode back towards the ditch again, while we trailed after him. He stopped beside the cart. 'These peasants here will guard the bodies till they can be collected by the proper agencies, at which time I will reimburse them as agreed.'

The woman bobbed a curtsey. 'And if the death-cart comes meanwhile?'

He gave her a look which would have withered leaves. 'Tell them that you're acting on my authority. Marcus Aurelius Septimus. Can you remember that?'

'I'll never forget it, Mightiness, as long as I draw breath. Or you either, citizen.'

I intervened. 'Tell them exactly what happened if they come. His Excellence stopped to look because I asked him to. I'd seen the bodies earlier and, despite appearances, I knew one was a miller, and thought the other might be a man of rank I knew. I wanted His Excellence's confirmation of the fact, before we reported to the fort.' I paused, then added, 'You needn't mention that you'd stripped the miller's corpse – simply that you'd seen him in the ditch and stopped here to investigate.'

This was an implied threat – given the punishment for highway robbery. She realised that at once. 'I'll tell them exactly what you say, citizen,' she answered, and stood aside to let us pass.

We walked slowly back towards the gig, where the driver and slave were waiting patiently. Marcus murmured thoughtfully. 'You thought there might be danger in their saying less?'

'I thought the army might conclude that you'd been involved,' I said. 'Unless they made it clear that you came at my request.'

'I almost wish I hadn't. A horrible affair.' He shook his head. 'Appius Corvinus was no friend of mine, but I'm more shocked than I can say.'

'One would not wish a death like that on one's worst enemy!'

He snorted. 'Worst enemy? That's exactly what he was. A threat to me, alive, and possibly a greater one now that he is dead.' He sighed. 'But, all in all, you were right to come and alert me to his death. And the manner of it. Lying here in that humiliating way, deliberately murdered and disguised!' He laid a friendly hand upon my arm. 'And I suppose, too, that you're probably correct in saying that I should tell the fort myself.'

'I'm sure that is your best defence. A man who sets out to disguise his victims in that way does not then report them to the authorities.'

'You think? It might be argued that it was a clever move.'

It was not wise to disagree with Marcus, but he'd asked for my opinion. And that hand was still upon my arm. 'Excellence, someone took considerable pains to make this look like two peasants dead of plague, or some other natural cause, so that the bodies would be picked up by the cart and disappear for ever in the pit. That person would certainly not, willingly, then go and tell the fort that Appius had been murdered – and where to find the corpse.'

He gave me a doubtful look. 'I sincerely hope you're right. You argue skilfully. Indeed, you make me think it would be wise for you to speak to the commandant first, despite the fact that you're not dressed for it. You can put the case on my behalf. Right, here's the gig. Slave, come and help us mount.'

And a moment later, we were on our way.

FIFTEEN

Speak to the commander first! By the time we reached Glevum I was quaking at the knees. Perhaps you'd feel the same, if you'd ever seen the fort. Vast quantities of stone and men – all armed and armoured – a formidable tower, and a general feeling of impregnable power. I'd been before: it terrified me then and the prospect terrified me now.

More so, when I found I was to walk there on my own. No sooner were we through the entrance arch than Marcus hailed a public carrying-chair. It wasn't difficult. There were throngs of litter-boys loitering about, desperate for business in these difficult times. Perhaps he expected me to call one too. But although they crowded round me offering unthinkably cheap prices, I had no money and – like Callidus – was compelled to follow the litter on my own two feet.

I could not match the bearers' pace, though the young page did so easily enough. I hurried after them as quickly as I could, fretting about the coming encounter all the way. I had not expected to be the chief informant about this, nor to be left ignominiously behind.

I tried to calm myself. After all, the place was less than half of what it was. After the previous legion was removed for its part in the Succession Wars, the garrison had never been brought up to total strength again. Severus had decimated so many rebel legions he did not have troops to spare. The fort perimeter has been reduced, and some of the area taken over by civilian enterprise. But it is still imposing. The walls are just as thick, and the army presence just as menacing. The new force may be smaller, but it is mobile, battle-hardened and highly suspicious of the local populace. And the legate commanding is very much Septimius's man.

Unhappily, I'd met him when he first arrived. Brought him on a fruitless hunt for rebels in a cave. Catching them would have earned him favour, but there were no rebels there. He was irritated with me, then, he made that very clear, and he's notoriously unforgiving to those who anger him!

So, what would happen if I turned up at the gate alone – in inappropriate dress – and had to ask the sentry for an audience? And – if granted – what reception would I get? Would the legate credit anything I said? But Marcus had decreed that I – not he – should tell the tale. And what Marcus ordered, Marcus generally got. There was nothing for it. I hurried to the fort.

I was not far behind His Excellence, to my surprise. Perhaps because there had been so few handcarts and people on the street – everyone doubtless still wary of the plague. So, by the time the litter-boys had stopped, Callidus was there ready to help his master down, and as Marcus paid the fare and approached the sentry at the entrance to the fort, I was able to come panting up myself.

The stout soldier on duty (being one of the new contingent and not a man I'd seen before) might not know Marcus, but he recognised the patrician toga stripe. The wearer is always a man of consequence. An escort soldier was obviously required.

'You!' He pointed with his spear at an olive-skinned young man, who was eating something from a bowl outside his barrack hut. 'Here! These two to see the commander instantly.' (He meant myself and Marcus: the army doesn't count an escort slave.)

The strapping young soldier came hurrying across, jamming on his helmet (which was a touch too large) to lead us proudly past the barrack area, and through the inner arch to the tower building where the commander's office was.

I recognised the downstairs room where I had been before, and where I expected to be forced to wait again – sitting on a bench, for what could be an hour, while military officials bustled in and out, organising rosters and bringing in reports.

But not today, at least for Marcus and myself. We were ushered up the stairs at once, though Callidus was left to kick his heels in idleness. Apart from an incurious military orderly of some kind, chalking up a list of names (presumably for a punishment fatigue, since it was headed LATRINAE) there was no one else in evidence.

We followed our escort up the stone steps to the commander's room. The soldier obligingly knocked the door and opened it a crack.

A sharp voice of authority barked out, 'Who interrupts me? Identify yourself.'

The soldier stepped inside and gave a smart salute, holding his upraised arm so stiffly straight it might have been a plank, and launched into the lengthy rigmarole of greeting, name and rank, and password of the day. Only then was he permitted to blurt out, 'Ave Caesar! Your pardon, Domine. Two citizens to see you, one of them the senior magistrate.'

'Very well. Admit them and dismiss.' The young *munifex* stood by to let us pass, gave another impeccable salute, and was about to leave when the legate added, 'On reflection, you may wait downstairs to escort them out again.'

'As you direct, Commander.' The young man closed the door. We could hear his sandals clattering on the stairs and we were alone in the presence of the commandant. My heart was thumping like a military drum.

The legate had been sitting at his desk – a large, high one, placed to face the entranceway – but he rose to meet us courteously enough. 'Marcus Aurelius Septimus? To what do we owe the privilege?'

His voice, though seemingly polite, had an edge of steel. He was tallish man with flinty eyes, a very Roman nose, and severely barbered hair which was beginning to go grey. The breastplate of his uniform was kept so burnished – by some unhappy slave, no doubt – that it reflected light from the numerous lamps and tapers set around the room. The very picture of a man accustomed to authority and to being instantly obeyed.

Marcus looked around for somewhere he could sit. There was nowhere obvious. The room was built of stone; unwelcoming and stark. (A contrast to the days of the last occupant, whose huge collection of battle trophies was the talk of every visitor.) It seemed now to be bare of everything except that heavy desk, a comfortable stool for the commandant himself (with arms and padded seat) the customary shrine and a rack of official-looking scrolls in canisters. And burning lamps and tapers on every surface and in every niche.

The legate indicated something propped up against the wall – a much less comfortable folding stool for visitors. He did not offer to unfold it for His Excellence, so I stepped forward and arranged the thing myself. Marcus settled himself on it, with a gracious wave, leaving me to stand awkwardly behind.

The commandant sat down on his own stool, facing us. 'It is good to see you, Excellence. It has been too long.' There was still no hint of warmth. And even less when he turned the stone-blue flints on me. 'I have seen you somewhere, once before, I think?'

I felt myself turn red. I was about to stammer something, but Marcus intervened. 'Of course,' he said, in his most silky voice. 'This is the Citizen Junio, a skilled mosaicist. You have indeed encountered him. A case of child abduction. You were kind enough to offer help, but the child was rescued before your troops arrived.'

That was one way of putting it – omitting the uncomfortable matter of the Celts – but I held my tongue.

I suspect that the commandant remembered anyway. His manner was as stony as the walls. 'And to what do we owe the honour of his presence here today? I did not realise we were seeking new mosaics here?'

It was a reproof about my state of dress, and scarcely veiled. My own fault, I thought miserably. I should have worn that toga after all!

I squirmed again, but Marcus went serenely on. 'Of course not, Legate. He isn't dressed for working here. He was on his way to offer his services to Appius Limpnus Corvinus when he encountered an emergency, and came to me to ask for my advice. Which was to report to you immediately.'

'Appius Limpnus?' The legate looked at me with curiosity. Marcus said smoothly. 'I believe you know the man?'

An unnecessary question, since of course he did. Appius reported to the governor through the fort. Marcus did not wait for the commander's nod.

'So you will have heard his plans to have a pubic shrine installed outside his property, with a decorative mosaic as a part of it? Junio was hoping to obtain the commission. He had worked for Appius before – entirely to his satisfaction, I believe. And he has a letter of commendation too, from another councillor.'

The commander did not even glance at me, but continued to talk to Marcus as if I were not there. 'A commendation? So shouldn't he be there presenting it?'

'Unfortunately, Legate, that will not be possible. But best, perhaps, if he explains that for himself?'

'I am all attention.' The commandant leaned back with folded arms, pursed his lips and glared at me.

There was no escape. I stammered out my tale – how I had seen the bodies dressed in peasant clothes, then recognised the miller and realised that the other corpse was Appius.

The legate frowned. 'But that's impossible! He was here, in this office, only yesterday. Proposing a civil banquet for the curia, around the Kalends of next moon, to commemorate the ending of the plague – and asking if I wanted to attend myself.'

'Then, Commandant, you may have been among the last to see the man alive. My guess is that he was killed last evening, from the condition of the corpse . . .'

'You seem remarkably well-informed about such matters! For a man who makes pavements.'

'I learned from my father . . .' I began.

But he interrupted me. He leaned forwards, suspicious suddenly. 'You found the bodies on the military road, you say? What were you doing there? From my recollection, that would hardly be your chosen route to town. You live beside the ancient forest track. Surely that would be the quickest way? Unless you have recently acquired a conveyance of some kind?'

That was intelligent and I was not prepared for it. 'I was in His Excellence's cart.' The very thing Marcus had not wished to advertise! I thought quickly. 'He'd sent some produce to the

SIXTEEN

This was proving even harder than I feared. I took a deep breath. 'Your pardon, Legate, but if I'd come alone, I might have found it hard to gain an audience.' I had an inspiration. 'At best, I would have had to wait for quite some time, during which the death-cart might have picked up the corpse. But with His Excellence, naturally, that was not the case.'

'I see – and you felt that speed was necessary?'

'Essential, Commandant!' I said. 'If it was Appius. But I wanted to be sure. His Excellence had seen him much more recently than I, so I persuaded him that he should come and see if he agreed it was the . . .' I was about to say 'delator' but managed to amend it to, '. . . the man I thought it was. It seemed so improbable – as you felt yourself.'

The legate turned his flinty gaze to Marcus now. But it seemed he'd been convinced. The manner was more cordial than before. 'And you are persuaded that it was?'

'I fear so, Legate, though it was hard to tell at first. A lot of flesh is missing from the face, and the seal-ring finger has been brutally removed. I doubt I would have guessed who it was if Junio had not suggested it. But then I saw an identifying mark, and now I'm sure of it.'

'But what is a man of Corvinus's high rank doing out there, dressed like that, and with a common miller, of all things?'

'Commander, I have no idea at all. It has to be deliberate, of course. My guess is that whoever put him there had killed them both and left them by the road, hoping they would be taken for victims of the plague, picked up by your death-cart and slung into the pit. If they were not eaten first by bears or wolves.' Marcus produced this argument as though he'd thought of it.

The commander had turned suddenly quite pale. 'Dear Mars! That would be an embarrassment for the garrison! The provincial governor . . .' He tailed off in horror at his thoughts.

market on a cart. The driver passed my door as I was setting out, and offered to drive me to the gates of town.'

Strictly true, and if anyone had seen us, there was nothing to deny. I felt, rather than saw, Marcus stiffen at my words, but it was the best that I could do.

The legate rubbed his newly barbered chin. 'A lucky chance for you!'

He did not believe me, I could see. I tried another tack. 'I confess I saw him coming and timed the exit from my gate to coincide. I called to him, in fact, and asked where he was going. I did not think His Excellence was likely to object.'

'Especially since he did not know!' He was sarcastic now but clearly satisfied – perhaps because this didn't show me in a favourable light. 'And on the way you made the driver stop because you saw the corpse of Appius? Or thought you did?'

Another rebuke. Giving contrary orders to someone else's slave! I tried to ignore it. 'Exactly, Commandant. At least, I saw the miller's corpse, and knew it was my civic duty to report. When we came closer, we saw Appius as well – on examination I was certain it was him. So I went back to Marcus . . .'

'Since you were in his cart, which he had ordered into town?'

'Since the cart-driver was shaken to his sandal-soles and terrified. He was anxious to return. We'd made his errand much more difficult by using the sacking which kept the load in place to cover Appius more decently. Besides, his master was the nearest person in authority . . .' I was quite proud of this, but I saw Marcus shake his head. Measured in distance it was marginally true, but given the condition of the respective roads, it would have taken less time to come into the town.

'Obviously my errand here was fruitless now,' I added hastily. 'His Excellence decided that the fort should be informed, and offered to accompany me in his fastest gig to ensure the news reached you as soon as possible.'

'You didn't think it better to come directly here – and permit the slave to sell his produce, as his master wished?'

'If it was discovered!' Marcus was at his smoothest once again. 'Though that's unlikely, if he went into the pit. The townspeople would simply think he'd disappeared on some official business. Though the governor might ask questions in the end.'

The legate drew a hand across his sculptured brow. 'You cannot imagine, Excellence! I have to thank you for alerting me. The problem is, what is it best to do?'

'Well, prevent the cart from bringing in the corpse, and arrange for him to have a proper funeral. That is the first thing, clearly. And we have left a guard – a family in a cart. They've been told to stop collection, on my authority, until some more appropriate arrangements can be made.'

The commandant nodded. 'Commendable forethought on your part, Excellence.' He stood up and strode briskly to the door. 'Escort! Where are you?'

The olive-skinned munifex came pounding up the stairs. 'You called, Commander?' He was panting but he stood to a salute.

'I have a mission for you. Mounted party to ride out on to the south road and relieve a group of peasants guarding corpses there, then wait for further orders. On no account are they to let the death-cart near.'

'The family were offered payment for their services,' I put in daringly.

Marcus shot me a furious look. 'Ah, the purse. I had forgotten that.' He turned to the legate. 'Could you have your party take a message to the family on guard, that – when I have finished here – I'll meet them at the Southern gate and ensure that they are paid?'

'See to it, soldier.'

'At once. Hail Caesar!' And he was gone again.

'That should avoid unfortunate disposal in the pit. A good thought, Excellence. What arrangements do you think that we should make? I'd be glad of your advice.'

Marcus accepted this as no more than his due, but he did turn to me. 'Citizen, you found him. Do you have views on this?'

'Well, I had been thinking, Excellence,' I said, addressing him and not the commandant, 'that . . . perhaps enquiries should be made at his household as to when he left and when they saw him last. And where he was going, if possible. They'll have to be informed about his death, in any case, since presumably that's where the corpse will be returned. It should be washed and dressed in proper clothes and generally prepared to have a fitting funeral. I don't know if a man like him would be a member of a guild?'

Marcus evaded this. 'The colonia should see to it, in any case. I'll ensure that the curia is informed. Only the best for a man with his connections and patrician rank. Paid mourners, dancers, instruments – and a handsome funeral feast.'

The commander nodded. 'A civic funeral. That is appropriate. He was not a military man, but I shall attend the rites, so we'll be represented. I could provide a trumpeter, in fact. And I'll have the body brought to town with dignity. So that takes care of that. But these enquiries you speak of, citizen?'

'If we can discover where he was last night, and who was with him,' I replied, 'we might work out who killed him. It's clear that someone did.'

'The man had enemies, no doubt.' The legate scowled and looked at Marcus doubtfully. 'You might know about that, Excellence?'

'I know that there were people who did not care for him.' Marcus was as silky as before. He shot me a look. 'But as to what company he kept, I could not say. I knew him, of course, but I avoided him as much as possible. There were rumours, you know, that he might have been a spy.' (The legate had the grace to look abashed.) 'But, as Junio says, the first thing must be to alert his slaves and tell them that arrangements will be made.'

'And the miller's wife,' I ventured. 'She will want to see her husband has appropriate rites. For which purpose, she may require his purse. Though perhaps the commandant should see it first.'

The commander looked at Marcus. 'Ah, the famous purse. Is it significant?'

Marcus produced it. 'It was found on the miller,' he explained. 'Quite a lot of money for a man like that. The corpse of Appius had no purse at all.'

The legate barely glanced at it. Instead, he made a face. 'So someone robbed Appius? Sufficient motive for the killing, do you think?'

I could not help myself. 'I don't think that's the question, Commandant. These men were wearing someone else's clothes. The question is – surely – not why Appius had no purse, but why the killer chose to give the miller one, and leave this money on the highway to be found. Especially one with a distinctive patch, like this, where someone has clearly mended it.'

He looked at it, and then at me appraisingly. 'You think it wasn't his?'

I shrugged. 'Nothing else that he was wearing was his own. I suggest we ask his wife, since she'll have to be informed in any case. If she doesn't recognise it, we'll know that we are looking for the owner of the thing.'

He looked at me shrewdly. 'And if she does – or claims she does? What trader's wife would not claim it, with the opportunity of a sum like that?'

I had not thought of that, although I should have done.

But Marcus had the answer. 'It should be hers, in any case, according to the law,' he said, suddenly adopting a magisterial tone. 'It was discovered on her husband when he died, so presumptively it's part of his estate, unless we have a counterclaim. And that I rather doubt. If it isn't his, presumably it was his murderer's, who will hardly wish to draw attention to his ownership.'

I had tired of all the talking and I wished to act. I risked a suggestion. 'I could take it to the widow if you wish and ask her if she recognises it – before I mention where it was, or how I came by it. That should extract the truth.'

'Before revealing that her husband's dead?' The legate looked appalled.

'I'll tell her afterwards, explaining that her husband has been killed and that – if it's not his – the purse might help to solve the death. It does suggest that whoever dumped the corpses by the road was rich enough not to worry about a few denarii.'

Marcus and the commandant exchanged a startled glance. 'Spoken like a tradesman,' His Excellence remarked. 'But you are right of course. We must be looking for somebody of means.'

The legate nodded. 'Take the purse and do as you suggest.' He handed it to me.

It was a dismissal and I had reached the door before a thought occurred to me. I turned to them again. 'Should I mention that he was found with Appius?' Silence, while they exchanged that look again. 'It might be helpful in establishing a link?'

The legate demanded, 'You think there was one?'

'A business one, perhaps? Appius has his own estate, of course, but it is mainly given over to his vines. He may buy flour sometimes or, if he grows a little grain himself, sell it to the miller, or arrange to have it ground. Craithaw's wife would know. It might explain why the two men were together when they died.'

The legate said, 'We don't know that for sure.'

'Use your judgement when you get there, citizen.' Marcus sounded weary, suddenly. 'But say as little as you reasonably can.'

'Is that wise? Gossip spreads in Glevum like a fire in hay.' The commander scowled.

'Exactly. And Appius's household must be expecting him, and may already be asking round the town. The miller's absence will be noted if he isn't at his post. All this won't be secret for very long. Better, surely, that the widow hears the news from us and doesn't suppose we were hiding it from her.'

The legate considered for a moment, then nodded brusquely. 'Very well, citizen, I suppose I must concur. But pay Appius the courtesy of telling his household first.'

'Me?'

'That would be the most convenient. His Excellence and I have other matters to attend to urgently – in connection with the rites. His household should be alerted as soon as possible. And you volunteered yourself as messenger.' The commandant had taken charge again. He turned to Marcus, who was looking quite surprised. 'More discreet than sending soldiers, don't you think? And from what you tell me, this tradesman was expected there today, about this mosaic. Isn't that correct?'

I bleated something about no official appointment being made, but the legate cut me off.

'You can make quite sure there's not been some mistake, and it isn't Appius's body after all. You'll soon find out if he did not come home last night. And if you've made an error – which is not unknown – you can come straight back and let us know at once. Perhaps you could send a message, either way, in fact, before you go to ask about the purse.'

He had not forgotten that confounded cave! I sighed. It must be well past noon, and I had earned myself a very lengthy task. 'His townhouse, or his villa?' It was miles to Appius's country house. Thank goodness I'd asked Tenuis to bring the mule to town! I might have to spend the night at the workshop, even so.

'Oh, townhouse first, I think,' the commandant replied. 'It's where you were to meet him, after all.'

This time I did depart, clattering down the stone stairs noisily enough for the orderly – who was still chalking names up on his list – to turn and stare at me. 'In a hurry, townsman? Can you find your way?'

No escort for a humble citizen like me, but Callidus was already on his feet. 'Citizen, I will see you to the gate.'

It surprised me. He was attending Marcus, not myself, and I was ready to decline but something in his urgent look dissuaded me. 'Thank you,' I said, and we went back together towards the sentry gate.

When we were out of earshot the slave-boy turned to me. 'Don't stop walking, citizen, in case we are observed, but there's something you should know. One of those corpses was Appius, I heard you say as much. Did you know he came here yesterday?'

'I did. The legate told us,' I murmured. 'Something about a civic banquet that's proposed, which he was invited to attend.'

'Exactly. They were gossiping about it in the waiting-room while I was there. Some excitement about who might form the guard, though the feast won't happen now that Appius is dead.'

'Dead?' I was so surprised I almost halted in my tracks. 'How did they know that? We only just told the legate.'

He gave me a wry grin. '*Parietes habent aures* – walls have ears – they say. Or rather, soldiers have been known to creep upstairs and listen at door-cracks when they've been told to wait downstairs.'

'That young munifex? The orderly did not intervene?'

'Encouraged it, if anything. I'd asked for the latrine. I saw the two exchange a glance, and the orderly decided he'd accompany me.'

'You? A slave?'

'I know! Unheard of! He did it to ensure I wasn't back too soon, and so catch the soldier in the act. I very nearly did. When we returned, he was tiptoeing downstairs, though he tried to pretend he was fastening his sandal-straps. But he'd been listening. They were muttering about it afterwards – I was not supposed to hear. Fortunately, my ears – like his – are very sharp. He was saying there'd be disappointment in the ranks at having lost the chance of being escorts at the feast – extra pay and maybe some leftovers as well. Unless the other man decides to hold one anyway.'

I did stop. 'Other man? Appius didn't come alone? The legate did not mention that to us.'

'Very likely he was not aware of it. Appius came here with some councillor. At the gate they asked to see the commandant, saying they wished to invite him to a feast. But, while someone was being summoned to escort them in, they had a bitter argument. I don't know what about, but apparently this other man stormed off and Appius went to see the commandant alone. I thought you ought to know.'

'Well done,' I said. We'd almost reached the sentry gate by now. 'But you'd best be getting back. You'll be wanted soon. Tell your master what you've just told me, but wait until you're well outside the fort. I'll try to discover who this other person was. The sentry on duty may have heard the name. Meantime, tell that young munifex – from me – if he wants to keep his ears, not to put them where they shouldn't be. If discovered, he'd be dishonourably discharged, and with nothing to keep his helmet up.'

Callidus grinned, though I knew he'd say nothing of the kind. He trotted back and I approached the gate.

SEVENTEEN

The stout sentry was not anxious to oblige. But I'd come in with Marcus – despite my workman's clothes – so he could not ignore me, or march me physically away. His reply was grumbling. 'More than my job's worth to tell you anything. That Appius has influential friends. Besides, if there was a quarrel, what business is that of yours?' His weather-beaten face had turned indignant pink.

'Appius is dead,' I told him.

'Dead?' He was scornful. 'Don't be ridiculous. He had connections in high places, as I said. If he so much as stubbed his toe, word would reach the garrison at once.'

'It's true, I assure you. It hasn't yet been officially announced but it soon will be – though, till then, I hope you'll be discreet.' (It hardly mattered – that munifex had heard and the news was doubtless spreading though the barracks as I spoke.) 'He didn't die at home. I'm on my way to tell his household now. We brought the news – that is why we came – and the legate has just dispatched a mounted party to go and guard the corpse. You may have seen them leave.'

He was persuaded. 'Appius? But only yesterday . . .'

'Exactly,' I said sharply. 'That's why I need to find out who he quarrelled with. I'm instructed to find out what I can. By your commander.' It was almost true.

'That puts a different polish on the shield.' It had certainly made a difference to him. He was suddenly confiding. 'It happens that I was on duty yesterday. Appius came here with a councillor. A proper purple-striper. If I heard the name, I don't recall – we're fairly new here and I don't know all the magistrates.'

'Could you describe him?'

He thought for a moment. 'Middle years, and stoutish is all I that I can say. Shorter than Appius, with thinning tawny hair.

Nice-looking fellow, but grumpy yesterday. He was looking doubtful when they first arrived, and while waiting for an escort to see the commandant, he abruptly changed his mind. Said he didn't like this and needed time to think. Appius lost patience. Started ranting and said he'd go in alone. The other man stomped off with Appius still calling imprecations after him.'

'You didn't catch these imprecations, I suppose?'

A grin. 'He was shouting so you'd think he meant me to.' He was relaxed now and leaning on his spear. 'I can't quote you word for word but it was on the lines of, "Don't think you can wriggle out of it. The agreement is binding under law, including how much you will be paid." Something like that. His final words, though, I won't forget: "And don't think of trying to cry off the meal tonight. This is going to happen, with you or without – and if you try to thwart me I'll make you rue the day. As you know I can." Really vicious, and so loud you'd think he meant the world to overhear.'

Perhaps he did. Letting Glevum know the man was in his power. 'To humiliate the councillor, no doubt. I wonder who he was.' Middle-aged and balding. That fitted half the members of the curia. But it was a start. And someone who clearly had a grudge. 'Did you see which way he went?' That might tell me something.

He pushed his heavy helmet back and scratched his grizzled head. 'Made off in the direction of the gate. Looking for a litter, I expect.'

Obvious. I should have thought of that. 'As Appius later did?'

He shook his head so fiercely that the cheek-guards slapped. 'On the contrary. He came out with an escort, who said he was taking him to the *mansio*.'

'The military inn? What was he doing there? Not looking for a room. Appius has a country house as well as one in town.'

A shrug. 'I couldn't tell you, citizen. Visiting, perhaps? We do have someone staying there, I hear, though we've not had many clients since the plague. Only the occasional official courier, who didn't have a choice. Not when there's a mansio every twenty miles or so.'

'I can see that people might avoid it. Your guest must have specific business in the town.'

He forestalled my question. 'I imagine that he does, since he's been here several days. And before you ask, I know nothing about him beyond the fact that he is interested in bees.'

'Bees?' I echoed. Was this the equivalent of Appius's claim that he had come to Glevum to plant vines? Another secret spy? I would need to tread with care, but all the same I asked, 'Could I contrive to visit him myself?'

'Nothing to stop you, townsman, as far as I'm aware. Though whether he'll consent to see you is another thing. I'd tell the man on duty that you've official business there, and that the legate sent you. That should let you in. But I mustn't stand here gossiping.' He nodded in the direction of the fort. 'There's someone coming. You'd best be moving on.' He straightened up into a military pose.

I thanked him and walked swiftly down the street towards the mansio without explaining I was not the owner of the purse which he'd been eyeing hopefully. (Even a soldier is entitled to a tip, but I hadn't one to give.) Round the corner was the entrance to the inn. Through the arch I could see the stable courtyard. Eerily empty, apart from a couple of horses in the corner stall, presumably for exchange to Imperial couriers. Only a bored man on duty at the gate.

When the fort was at full strength, this had been a thriving place. Of course, to stay here, even for a night, demanded rank and preferably an official travel warrant, signed and sealed. It was awkward for a man in tradesman's clothes to request admittance.

But I did so, heeding the sentry's advice. That got me through to the heavy entrance door beyond. There did not seem to be a doorkeeper and there was nothing for it but to knock.

The *mansionarius* himself came bustling out, but his smile faded when he saw me. He looked me up and down. 'What do you want? Since clearly you have no valid travel documents?'

I explained why I was there.

'Official business? I will send to Gaius Valerius and see if he agrees. In the meantime, you can wait out here.' And he shut the door.

I expected to be left to wait for hours, and was beginning to regret that I had come at all, but it was only a few moments before he reappeared. 'It appears that I was wrong.' His tone did not suggest apology. 'Evidently he is expecting you. I am to show you in. If you would follow me.' He led the way along the corridor.

How could this Valerius be expecting me? My heart was beating fast, but there was no retreating now. 'Thank you,' I said, and hurried after him.

It was not as I expected. Evidently, as the garrison had shrunk, the accompanying inn had done so too. On the right, some of what had clearly once been rooms for guests were now reserved for stores. There was still accommodation on the left (presumably including the 'Emperor's room', which every inn must keep in case the Imperial purple decided to call).

At the end of the passageway the mansionarius pushed open the last door, revealing a large dining area. There were several tables and a feeble fire, but there was only one man to be seen – toga-clad, so clearly a Roman citizen. He was seated with his back to us, on a bench at a trestle by the fire – a balding man with a fringe of silver hair, scooping something from a bowl with a large chunk of bread.

'Late lunch,' my escort murmured unnecessarily. 'He hasn't heard us come.' He raised his voice. 'Citizen Valerius? Your visitor is here.' And with that he backed away and closed the door again.

The diner turned his head and got slowly to his feet. He had a gap-toothed smile, which faded to a frown as he realised that I wasn't the expected visitor.

'Gaius Valerius?' I gave an awkward bow. 'I am sorry to interrupt your *prandium* . . .' I tailed off in surprise. I had seen the wisps of silver hair and guessed that he was slightly deaf, but I had not expected anyone so old. His face was not haggard – clearly he'd not suffered from any lack of food! – but it was white and wrinkled, and his pale eyes were overhung by eyebrows that looked like icicles. Only his hooked nose was rather pink. But his most striking feature was his chin, or lack of it. It made him look feeble, though his greeting suggested otherwise.

'And who might you be?' His voice was high and not exactly strong, but it still offered a purposeful rebuke.

'Junio, a humble citizen and tradesman,' I replied. I made a daring guess. 'You were expecting Appius Limpnus Corvinus?'

A nod. 'I was. Or possibly his slave. But you are clearly neither. Have you come on his behalf?'

'I'm not here to represent him, but I do bring news of him. Not good news, if you are a friend.'

'Hardly that.' Valerius was curt. 'I only met him a day or two ago. I have agreed a settlement with him, that's all.'

'Yet you were expecting him today? Though your business was concluded?'

'Not exactly that. He suggested terms, which I accepted yesterday. Informally, of course. When I heard there was a visitor, I imagined he was bringing a document to sign, or was arranging witnesses to seal a verbal deal. I should have known it wouldn't be as easy as it seemed. I was warned that he is very difficult. But I hadn't found him so – until he didn't come last night as he'd arranged. At first, I thought he'd simply been delayed. But I'm beginning to wonder if he has reneged.'

'Whatever the contract was to be, it is invalid now,' I told him. 'Appius is dead. Murdered, almost certainly. No fatal wounds, so poison, I suspect. I came to tell you, as you may have been one of the last people to talk to him alive.'

Valerius sank heavily onto his bench again. 'Great Mars! And his estate will pass directly to the Emperor. He told me that it would – and there'll be no appealing that. A total waste of time to come and risk my health. I'll tell Honoria so. She was the one who insisted I should come. She can rant all she chooses.'

It was a strange response. I'd meant to hint that I suspected him of some involvement in the death, but he seemed oblivious to that. 'Honoria?' I echoed.

He looked at me and heaved a heavy sigh. 'My wife. Let me advise you, citizen, if you choose to wed, never permit yourself to be ensnared by youthful curves and dimpled smiles. You may find yourself dancing to the lady's lyre. In ways that you might not choose yourself.'

I thought of my Cilla and could not restrain a smile. He noticed. So, lest he think that I was mocking him, I murmured, 'I have a wife myself, and she is forceful too – though I'm very fond of her, and she of me, I think.'

His old eyes were searching. 'You have a family? An heir?'

'Four fine children,' I replied. 'Two of whom are sons.'

Somehow that seemed to form a bond. He gestured me to join him on the bench. 'I do not have that consolation,' he muttered mournfully. 'I had high hopes, but it was just a girl. The birth was difficult, and the babe did not survive. There have been no others since. Honoria was ill, and we ceased to try. I've thought of a divorce, but I'm too old for all of that. Besides, I do not wish to lose the dowry that she brought.' He waved at the table. 'I was lunching, as you see. I would not recommend it: horrible coarse army bread, tough meat and disappointing cheese. But you are welcome to join me if you choose.'

I muttered that I hadn't eaten anything since dawn and would be glad to do so, but I was on an errand for the commandant. 'Making enquiries about Appius,' I said.

'Of course, you wished to speak to me. But you can do that as you dine!' The smile appeared again. 'Help yourself, there's plenty. The nuts and apples seem all right, and I believe there is some sort of army gruel available. I could summon some of that, if you prefer. I'll have them bring a bowl and drinking cup for you. The wine is fairly decent, if you water it enough.' He clapped his hands sharply and an aged slave appeared. 'Another cup and plate and spoon for my companion here. Be quick about it too.'

The fellow bowed and tottered off to do as he was told. Though 'quick' did not describe it.

'Not a mansio orderly?' I said with some surprise. 'Don't they detail somebody to wait on you? He is clearly not of military age.'

'I've shooed them all away – far too eager to interrupt if

one intends to work. This is my personal attendant. Honoria insisted he should accompany me. Too dangerous to travel on the roads alone these days, she said. Though Jove alone knows what use he'd be if we encountered trouble!' The old slave had returned by now carefully balancing the items that he'd brought. But Valerius continued blithely, 'I call him Lentus, because he is so slow.' He gave a bray of laughter. 'Fortunately the carriage-driver that I hired is young and strong. Now, you wished to talk to me?' He selected an apple and took a bite of it.

I waited till Lentus had retired before I spoke again. There were a hundred questions, but I chose a simple one. 'You hired a carriage? You have travelled a long way?' As I spoke I helped myself to food.

'From Eboracum.' He took a sip of wine. 'It's only chance that I am here at all. We went to dine with friends one night and met a man from Glevum. He had escaped the plague by fleeing to our host, a distant kinsman. When Honoria heard about the pestilence, she enquired for the health of a distant relative of mine, and learned that he and his whole household had succumbed. Name of Fortunatus. You may have heard of him?'

I swallowed my mouthful of soft cheese (which, like the meat, seemed more than satisfactory. No doubt Valerius was used to finer fare). 'Indeed! He owned the house that Appius acquired.' I put two and two together on my mental abacus. 'Your wife had hopes that you might profit from the will? Since all Fortunatus's other known relatives were dead?'

He gave me a wry smile. 'You judge her perfectly. It was not a close connection – my father died when I was very young, and another man took my mother for his wife, and then adopted me. It happened that he was a remote cousin of Fortunatus's. Only by marriage, even then, but you know how these things work.'

'So in the absence of any closer living heir, there might have been a claim?'

'But I came much too late. By the time I got here, not only had the will been read in the forum as the law demands, but the assets were already distributed and sold. It must have been dealt with very fast indeed, especially considering there was plague about.'

'It all defaulted to the Emperor,' I said. 'Which would account for the speed. And Appius Limpnus Corvinus had contacts with the Imperial Courts. I believe he acquired it at a favourable price.'

He nodded. 'So I understand. But it was not the property Honoria coveted. Though we could have sold it on for considerably more than Appius paid for it.' He gave me a sharp look. 'Honoria has a penchant for expensive jewels.'

'So did the wife of Fortunatus,' I said. 'She was renowned for it. Perhaps . . .'

That barking laugh again. 'Those will be in the empress's coffers by this time, no doubt! There is no hope of those. Indeed, when I discovered what had happened, I had little hope of anything. But, all the same, I called on Appius . . .'

I paused in the act of mopping up my cheese using the last remaining hunk of bread (despite his complaints, he'd eaten all the rest!). 'But I thought that Appius had called on you!' I realised it was imbecilic, even as I spoke.

'But, of course, I visited him first, otherwise he would scarcely have known I was here.'

Knowing Appius's profession, I rather doubted that. But all I said was, 'What did you hope to gain? The moment that you made enquiries, you must have learned that Fortunatus had named the Emperor as default.' Most wealthy Romans do so – hoping that it will reach Imperial ears – though obviously they don't intend it to apply. There's usually some family, somewhere, who would have a claim.

'I did not hope for much. Appius had acquired the house – I'd discovered that, or I could not have called on him. But there was a small dyeing business with it, I believe – and Appius has no interest in that beyond the rent. I wondered if he might consent to some sort of arrangement over it, especially if I threatened to contest our claim in court.'

'What did he say? I don't imagine Appius would easily be cowed.'

'So my informant warned me. But I tried it all the same. And to my surprise he offered settlement. A lump sum – not a large one – paid in silver now, in return for which I would withdraw the claim. Honoria will no doubt tell me it is nothing like enough, but it would buy some pretty trinkets and I felt it more than fair. If we'd gone to court we would certainly have lost – Appius apparently has influential friends, though I didn't know that at the time. But I wouldn't have pursued it, probably. It would have cost too much to ensure he came to court – and to find ourselves an advocate who wouldn't cause the case to fail by making some technical mistake. I would have gained nothing. Which, as it happens, is exactly where we stand.'

'Except that you may be the last man to see Appius alive.'

This time he saw the implication. 'You can't imagine I had anything to do with killing him? He was alive and well when he left here yesterday – the mansionarius will vouch for that. And I have not since left the premises. Appius even promised he'd come back to me later and take me out to dine. Said as a visiting patrician, it was no more than my due. I have been waiting ever since for his return.'

'You spoke of working? Didn't that require you to go into the town? Or at least meet the people you were doing business with?'

He shook his head. 'Not that kind of working. Making notes for my treatise about bees. When I've finished, I hope to have it copied once or twice, and send the scrolls to other apiarists. It should make my reputation – though it will cost, of course.'

'So Appius's money was important to you too? Which might make you very angry if he changed his mind. One does not have to be personally present at a poisoning.' (Though it might be difficult, I thought, to change the corpse's dress and leave it by the roadside for the army cart to find.) 'By your own admission, you sent the mansio staff away. Was that because you did not wish for witnesses?'

The faded grey eyes looked at me appalled. 'Because I did not wish to be disturbed! As I said, I have not left the inn since Appius called on me. Oh dear Mars, you think I contrived to give him something poisoned to take home? It's true I sent him a small flask of wine. I bought it in the town after he left. Or Lentus did, on my behalf.'

'And he no doubt delivered it as well.'

The old man was starting to look seriously disturbed. 'Well, naturally. I was hardly likely to take it there myself! Just a friendly token, to thank Appius for the deal.'

Supposing that the spy had meant to honour it, I thought. If such a deal existed anyway. It was unlike Appius to be so generous, and I had only Valerius's word for anything. Meanwhile, he'd the chance of poisoning the wine. And of being unattended in the mansio, even by his slave.

'And when was this?' I asked. (If it proved to be this morning, I could cease my questioning – Appius was already dead by then.)

But Valerius answered, 'Late yesterday. About the time I'd hoped he would return. A compliment and a reminder about his promise to take me out to dine, you might say.' He brightened suddenly. 'If he did go out to dine, I doubt he tasted it. You could ask his household – no doubt they would know.' He gave that gappy smile, a little doubtfully. 'Look, Appius is dead. I understand you're sent to question me. But you can't suppose that I had a hand in this? If anything, I wanted Appius alive. If he kept his bargain – which I had no cause to doubt – Honoria and I had everything to gain. Besides, do I look like a murderer to you?'

'Frankly, you don't.' I pushed away my bowl and got slowly to my feet, feeling I'd abused his hospitality. 'But murderers come in some most unlikely forms, and I'm obliged to follow all lines of enquiry. I'll call on Appius's household and ask about the wine. I was about go there anyway, and I've lingered far too long.' I hoped that I could prove that Appius had not tasted it. 'But, just in case, I need your word that I will find you here if I need to speak to you again.'

'You will.' I'd been apologetic, but his response was brusque. 'I shall have to attend his wretched funeral, no doubt, if it's to be a civic one. Having dealt with him in public recently, it would be discourteous to leave.'

'Not to say suspicious,' I agreed. 'Well, citizen, I will leave you to complete your prandium. Thank you for having agreed to talk to me, for lunch and for your considerable help.' I was about to say that I would see myself out, but he had already clapped his hands and Lentus appeared.

He accompanied me in silence to the entry door. I could not tip him, though he eyed my purse, but I mumbled thanks.

'Nothing the matter with that wine, I promise you,' he said. 'I picked it out myself. And my master is an honourable man.' He turned his back and shuffled off.

I nodded to the guard as I went out through the gate, and found myself on the streets of Glevum once again.

EIGHTEEN

I had only the vaguest notion where Appius's townhouse was, except that it was somewhere on the eastern side of town. That was no problem, though, I thought – I would simply ask people in the street. In a town like Glevum somebody would know.

But I'd reckoned without the aftermath of pestilence. There had been few enough pedestrians when Marcus and I arrived, but now there seemed to be nobody at all. I spent several moments looking up and down, without success, and was considering going back to make enquiries at the fort. Then I spotted the pair of litter-boys who'd carried Marcus earlier. They were loitering round a corner, clearly hoping for another fare when he came back.

But a certain customer is better than a potential one. They straightened up and smiled encouragingly as I approached. 'Take you somewhere, townsman? Very cheap and fast. Safer than walking when there's plague about.'

'You know the house of Fortunatus?'

They exchanged a glance. 'Of course. But you know that he's dead, and someone else has taken on the place?'

'I do.'

'But you still wish us to take you?'

'If I had money I would seize the chance,' I said. 'But despite that purse which you are eyeing, I have nothing to pay you with. This belongs to someone else, and I am simply delivering a message.'

They looked disbelieving. I had to mention that Marcus had commissioned me before I could persuade them to tell me anything.

However, their directions were concise and clear. I set off at a trot. I crossed the forum (a technical offence, since I was a citizen and had neither toga nor attendant slave. But that law's not much enforced except on holy days, and there was no one in authority to see me anyway). Not a councillor in sight. Of course, this morning the curia hadn't met, otherwise Marcus would have attended it. Maybe, since I'd lost track of the official calendar, the day was ill-omened before noon. Either way, the magistrates weren't here. Probably either in the baths or – more likely – safely in their homes, well away from dangerous disease.

The day was not totally nefas, clearly. That would mean no business, but there were some stalls about. A few of the usual tradesmen had set tables up, though they were hardly overrun with customers. A slave was haggling with a skinny man for some of the wilting pile of goosefoot on display; a few sad eels lay barely wriggling in a pail outside the fish-market, which otherwise seemed closed, while half a dozen women were squabbling over what might be exchanged for a pair of scrawny chickens and a basketful of eggs.

No street-vendors with trays of oatcakes or hot pies, no women with pails selling dippersful of milk, no men with braziers offering crispy pork skin or fresh-cooked salted beans. I wondered how the poor survived with no means to cook. But things were better than the farmer had last reported them. The old-clothes stall had ventured back, with just one small trestle table. It was doing a desultory trade, mostly in children's tunics by the look of it.

But it made me think. What had become of the proper clothes of those bodies by the road? No one would dare try selling a toga to the stall – they would have been reported instantly for theft – but Appius's fine undertunics, or Craithaw's working clothes? They must have gone somewhere. And they had value too.

I went across to the grizzled stallholder. 'You haven't been offered adult tunics of quality, I suppose?'

The man bared yellow teeth in a knowing smile. 'If you are hoping to find a bargain upgrade, townsman, you won't find it here. We're not taking any clothes that haven't simply been outgrown. You'd never know who wore them last and whether contagion might be lurking in the folds. We only buy from people who are clearly fit and well, and preferably customers we recognise. We need to eat, but there's no point in risking death.'

'No adult clothes at all?'

'The only things we've taken recently were a couple of slave tunics, which had grown too tight and short. Even then I only took them as a part exchange – we don't have the cash to buy fresh stock outright.'

Slave tunics! I scanned the table, but could see no sign of them. Coarse ochre tunics are occasionally worn by land-slaves with thrifty owners. Those peasant outfits must have come from somewhere! 'What sort of size?' I asked.

The fellow gave that yellow grin again. 'You're too late, townsman. Sold those on within half an hour – and for a decent price. I doubt you would have wanted pink in any case.'

Pink, so no chance they were the ones! 'No peasant outfits, either, I suppose?'

He glowered at me. 'We rarely touch the things. Those that need them wear them into rags, and when that happens they don't buy from us – they weave and make their own. Anyway, I thought you wanted clothes of quality? What makes you ask for those?'

'I have a friend who might be interested,' I said mendaciously. (Though true, in the sense that Marcus would!)

'Well, he'll have to find them somewhere else. I did take some, before the plague, from a wealthy landowner who was moving back to Rome. When we reopened we had a couple left, but they went long ago.'

'I don't suppose you recognised the purchaser?' I was more alert than a sentry in the night. 'You wouldn't know his name? And you didn't happen to sell two pairs of country boots as well?'

The smile had faded. I'd offended him. 'Why all this interest, tradesman? I told you they were gone. I've no idea who bought them – it was half a moon ago, and I believe it was my wife who sold them anyway. A patrician customer, no less. And before you ask, she wouldn't know the name. We don't interrogate our customers. And don't expect to be interrogated by them, as a rule.'

'It doesn't matter,' I said bitterly. If it wasn't yesterday, it wasn't relevant, I thought. 'I wondered if the buyer might be somebody I knew.'

'I hope you're not proposing to go and call on him. Can't have you pestering our customers. Not that it would do you any good. He'd bought some land-slaves from the slave-market, he said, and they're sold naked, so he'll be needing them.' He brightened suddenly. 'Now, did you want a tunic? I've got some children's sizes.'

I shook my head.

He spat disgustedly. 'In that case, if you've finished asking questions, I've got work to do. Deal with people who really want to purchase things.'

I made apologetic gestures as I backed away. 'I didn't mean to press. And as I say, it's not important now.'

The stallholder had not finished his tirade. He shouted after me, 'And if your so-called friend is looking for footwear for his slaves, tell him to get new ones. The sandal-maker's back.'

He was. At least, the older one. Looking still more thin and wizened, but squatting on his accustomed stool against the wall. But he wasn't making sandals. He was hammering new hobnails into the soles of a pair of ancient ones, while the owner loitered – barefoot – patiently nearby. The old man would be glad of that commission for my son, if I only had the means to offer it!

But I didn't, and I resumed my interrupted search for Appius's house. Here was the Street of the Dyers and Weavers, which had seen early victims of the plague. One or two of the premises had opened up again – now the worst was over – but there was still the danger of the smell. I pulled my cloak across my face and hurried on, shaking off the grasp of hopeful tradesmen at their doors, past a fountain and a crossroads, till I found the place I'd been directed to.

It was a handsome house, set back a little distance from the road, though hemmed in by beetling apartments the left and rear. To the right was what must be the 'dyeing business', though it was closed and hidden behind by a high surrounding wall. The house itself had a front wall of its own and a burly gatekeeper who barred my way. But when I announced myself as 'Junio, the mosaic maker. I was told to call about the decorations for a shrine,' he reluctantly admitted me.

'You have had a wasted journey, I'm afraid. The master isn't in. But you can leave a message at the door.'

It was a fine door, too, with a charming open courtyard at the front of it, a little garden with statues and a bower, and a pool with two stone fishes spouting water from their mouths. Appius Limpnus had made a handsome buy – if one didn't mind the stench.

I expected to be greeted by a lowly page, but the servant who appeared was no ordinary slave. He wore a long wine-coloured Grecian robe – rather than a tunic – and a pair of decorated sandals under it. He seemed vaguely familiar – a small, balding man with a worried expression and enormous ears – but it was not until he spoke that I realised who he was.

'Can I assist you, townsman?' An educated, rather high-pitched voice.

Of course! This was Appius's steward whom I'd met before, when I relaid that pavement in his master's country house. A little older, with more wrinkles and a great deal less brown hair, but clearly the same man. Evidently he'd been transferred to town. I could imagine why. He was both literate and numerate, and a first-class organiser too, judging by the speed at which the abandoned villa had been readied for reuse. For a moment, I struggled for his name. But then it came to me.

'Steward Sylvanus?' I murmured with a smile.

The worried frown deepened. 'I don't think I know you? Have you business here?'

'Junio, the mosaic maker. I met you at your master's villa when he first moved in. I was called on . . .'

'The mosiacist, of course!' The wrinkles softened and he looked relieved. 'Doubtless you have come about the shrine? I think my master was expecting somebody. Who had been recommended, I believe?'

'I have a letter with me,' I replied. 'But—'

He cut me off. 'I'm afraid he's been delayed. He went out last night to dine and he has not returned. Too much Falerian wine, perhaps. Or too little water to accompany it. It can't have been the weather which decided him to stay. We watched for him all night, and it was cold but fine.'

I thought of blurting out the news, but recalled my father's methods, and asked some questions first. 'You don't know where he went?'

Sylvanus shook his head. 'He does not confide in me. It must have been someone important or he would not have gone. Someone with a household full of slaves, since he did not take one from here. A covered litter came and bore him off, and that is all I know.'

'No page or bodyguard?' If I'd been Appius in this town I would have been careful to have someone guard my back.

'That was not unusual,' Sylvanus said. 'My master is . . .' he paused, '. . . careful not to advertise his movements, as a whole.' He had no illusions about Appius's trade, and did not love him for it, I could see.

I said daringly, 'A secretive man?' (After all, Appius could not hurt me now.)

He did not quite smile. 'Some might say that, citizen. I prefer to say "discreet". I keep his books and run his household here but know very little of his outside life. He often dines with men of power, and very often here, but when it comes to conversation afterwards, he always chooses to send the slaves away.'

A perfect servant, speaking of his master with respect, but still contriving to convey the truth. But he'd given me a thought. 'So, he was dressed for a banquet?'

The man looked mystified. 'Naturally. My master prides himself on how he looks. He has his togas laundered every month and had two tunics sent recently from Rome to ensure he has the latest fashion in embroidered bands. He had one under his toga, when he went out last night.'

I could imagine that. The first time I'd seen Appius at the villa he was dressed in a way which, at the time, seemed quite effeminate – a long white woollen tunic, with embroidered hems and matching multicoloured woven belt. He'd brought the fashion from the capital and it spread through Glevum quicker than the plague. I've seen even Marcus in something similar. Last night, Appius would have worn a toga, too, arranged to show those ornamental hems.

Which raised again the question which I had not solved. If Appius was dressed to dine, what had happened to all that finery? He must have arrived in it to meet his host, expecting to be fed and wined extensively. And found himself murdered? By the food perhaps? Or had he already sampled Valerius's wine? That was something I would have to ask.

But one thing at a time. 'If I could find out where he went . . .'

Sylvanus shook his head. 'He would not thank you, townsman, for attempting that. You'd anger him by arriving at his host's and trying to discuss the contract for the shrine – especially if he has a headache, as I suspect he does. Better come back tomorrow and have another try. I'll tell him that you called. You're not the first to ask for him today.' He seemed about to bow away and shut the door – he had kept me standing at the entrance – when he stopped suddenly and said, 'Though if you do find where he is, perhaps you'd let me know. We don't know what meals to prepare, or whether he intends to bring a guest, and he is apt to be angry if things aren't exactly right. I would have expected a messenger by now. That's why I came to answer the door to you myself. I'm beginning to wonder if he's been taken ill.'

So, finally, I told him. A detailed account, including the fact that Marcus and I had already reported to the garrison. 'We had to tell them first. To prevent the bodies being flung into the pit as simply peasant victims of the plague.'

He was shocked to his fancy sandals, you could see it in his face. 'Like a pauper? And dressed like one as well. How my master would have hated that!' What might have been amusement flickered in his eyes, but it was gone in an instant and he was all solemnity. 'Then we must thank you, mosaic maker, for bringing us the news. I'll prepare the household to receive his corpse.' He frowned at me in that worried way again. It made his ears look even bigger. 'Should he be laid in state for visiting, you think? Or with those injuries . . .? And considering the plague so recently?'

'The curia is offering a civic funeral,' I said. 'I should ask them for advice. And perhaps you should send a servant to the fort to tell them that you are preparing to receive him here. I'll have done my duty, then.'

'Of course! So, if you'll excuse me, townsman . . .'

I made one final effort. 'You have no idea at all who was his intended host? Could it have been the person who called earlier today?'

He shook his balding head. 'Pavement maker, as you said yourself, my master was a secretive man. And the caller this morning refused to leave a name. Just said he was a magistrate and would return. Typical purple-striper, middle-aged and middle height, with his own litter and a handsome, brown-skinned page. I only glimpsed him as he left – it was the doorkeeper who spoke to him. Said he thought the person might have dined here once or twice.'

'That's true of most of the curia, I believe. There's nothing else that you can tell me that might be of any use?'

Sylvanus thought a moment. 'Clearly wealthy, as you might expect, wearing a fine blue woven fur-trimmed cloak. It was hooded and I didn't see his face. That is all I know.'

'And what about the man that he met yesterday, when he went to the fort?'

'My master did? I was not aware of that.'

'The legate told us. Appius went there with a councillor.' (In the end he'd called alone. But I did not mention that.) 'Could that have been the same man who was here today?'

'I've no idea. Whoever he went with, they did not start from here.' Sylvanus seemed anxious to close the door again.

I put my foot against it. 'Help me, Sylvanus. I'm a citizen, here by order of the fort. Appius was killed and his killer must be caught. I am trying to establish who might have seen him last. That's probably his host. One of the friends who came to dine, perhaps?'

The plea had done the trick. He let go of the door and the look he gave me was an answer in itself. 'Friends? A man like Appius does not have them. He trusted nobody he could not blackmail or bribe. But men who might be . . .' he hesitated,

'. . . advantageous, shall we say, he did invite here, and they returned the favour as a rule. Though if he was murdered, as you seem to think, shouldn't you be looking for his enemies?'

This was something I wasn't anxious to pursue, since it would surely lead to Marcus. But I could not ignore it. 'Is there anyone who had a special grudge?'

Sylvanus said doubtfully, 'Not that I know of, citizen. Unless you count that fellow who turned up at the door and said he was some relative of Fortunatus's.'

'Gaius Valerius?'

'You've heard of him?'

'I spoke to him today.'

'Then you'll know he felt he had a claim on the estate.'

'Hardly a convincing one,' I said. 'Everything passed to the Emperor, moons ago. No one could hope to overturn that in the courts.'

'As Appius explained! Valerius was disappointed, as you might expect, but accepted that it was too late.'

'Yet you felt he was nurturing a grudge?'

'Not really, citizen. My master made an offer to compensate his loss.' The steward smiled. 'He always said that all men have their price. Not, in this case, a very handsome one. But Valerius seemed satisfied. In fact, he sent a handsome flask of wine as thanks. My master seemed to be content as well.'

'This flask of wine . . . Did Appius sample it before he left the house?'

'I assume so, citizen. He was contemptuous. Poor stuff, he told me. Though whether he actually tasted it, or simply sniffed . . .' He looked at me sharply. 'You think that might have killed him?'

'I think it's possible.'

He looked doubtful. 'Surely Valerius can't be your murderer. What would he gain from killing Appius? The whole estate will go back to the Emperor, and he would lose all hope of anything.'

'Perhaps he thought that Appius would renege on their agreement. It is not formal yet, I think?'

'I couldn't tell you. I imagine not. Appius would want firm proof of his identity. But I cannot credit that Valerius . . .'

I cut him off. 'There's one way of finding out. Do you still have the flask, or was it thrown on to the midden heap?'

He shook his head. 'Neither, citizen, I think my master took it to his host last night, as a sort of contribution to the feast.'

Most hosts in Glevum would take affront at a suggestion that they couldn't provide excellent provisions of their own. But Appius made his own rules, clearly. 'Because he preferred to eat things that he'd brought himself? You said yourself, he trusted nobody.'

'With reason, it appears. Since someone murdered him.'

It was a rebuke that I deserved. 'Almost certainly his host of yesterday. And we don't know who it was. The councillor who was at the fort with him would know. I hear he was to attend a meal with Appius that evening as a guest himself. But you don't know who that was?'

'Appius never discussed his plans with anyone.' He shook his head. 'I am sorry that I cannot be more help.' He brightened suddenly. 'Though I could supply you a list of councillors who've dined here recently.'

'Recently? When there was plague about? And food has been so scarce?'

'Not while the contagion was prevalent, of course. But in recent days, since it began to ebb. On several evenings different councillors have been. And as for food, I think that was the draw. He has supplies sent specially from Londinium. Very good food too. Fine enough to make gifts of at a feast. After all, they were a gift to him from the governor himself. That's why, if Appius asked you, people always came. And why his contributions didn't give offence. Supplies have not been easy in Glevum recently.'

Two reasons why, I thought. Fine food and an unwillingness to cross the delator.

The steward was still speaking. 'He used to hold dinners at the villa, long before the plague. Those names are on the list as well. He seemed to be working through the curia. Look for the ones that were asked back several times – they're most likely to have invited him.' He gave me a sideways look. 'Your friend Marcus Septimus isn't listed, I'm afraid. Of course, he has been out of town. Though I understand he has recently returned . . .?'

Exactly what Marcus predicted. My turn to shake my head. 'Marcus did not invite him out to dine. Or kill him either, I can vouch for that.'

'In what way, vouch?'

I thought quickly. 'I live close to Marcus and I know for certain that he had no guests to dinner yesterday. I called on him, myself, early this morning. There were no visitors. Indeed, he was being very careful to keep himself apart, for fear of pestilence. And I would have heard the horses if he'd gone out last night. They go straight past my gate.'

Sylvanus still looked cynical.

'He was alone this morning. After I found the corpses, I went back to him, as senior magistrate, and asked him to identify your master formally. He was as shocked as I was – and as you were yourself. He helped me to report it to the fort.' Strictly true, though not a full account. 'So be very careful what you say, lest you start unfounded rumours which harm his *dignitas*. The punishment's severe.'

He looked chagrined, and hurried off to get the list. It was written in a careful hand, on a handsome writing-block. At a glance it seemed to cover half the curia. I made a mental note of the repeated names. Among them, I noticed, was Titus Flavius.

I sighed and thanked Sylvanus, then made my way outside.

NINETEEN

I had visited Craithaw's mill before, so this time I knew where I was going – towards the riverside warehouses and docks on the other side of town.

It is not the most salubrious of areas, riddled with narrow lanes and alleyways, full of busy workshops offering everything a ship might need, from iron nails to anchor weights and ropes, pitch for waterproofing hulls and hempen cloth for patching sails. There are also enterprises providing for the crews: shady tavernas and steamy hot-food stalls, and even steamier *lupanaria*, with paintings depicting the specialities offered by the girls (not only for the benefit of customers who cannot read!). And, in the upper storeys above these businesses, the rickety apartments of the people who provide these services, together with their families, apprentices and – in some cases – slaves.

It was also very noisy, even now. Apparently river trade doesn't stop for plague – or perhaps news had spread that the worst was past. I could soon hear shouts and hammering, and the groans and creaking of the wooden cranes. The area is prone to flooding when the river's high, which must have happened recently, because the streets were full of mud and detritus which had washed up ashore.

I picked my way across this sticky mess. It smelt appalling, adding to the already powerful reek of midden heaps and pots of heated pitch or acrid oak-gall cutch. Rents for residential property are not expensive here, though the riverside warehouses command quite hefty ones.

Yet not everything is noise and industry. Ships also need provisions and round the corner from the docks there is a row of victuallers, one of which is – was – Craithaw's premises. As I approached, I could see the front court and its donkey-mill. But the heavy cone-shaped grindstone was idle, the holes for the turning bar were empty, and no donkey was in sight.

Only a circle of faint dust around the base showed that any milling had ever taken place.

'Been like that all day. No answer when you call. What am I supposed to tell my master?' a disgruntled balding slave told me as I approached. 'Don't waste your time here, townsman, there's nobody about. I've been back several times. No sign of anything, not even of the ass. All this way for nothing!' And he grumbled off, leaving me alone in the empty mill-court.

The absence of the miller was hardly a surprise, but I had expected to find at least his wife. Perhaps, though, she'd already heard the news and retired upstairs in grief. No secret in Glevum is safe for very long. Either way, I had to find her, if I could. And if calling to her from the court brought no response, I would have to venture a little further in.

'Anybody there?' I murmured, peering into the lean-to area in the rear corner of the court, but there was nothing there to see. Only the domed brick furnace-oven at the side, where the bread was cooked. It must be desperately hot when it was fully fired, because – although it was clearly cooling now – it still gave off sufficient sullen heat for a pot of something (it smelt like spicy stew) to have been burned and set, still bubbling, on the sill.

And there had been baking fairly recently. There was a sort of mixing vat, complete with wooden paddle for stirring dough, and several round segmented loaves on a trestle top nearby – together with a large uncovered bowl. A glance revealed a 'starting mixture' (which I recognised from Cilla's baking days at home) kept back to cause tomorrow's loaves to rise.

There was still no answer to my call. But there were sounds of something moving in the building at the back. I had never penetrated further than the court, but now I tiptoed towards the building and the sounds.

It was a strange edifice, the front part made of wood (which in Glevum is quite unusual), filling the angle between two high neighbouring walls. Oddly triangular, but respectable enough. The wide doors were half-open to reveal a storeroom-cum-stable on the lower floor, with a ladder to what was presumably a living space above. The flagstones appeared to be newly swept and scrubbed – nothing left behind by donkeys, or split trails of grain.

'Is anybody there?' I peered in through the doors.

The air was dusty, and when the door was shut it must be gloomy here. The only window space was on the upper floor – presumably in order to ensure that when it rained this whole area could be closed and the contents of the storeroom kept dry. In the shadows I could see the ass in residence, on the left, contentedly chewing on something in its stall. Perhaps it had made the noise. There seemed to be an empty stall beyond it – probably a sleeping space for slaves, though in the gloom I couldn't really see. In front of me were several sacks of what looked like flour, ready-milled and loaded for delivery on a cart, which took up most of the remaining space.

I edged around it, dodging the hook of the wicked-looking hoist dangling from the ceiling, evidently used for loading the vehicle below. On a bench beside the wall were scoops and measures, heavy scales, an abacus and other equipment of the enterprise, while underneath were sections built for holding grain. One held a small heap of rye, and another a slightly larger pile of spelt. For a moment I could see nothing else. But as I became accustomed to the light, I saw in the back corner an open storage bin. I tiptoed over to peer inside.

I don't know what I hoped to see – perhaps proof that Craithaw used contaminants to bulk his own flour (as he'd accused his rival of doing) – but these were clearly provisions for the house: an amphora of oil, rather less than half of a round loaf of bread, an end of cheese and a couple of wizened apples in a wooden bowl. There were also fresh turnips and a bucket of dried fish, along with a bag of coarse milled spelt and one of fine flour, both open and half-used. Even in plague-times a miller can do well.

I closed the lid, and so revealed a cupboard niche behind, in which a row of stoppered jars had been concealed. It was open, and the lock hung from the hasp. I glanced around. There was nobody in sight. I took the stopper from the smallest jar. Salt, disappointingly, as a quick taste confirmed. Another held a bunch of seasoning herbs. I turned to the largest and found a ground-up powder which I felt sure was chalk. Aha! I dipped my finger in. It came out covered in a fine white dust. I was about to test my theory with a lick, when . . .

'Can I help you, townsman?' An unexpected voice. It came from the corner nearest to the ass, and – since I had turned my back to look into the store – it startled me.

I whirled around, guiltily rubbing my prying fingers against my tunic-hem. If she had noticed she did not mention it. She was kneeling on the floor, busy with a bucket and a piece of rag. This must be Craithaw's wife. Or even, given the soiled ochre tunic that she wore, possibly a slave?

She resolved that question. 'If you've come to see my husband, I'm afraid that he's not here. I can sell you a very little flour, if you want. Not much. Most of what you see is already spoken for – I've managed to get a load on to the handcart, as you can see, but there won't be any milling till that wretch gets home. Out drinking with his fancy friends at the bakers' guild last night, and never mind what happens to the business. Or to me. I do my best, but I can't do everything myself.' As she spoke, she struggled to her feet.

She was a weary-looking woman, wispy-haired and thin, though probably not as aged as I'd thought at first – drudgery had drained her of her youth. Her hands were calloused and reddened with hard work, and there were knotted muscles on the scrawny arms and bruises on the legs. They might be from pushing carts and moving heavy sacks. But the telltale welts on face and shoulders were not inflicted by any accident. You could see the fingerprints. A bloodied piece of rag was wrapped around one wrist and hand.

I was beginning to like Craithaw less and less. I hadn't liked him very much before.

'A quarter of a *modius* of spelt, perhaps? I could spare you that.' There were dark rings around her eyes as if she hadn't slept for weeks, but she managed a tired smile. 'Otherwise, I fear, you'll have to call again. I cannot even sell you bread – the batch outside is for a customer. There may still be a little corn in the bottom of the mill, Craithaw rushed off last night before we'd cleared it out. But I'm not strong enough to lift the grindstone on my own and I'm not about to try – that's how my husband lost half his hand.'

I gestured to the wrist. 'What did you do to yours?'

She flushed. 'It's nothing. Generally Craithaw operates the hoist, but today I had to do it on my own. We've got a few rich houses that we deliver to, and I thought it would be a little income, even if he came home unfit to mill today. But now look what I've done!' She raised her wrist to show the bloodstained cloth. 'I caught it on the hook. I had to bind it up before it dripped into the stock.'

I wondered if that was accurate, judging by her other injuries, but all I said was, 'Even with that, you were going to pull that cart yourself?'

She put the hand behind her back, as if embarrassed to have said so much. 'It's nothing, really. Just a nasty scratch. I'll manage with the cart; I generally do.' She flushed again, 'We can't use the donkey until after dark, you see, because of the ban on horse-drawn transport during daylight hours in town. We used to have a couple of young slaves to help, but Craithaw sold them just before the plague. Not working hard enough, he said, and playing dice instead. I hoped he'd replace them. But the contagion came, and now he says that – having lost a lot of customers – we can't afford another pair of hands. So it all falls to me.'

'While he's busy milling?'

She gave me a wry smile. 'He maintains that with only one good hand he cannot push the cart. Though he could pull it, just as well as me, with a rope around his shoulders, as far as I can see. But it does no good to argue.'

I looked at the bruised place on her face. Poor woman – and I had such dreadful news for her. Still more would fall upon her shoulders now, if she were not to starve. 'And you bake the loaves as well?'

She shook her head. 'Not many nowadays, and he mostly makes the dough himself. Insists on it, in fact, in case I do it wrong. Just a few for selected customers. Enough to gain him membership of the bakers' guild – it's very prestigious, as I'm sure you know. But mostly we just mill flour for private customers, or for people who sell baked goods in the street. Without a slave, that's all there's time for. When my father had the mill, we did everything ourselves. My brother, if he'd lived, would have carried it all on. But only I survived, so the business fell to me. Craithaw and I have no children to assist, or hand it on to.' She wiped the bandaged hand across her brow. 'My fault, he tells me, so I have to compensate.'

'By doing all the extra work?'

'So much, there's hardly time to cook and clean for him. He complains, of course. And I fear it's getting worse. Craithaw isn't young. I'm expecting any day that he's about to say that with one good hand he can no longer cope with everything at once – feeding the mill with grain, keeping the grindstone balanced and leading round the ass. But I can't do it with deliveries to make. And you must excuse me, townsman, because I'll have to do that now since I've finished cleaning here. You're lucky to find me. Another moment and I would have gone.'

'But cleanliness comes first?'

She gave me a strange look. 'I dared not go until I'd done the floor. He gets furious if things aren't clean.' Unconsciously, she touched the bruise again. 'But enough about my woes. Did you want a little flour?'

I shook my head. 'That isn't why I'm here. I bring important news. It concerns your husband . . .' I began.

'Well, as I say, he isn't back . . .'

I saw an opportunity. 'You don't know where he went?'

She gave me a telling look. 'Me, townsman? Craithaw doesn't tell me anything. Never did, and even less so, now. Just goes off, looking smug, to meet his baker friends. I understand they feed him – he often doesn't eat what I prepare. Certainly they drink.' She picked up her bucket and dropped the cleaning rag inside. 'So if you discover where he is, perhaps you'd send him home. Tell him, if he doesn't want to starve . . .' She broke off as she saw the purse that I was disentangling from my belt. Her face turned ashen. 'Where did you get that?'

'You recognise it?'

'Of course. It's Craithaw's. I made that patch myself.' She

frowned at me. 'Don't tell me he lost it somewhere? Is that what he gets up to while he's out in town? Playing dice in some taverna? That would make sense, I suppose. I've known him come home self-satisfied with silver in his purse – though when I asked . . .' She raised that bound hand to her face again.

Gambling? I hadn't thought of it. Not strictly legal but it might explain a lot. 'There's silver in it now. Not a great deal . . .'

She shook her head. 'If you won and he still owes you, townsman, I cannot really help. I have a little money – he allows me that – but not an *as* to spare—'

I cut her off. 'I was looking for the rightful owner of the purse, that's all. And you have answered that. So it should come to you.'

She frowned. 'How did you come by it? He can't have dropped it? It attaches to his belt. Or have you caught a robber who confessed?'

'Goodwife,' I said, 'I'm sorry. I do not know your name . . .'

'My father called me Pulchra, I was very pretty once.' Her voice was dull, as though she were speaking in a trance. 'There's trouble isn't there? With Craithaw . . . I can see it in your face.' She dropped the pail and sat down heavily on a ladder rung. 'He's been taken ill or hurt, and they have found his body in the street? Badly injured? Or dying of the plague?'

'Worse,' I said, 'I am afraid he's dead. And discovered not in Glevum, but some way outside, lying in a ditch beside the road.'

'Dear gods!' She buried her bruised face in both her hands.

I let her sob a moment, and, looking for words of comfort, which I failed to find, I did what a Roman citizen shouldn't do when the woman is not a relative. I laid a hand on her shoulder, careful not to put pressure on the bruise. 'Try not to grieve too much . . .' I murmured stupidly.

She raised a stricken face, and murmured through her tears. 'Townsman, you don't understand. I made this happen. It is all my fault.'

TWENTY

I moved my hand as though I had been stung. 'You murdered him?' I could almost understand it from the way he treated her, but the penalties for mariticide are terrible.

She looked at me dully. 'Murdered? That makes it even worse. I assumed there'd been some sort of accident.' Her damaged shoulders shook and she hid her face again.

'But if you killed him, surely . . .?'

She made no answer, just continued burying her head.

I tried again. 'Pulchra? I can see you might have cause. He wasn't kind to you. If he attacked you first, the court might pardon you.' Of course, they wouldn't, not without witnesses that he was threatening her life – and even then, there might be punishment. The law does not encourage mariticidal wives. But there was clearly no such witness, not even a slave (whose testimony would not count, in any case, unless extracted by the torturers). But if she confessed like this, there'd be no hope for her.

She looked up at me. 'I did not say I killed him, townsman. I said it was my fault. I brought this on him at the temple, yesterday. You're right. He wasn't kind to me.' She gestured to a bruise.

'He beat you?'

'Often. Everything I did offended him, of late. In fact, I've wondered if he wanted to get rid of me.'

'Put you aside and marry someone else?'

'Kill me, even, since the mill was mine – part of my dowry, which would revert to me if we were divorced. But if I died, it would be his, of course.'

'So you went to the temple, and did what? Prayed to be delivered? Appealed for sanctuary, perhaps, since all your family were dead?' People do, when they are seriously ill-used and there is nowhere else to turn. Protection is occasionally given to a slave. Not generally to wives.

She shook her head. 'Worse than that. I did make an offering to Juno – because she protects women, especially married ones. Only a pigeon – it was all I could afford, but of course, as a female I couldn't perform the sacrifice myself. I didn't know when the offering would be made, being such a small one, and of course I couldn't tell the priests what I wanted from the gods. So I went further . . .' She gave me a piteous look. 'You know the curse-tablet makers who have stalls nearby?'

I did. Rogues, in my opinion, most of them. They set up tables by the temple steps and offer little pieces of soft lead on which a curse – or votive message – can be scratched, then offered to the gods. Tightly rolled, so they cannot casually be read.

'You had them make a curse-tablet for you?'

She nodded ruefully. 'They offer a service for those who cannot write.'

'For a price,' I murmured.

'Indeed. But they'll take anybody's money. You don't have to be a man. I had to have the cheapest one, of course. And just word or two. Asking to be freed of "my tormenter". I didn't dare to mention him by name – and the tablet is anonymous. But I thought the gods would know. I slipped a coin to a temple slave to have him nail it to the sanctuary door, and it has clearly worked. I didn't expect it to take effect so soon. I only went there yesterday when I'd finished the deliveries.' She buried her poor head in both her hands again.

If she'd been very old, or very young, I could have given her another sympathetic pat, but I had already overstepped the mark.

'Pulchra,' I said solemnly. 'You cannot blame yourself. Craithaw was not struck down by any deity. He was killed by human hand. I'm certain about that. My guess is he was poisoned. Eating and drinking with his baker friends, perhaps?'

'But great Juno may have had a hand in it, prompting the murderer,' she said.

'Perhaps, but a mortal can't be responsible for the actions of the gods.'

She wasn't comforted. 'If the authorities find out, I'll be

indicted for using sorcery. Against your husband, that's a death sentence. Oh, great Mars!' She broke off with a sob.

'Did you use incantations, or spells, or summon spirits up?'

Her tear-stained face was startled. 'Of course not, townsman.'

'Then what court could find against you on that charge? Votive prayers addressed to gods aren't sorcery,' I declared. 'But it might be wise, in future, not to blame yourself in public for your husband's death. Besides, I assume you didn't write a curse on anybody else?'

She was so shocked that she scrambled to her feet. 'I certainly did not! Whatever makes you ask?'

'Because Craithaw was not the only corpse I found,' I said, and saw her turn paler still, if that was possible. 'There was another man. A very wealthy one. Appius Limpnus Corvinus – you may have heard of him?'

She looked at me aghast. 'Corvinus? But he was—' She broke off, clasping her undamaged hand across her mouth. Decorum or not, I seized her by the arm, if only to stop her collapsing to the floor.

'He was . . . what?' I prompted gently. 'You clearly know the name. A friend of your husband's, were you going to say? I know that Appius went out to dine last night. Could it have been him that Craithaw went to meet?'

She had recovered now, and snatched her arm away. I saw that it was the bandaged one, and cursed myself for having been an idiot. I'd not only behaved improperly – as though she were a slave – I had probably hurt her. I was unlikely to get any further information from her now.

But I'd misjudged her. She gave me a shaky smile. 'That was not what I was going to say. And it's impossible. Appius would never have been seen consorting with a tradesman anywhere. He was too conscious of his rank. He was an occasional customer of Craithaw's, that is all. I was going to ask . . .' She shook her head. 'One must be so careful nowadays. You never know who's listening.' She gestured vaguely at the ass, as if its long ears might have overheard, and it might go braying news around the town.

I gave her a reassuring grin. 'You're safe enough in here. I'll just make sure there's no one in the court. I suppose it's possible to overhear from there.' I went and looked around, but there was nobody in sight. 'No one out there. The news has clearly spread that the mill is shut today. But you're right to be cautious; the Emperor has informers everywhere – I can only swear that I'm not one of them.'

'I believe you. But Appius Limpnus was?' She saw my startled look. 'That was my question. That's the general rumour and I'm inclined to think it's true.'

A woman with opinions of her own! 'Why, in particular?'

'Most people who retire from the provincial court and move as far away as possible generally do so because they're in disgrace. But Appius doesn't hide from the authorities. On the contrary, he's always visiting the fort. He seems to positively relish being feared, from what I hear, and boasts of having presents from the governor. What does that suggest to you?' A shamefaced smile. 'You understand why I was hesitant? Such talk is dangerous.'

'Less so now, perhaps, because the man is dead!' I was impressed by her intelligence. 'But I agree, I think he was a spy. You are right about him being in constant contact with the fort and receiving presents from Virius Lupus, who has no love for Glevum. You have heard the tale, no doubt?'

'What our local legion did to Virius's own, and how they captured him, so he was lucky to be ransomed and escape alive? Everyone knows that. He sent Appius Corvinus here, you think? To keep an eye on Glevum, in particular?'

'And send reports back to the Emperor, so dissidents could be exiled, if not worse. Probably with instructions to dig out everyone who secretly supported Clodius. Appius was planning to stand as magistrate. As a member of the curia, he'd know all the business of the town and hear all the gossip – who supported Virius and who did not.'

She looked at me, appalled. 'And he would have been elected, wouldn't he? No one would dare to vote against him, even without his offering a bribe.'

'But that hardly matters now. The man is dead, just as your husband is.'

She gave a sigh. 'But don't you see, it makes things worse for me. If Appius was murdered – like my husband – there'll be a dreadful fuss. The authorities won't rest until the culprit's found. They'll be looking for somebody to blame. If they find out about that tablet . . . Oh, why did I go to the temple yesterday?'

'Pulchra,' I said, severely, 'your prayer tablet . . .' I avoided saying "curse", '. . . even if they found it, only showed that you wanted to be free. From what you say, it did not even wish your husband dead.'

That earned a sideways glance. 'Not specifically. But I did request a curse. To tell the truth, I hoped he'd catch the plague before contagion passed entirely from the town. When you first told me where you found him, I thought perhaps he had. It can strike very quickly, I believe. Or, if not that, been killed by bandits, or by wolves – these things can happen on an empty road, especially near the forest. But poisoning . . .!' She shook her head again, despairingly. 'They'll want to come and talk to me, for sure.'

'Pulchra,' I said, 'I doubt that they'll even bother about you. You're quite right – there'll be huge efforts to find Appius's murderer. But that's to your advantage, isn't it? It will identify who killed your husband too. You may even be able to claim *compensatio*. A court would be sympathetic to a plea against the killer of the Emperor's protégé.'

The look she gave me was withering. 'Spoken like a man. How could I afford an advocate to speak for me? Or even gain admittance to a magistrate? I am a woman, a simple tradesperson, and now I am a widow, with no male family – not even the most distant relative.'

'But your husband was born free within the walls, so was legally a citizen, I think? As his widow you will have some rights.'

'If I could afford to claim them, which I can't, though I'd qualify by birth. On my own I cannot even run the mill. The gods alone know how I'm going to live.'

I said rather sheepishly, 'I'm a citizen, myself, but I know what it is to be in want.' There was no more comfort I could offer her – except to promise to speak to Marcus Septimus on her behalf. That made her panic as much as it impressed.

'Don't do that, I beg you, citizen. I apologise for calling you "townsman" all this time. And that is just the point. A woman of my rank, asking His Excellence to intercede for me – that would be impudence.'

'He sent me to see you,' I said. Well, it was almost true. 'I was to tell you of your husband's death, so you could make arrangements to have his body brought back home and start preparing for his funeral. I think you said Craithaw was a member of a guild?'

'The bakers' collegium. That's where he paid his dues.'

'Then they will see to everything,' I said, and hoped that I was right. Most guilds ensure a proper funeral, providing everything from the undertaker to the pyre. Women to wash the body, herbs to burn and cleanse. Professional mourners, even, if – like Craithaw – there's no family to tear their clothes and wail. (The widow is not generally expected to attend – it's assumed that she'll be prostrated with grief.) 'Certainly they'd provide a bier to bring him here and take him to cremation afterwards. All you have to do is contact them. Now, if you'll excuse me, I have other messages to take. But try not to worry – all the attention will be on Appius. And even if your husband knew him, you did not, I think? I imagine that could easily be proved.'

There was a moment's hesitation. She gave me strange look. 'What makes you say that? Such a thing could not be proved at all.'

'It's always hard to prove a negative,' I agreed, remembering my conversation with Marcus earlier. 'But Appius has a household full of servants, both at his country house and at his new one here in town. If you'd ever been there – with a delivery, perhaps – they'd be sure to know. And if a man of Appius's rank should ever come down here, half the street would talk of nothing else.'

'Indeed they would,' she said emphatically. 'But that's not what I meant. About me knowing Appius . . .'

I frowned. 'But I understand that even though Appius was

your husband's occasional customer, he would not come here to collect his order. He would surely send a slave.'

She shook her head. 'I didn't know him. But I've seen him. Because he did come here. Once at least, before the plague broke out, wanting my husband to bake some special bread for a feast he was giving for an important guest.'

'He came in person?' I was utterly amazed. Patricians like Appius send slaves to place orders and make purchases. Or they summon the vendor to come to them, if there are special arrangements to be made. It is not entirely unknown for such men to visit trade premises themselves, but I was surprised at Appius doing it. Even if he had other reasons to be in this part of town.

She knew what I was thinking. 'I was surprised myself, at first. He came in a litter, naturally, and only to the entrance of the court. Craithaw was so proud that he was fit to burst. He shooed me off to sweep the yard, and went to talk to him, all fawning smiles and wringing hands and bows.'

'You didn't speak to Appius yourself?'

She gave me that look again. 'Citizen, I am a woman. I doubt if Appius even noticed me. I was curious, but I dared not stray my sweeping near enough to listen in.'

'So you don't know what he wanted?'

'I do. I was the one who had to bake the loaves – although my husband prepared the dough.'

'Appius placed an order?'

'Quite a handsome one. A dozen special loaves that he wanted for a banquet honouring an important guest that night. Must have been someone really important, because he looked at samples of our grain and then decided it wasn't good enough. He sent some round, by slave, a little later on. A present from the provincial governor, sent down specially from Londinium.'

'And was it better?'

'Some of the finest flour I ever saw. White as snow and baked up beautifully. Just as well – I dread to think what Craithaw would have done if I had burned the batch, or failed to let it rise sufficiently.' She spoke bitterly. 'In fact, my husband was so pleased he actually made that delivery himself, though that might have been to make sure that he was paid.'

'A handsome sum, no doubt?'

'Very handsome, I believe, for just a dozen loaves. My husband boasted that he'd made a splendid bargain – though he never told me what it was, and I saw no part of it. And it did involve a lot of extra work. We had to get the oven hot again, make new dough and let it rise, then bake it in a hurry before the sun went down.'

'All so that Appius could serve fresh loaves to friends? To show off his affluence,' I said.

'There were different flavours too – some plain, and some with herbs and one with honey, dates and nuts. Appius provided the ingredients himself so we had no problem there, but naturally each batch had to be separately prepared, and scored in different ways to show which one was which.'

'Like the ones I saw outside?' For a moment, I thought I'd made a link.

'It has become a fashion since with other customers,' she said. 'More work for me, of course.'

A fashion. Just like Appius's taste in clothes! 'But at least you didn't have to deliver them that time,' I murmured sympathetically.

She gave me that wry smile. 'It was out of town, of course. Appius did not have his townhouse then. Craithaw had to take the ass, with panniers, while I rushed round town with our usual deliveries, pulling the cart with a rope around my waist and getting grumbled at because the loaves were late. But I could not explain. That would be blaming Appius, Craithaw said, and if that got back to him, as it very likely would, it might stop him using us again.'

I could imagine that. The man would expect such service as his due. 'And did he come again?'

She thought a moment. 'If he came in person, my husband didn't say as much to me – though he could have called, perhaps, while I was on my rounds. I know that he sent slaves. There have certainly been further orders from him for the same thing since.'

'Often?'

'Whenever Appius proposed to have a feast, I think. I always knew when orders came, of course, because I had to bake the loaves, though Craithaw insisted on making up the dough. And delivering the order himself.'

'Has there been another order recently? Yesterday, perhaps?' That might explain how Craithaw came to be with the delator, I thought. 'I know Appius sometimes takes presents to a host, and he was proposing another banquet soon. A very big one, by the sound of it, probably in the victuallers' banquet hall. All of the curia were invited to attend. Or would have been, if Appius had lived. For a feast like that he'd need a lot of loaves – so, if he wanted you to make them, he would have to warn you in advance.'

She was frowning doubtfully. 'But don't the victuallers provide their own for these events?'

'Not if he wanted to show off his Roman flour to selected guests.' I took a risk. 'I gather he had special allies in the town.'

'You think one turned against him yesterday? Gave him a gift of poisoned wine, or dates or something of the kind, which he then shared with Craithaw, who was killed by accident? Unlikely, but that might well be the doing of the gods.'

Intelligent again. It was the obvious solution, considering what I knew, though I didn't tell her so. 'That's possible. So what I need to know is if they met last night, where they went – and if they were seen together afterwards. Whoever was Appius's host is probably to blame. Can you think of anyone who'd know? Your husband never mentioned anyone at all?'

She bit her lip. 'Never. He liked to keep things secret. It made him feel important. And made good money too. You've seen his purse. A miller does not usually have silver coins to spare.' She looked at me again. 'I can trust you, citizen?'

'Of course,' I said.

'Then,' she said slowly, 'there is one thing perhaps you ought to know. But I don't want to delay you. I'll have to go and see the guild to make arrangements for Craithaw's funeral. If he's dead, no one will want deliveries from the mill, for fear of bringing down a curse. Are you proposing to go back into town? If so, with your permission, might I walk some way with you?'

'Of course,' I said. It is proper for a widow to be accompanied in the street. And thanks to her husband she didn't have a slave. 'I was thinking of calling on the victuallers, anyway, in case they had contact with Appius yesterday.'

She gave me a wan smile. 'Then let me slip up and put a cleaner tunic on and fetch my cloak. I can't go out like this. I won't be a moment.' And she disappeared upstairs.

TWENTY-ONE

It was much more than a moment. I had nothing to do but stand and gaze about. I found a pair of folding stools propped against the further wall, so I pulled one out and sat there, looking at the ass. It looked blandly back at me and went on eating hay.

It was well-nourished, I thought idly, for an animal kept in town throughout the plague. Arlina had an enclosure full of grass and weeds, so – even when we went hungry – she had a little food. But this one didn't have a field. Yet it looked better-fed than Pulchra. An indication of which Craithaw valued more?

My musings were interrupted by a clatter overhead. I looked up and saw Pulchra coming backwards down the ladder rungs. She was totally transformed: now washed, in a neat, dark-coloured tunic, with newly braided hair just visible under a square brown *palla* draped around her head and shoulders. Even the bloodied cloth around her wrist had been replaced by a clean strip of linen, neatly tied.

She noticed my approving glance. 'Suitable for a widow, citizen, you think? I had this tunic from the clothes stall when my father died, and haven't used it since. There are some moth-holes round one shoulder, but that doesn't show with this.' She gestured to the shawl. 'I want the guild to think that I'm respectable and not fob me off with less than we should have. Especially since they have to go and pick the body up.' She gave me a wry smile. 'You must give me directions to exactly where that is.'

'I'll come with you and tell them where it is myself,' I promised gallantly. 'I think I know the building and it's almost on my way. Though I can't be long – the afternoon is getting on and I have much to do. But I will see that your husband gets whatever's due – assuming that his payments to the guild are up to date.'

That rueful smile again. 'I think so, citizen. During the plague he got behind because he rarely left the mill. I had to go out, if anybody did. But he paid what was owing to the guild a day or two ago – when he came home with money, I don't know from what. Gambling again, perhaps. So his fees should all be paid.' She dropped her eyes. 'Thank you for agreeing to come with me. They'll take more notice of a man. If I had a slave, he would have gone, of course – they won't be expecting anyone like me.'

She led the way outside and softly closed the door, murmuring a farewell to the ass. 'Oh!' She stopped. 'You were wrong in your prediction, citizen. I do have customers.' She gestured to the street.

Two men, evidently slaves, were standing at the entrance to the premises. When they saw us, they rushed into the court to accost the miller's wife. 'Where have you been? What's happened to the mill? We have been sent for flour.'

They were angry but Pulchra spoke with quiet dignity. 'I'm sorry. There'll be no trade today – nor for a little while. There's been . . . an accident.'

She glanced at me, but I didn't contradict. Gossip travels fast enough without my fuelling it.

'I'm afraid my husband's dead. This citizen has kindly come to tell me so. There's no one else to run the mill today. Apologies to your owners, naturally. But now, if you'll excuse me, we're on our way to arrange the funeral.'

The two servants went off, muttering. I saw one spit into his hand and rub behind his ear to ward off evil, then hurry off as if the miller's ghost were at his heels. We followed him, sedately, back towards the town.

Pulchra said nothing for some time, just concentrated on picking her way among the slime. There was hardly silence with the constant creaking and shouting from the docks, but she didn't speak, and eventually I had to prompt. 'There's something you wished to tell me, I believe? Perhaps about Appius Limpnus Corvinus?'

She looked at me abashed, and looked away again. 'There is. I confess that I misled you, citizen. I told you that if Appius ever visited again, in person, when I wasn't in the house, then my husband didn't tell me . . .' She trailed into silence.

'That wasn't true?' I was surprised at her.

'It's strictly accurate,' she said. 'I chose my words with care. He did come here again, as the neighbours would no doubt tell you. And I was out. And my husband never mentioned it. But I chanced to see him.'

'Why didn't you tell me this before?'

'I feared to be involved,' she told me candidly. 'The authorities would come asking questions if they knew, and look for somebody to blame. You won't pass this on to them?'

'Not if I can help it,' I replied. 'What happened?'

'I'd been sent to fetch water. On purpose, I think now, because my husband must have known that Appius was to call, though I didn't suspect that at the time. But the paving stones were slippery, even worse than now, and on the way I fell and broke the jug. I went back to fetch another one, expecting a beating for my clumsiness. Then, as I turned the corner, I saw a litter drawing up and Appius Corvinus stepping out of it. I don't believe he even noticed me. My husband almost did. He came out and looked up and down the road, obviously checking there was nobody nearby.'

'And was there?'

'Not at that moment, citizen. Things have not been normal since the plague. Look around you. It is empty now, apart from that fellow scraping up the muck.' She gestured to a peasant, who was piling his handcart to fertilise his fields. 'There was nobody but me, and I managed to nip into an alley just in time. I didn't want to go home to a domestic row while Appius was there.'

'And when was this?' I prompted, as we turned down an alleyway ourselves.

'That's the point. It was just yesterday, and shortly after dawn.'

'And no one saw you?'

She thought for a moment. 'On my way to the fountain, I passed a few shops which have opened up again. There were slaves taking shutters down or sweeping the pavements outside their master's premises. You might find one who saw me passing – or even saw me fall.'

I might do that, I thought privately, but all I said was, 'So he got out of the litter and that is all you saw?'

She shook her head. 'By no means, that's why I'm telling you. My husband disappeared inside, and Appius followed him.'

'Appius went inside?' I was astounded now. 'Into that storeroom with the ass, and everything?'

She shrugged. 'I thought it was untypical, but obviously whatever business was in hand they did not want it overheard. Even the litter-boys were sent away. I came out of the alley when I judged that Appius had gone, but he was still in the street. He'd turned back to shout instructions to his litter-boys. He glanced up and saw me, so I dared not duck away – I would have drawn attention to myself. But he showed no sign of recognising me. So I walked straight past and he did not look at me – a lowly woman. But I was curious enough to listen to what he told the litter-boys.'

'Which was?' We were almost at the headquarters of the Guild of Bakers now.

'They were not to wait for him, but hurry to the basilica, and see if there was someone waiting on the steps. He would be carrying a scroll. If so, they were to take him to the southern gate where Appius would join him later on. If no one came before the shadow on the forum sundial had moved a single notch, they were to come back here, and carry Appius to the southern gate himself. To go to his country villa, I presume.'

'If he was planning a visit there, he hadn't told his Glevum slaves,' I mused. 'And he was certainly at his townhouse yesterday. He left from there to dine.'

This time it was she who clutched my sleeve. 'So he wasn't going to the villa. He wouldn't abandon a visitor there overnight, alone.'

I was puzzled for a moment. And then the obvious occurred to me. 'Of course! Yesterday morning! The southern gate. The fort's not far away.'

She looked at me sharply. 'What has that to do with anything?'

'I mentioned that he planned to hold a civic feast. He called at the garrison yesterday with an invitation to the commandant. It was officially a thanksgiving banquet for the passing of the plague, but he meant to use it to canvass for a curial seat, I think. And he didn't go alone. He had a joint-sponsor for the enterprise – someone who was already a councillor, and therefore much harder to refuse without offence. This could have been the person. You didn't hear a name?'

She shook her head. 'He didn't mention one, just said that the man was a purple-striper. That's all I know.'

So, a patrician or a magistrate, or both. Or just possibly a priest. It would hardly be a boy-child of less than fourteen years – the only others who wear the purple stripe. That tallied with what Callidus had told me at the fort, and – it suddenly occurred to me – also with what Appius's steward had said, about a man who'd visited the townhouse earlier. I was all attention, though I tried to keep my question casual. 'The person with whom he was to dine, you think?'

She made a little face. 'Perhaps. Supposing there was anyone at all. I supposed it was a ruse to send the litter-boys away. Anyway, I've told you what he said. He went into the house. I walked around the docks a little while and then came back again.'

'And by that time he had gone?'

'I made certain that he had,' she said, as though I should have guessed this for myself. 'Naturally I loitered till I saw the litter come again and did not hurry till I saw him leave in it. I did not want a beating in front of Appius. I'm sure I was not supposed to know that he had called.'

'Craithaw did not mention it?'

'Not that Appius had been. He did say there'd been an order for another dozen special loaves, because of course I had to help him, but implying that a slave had come with a message. Very proud he was about it too, as usual. Even forgot to punish me for having dropped the jug. That tells you how self-satisfied he was. And now, citizen, we seem to have arrived. Are you still willing to come in and speak for me? It should not take you long.'

It didn't. Our first reception was not welcoming – I looked like a tradesman, and not one of theirs – but when they learned I was a citizen, and that 'Marcus Aurelius Septimus had an interest in the case', they were suddenly helpfulness itself. Craithaw was indeed a member of the guild, 'a citizen by virtue of his birth within the walls, and fully paid to date', according to the clerk, who found the entry on a roll of bark-paper. 'Of course, we'll send some bearers out to bring his body home at once.'

'Can you keep him here until the funeral?' the widow said to my surprise. 'At the mill, we'd have to put him in the slaves' old sleeping place, next to the donkey. Hardly fitting for the master of the house. You couldn't haul him up the ladder with any dignity. Besides, the whole premises would need ritual purification by a priest – and even then the presence of the dead would be thought to contaminate the stock, and I couldn't sell it afterwards.'

Put like that, I could understand, and the clerk did too. 'We do have a facility for storing those who have no family to mourn. We can take him there.'

'Then I'll send some decent clothes to dress him for the pyre.' She turned to me. 'He was a brute, but he was a baker and a citizen. This way, he'll get a respectful funeral – if you tell them where to find him.'

I gave directions, then left them to discuss the rites, saying as I hurried off, 'There's another corpse, but separate arrangements are being made for that. Craithaw's is the body in the ditch.' (I didn't mention Appius's name. That story would be round Glevum soon enough.)

But when I reached the victualler's hall, I had to mention him.

TWENTY-TWO

A tall, hook-nosed slave (who appeared to be some sort of record-keeper), looked up from the table where he was consulting something on a scroll and gazed scornfully at me. 'How can I help you, tradesman? This is the collegium of the Sutlers and Victuallers. If you want the builders and tilers, their office is in another part of town.' That was pointed, implying that in arranging matters for the guild (including the festive banquets for which it was famed), he was accustomed to dealing with customers of quality. My working tunic had offended him.

I gazed around. More outwardly prestigious than the bakers' guild, with painted murals on the walls, and equipped not only with squid ink and linen scrolls, but also with this expensive amanuensis slave.

'I'm not a member, but I am a citizen,' I said. 'And you're the guild I want. I've come to make enquiries about a civic feast for all members of the town curia. Appius Limpnus Corvinus was arranging it, I think – and you were to supply the food and drink at his expense.'

He sighed, put down the scroll and rose to his full height, which was almost as lofty as his tone. 'Citizen or not, I cannot disclose the private business of our customers.'

'I'm making enquiries at the express request of Marcus Aurelius Septimus and the commander of the fort,' I said. (Strictly true, though they had no idea that I was here.) 'Both were to be invited, I believe. Indeed, the legate has already accepted. He told me so himself.'

Rank is everything in Glevum. The illustrious names had the desired effect. The haughtiness melted like snowflakes in a fire. 'In that case, citizen, I apologise. Of course, I will investigate. Do you know when this banquet was to be?'

'I was hoping you could tell me that,' I said. 'Neither of the invitees appears to know. I believe it was around the Kalends.'

'Then it shouldn't be too difficult to find. There've not been many private feasts since the outbreak of the plague.' As he spoke, he went over to the crowded shelf behind his stool. He consulted the labels on the storage pots, selected one and shook out the linen scroll. He partially unrolled it on the desk and ran his finger down the latest entries. (Smudged, because the ink had seeped a little through the cloth – even the victuallers did not aspire to vellum or papyrus for their record rolls.)

'Here we are!' he said triumphantly. 'Three days before the Nones. Five days from tomorrow.' Suddenly he frowned. 'Wait a moment, though. There is another note.' He shook his head and rolled the scroll again. 'It was cancelled by its sponsor earlier today.'

'Today? That isn't possible!' Appius had been dead some hours when I discovered him.

The amanuensis shook his head again. 'This can't be the banquet that you want, in any case. The sponsor wasn't Appius Corvinus, and I cannot find his name in any other entry here.' He rerolled the scroll and stood to put it in its jar. 'Whoever told you must have been misinformed. I'm afraid I can't help you any more. Please convey my apologies to those who sent you here.'

I was bewildered. I muttered thanks and was about to leave when an unlikely thought occurred to me. I turned around. 'It wasn't citizen Craithaw who arranged it, I suppose?' A stupid idea – of course it wasn't. He couldn't have cancelled anything today.

The scribe's reply suggested I was an idiot. 'The miller? Naturally not. Such a thing would be beyond his means. We rarely deal with tradespeople, even if they're Roman citizens.'

'Or a patrician visitor from Eboracum, possibly?' That was a better thought.

The slave was losing patience, but he controlled himself. 'A local man – a member of the curia. That much I can disclose. Nothing to do with Appius Limpnus.'

It must be the same banquet – there couldn't be two in celebration of the same event. One of Appius's councillor cronies, perhaps (those that Marcus had been warned of by his dying friend), sent to act on Appius's behalf.

It would make sense. If Appius was named as sponsor for a feast, dignitaries who were not his friends would have found excuses to decline. (Marcus, almost certainly, for one.) That might make Appius a more dangerous enemy, but officially he had no civic role. He had retired here simply 'to grow vines'. An invitation from a town councillor would be more socially appropriate, and much more socially improper to refuse.

Of course, Appius hoped to be elected to the curia himself. This banquet was probably a ploy to win support from other councillors, so he would have wanted all of them to come. Which was much more likely if the invitation appeared to come from a fellow magistrate.

And I realised who that must have been. The man who'd accompanied Appius to the garrison! Even more essential to find out who he was.

I was about to press the record-keeper again when he cut across my thoughts. 'Is that all, citizen? I have work to do. I'm sorry that I can't assist you more. But even if this were the feast you meant, it cannot matter now. The sponsor called this morning – personally – to say he'd changed his mind. It was to be a celebration of the passing of the plague, but he'd decided there was still a threat of it.'

That tallied precisely with what the sentry said about the two men having a heated argument about the feast. So this was almost certainly the person that Appius had quarrelled with so violently. And threatened publicly with ruin if he did not do as he'd agreed. A blackmail victim who might well wish Appius dead! But the slave was already rolling up the scroll.

'I must've been mistaken, as you say.' I'd decided on a little flattery. 'I'm sure your records are impeccable.'

He turned back from the shelf where he was putting back the document, and I was rewarded by the faint ghost of a smile.

It was encouragement enough. 'You could not tell me who the sponsor was?'

'The feast has been cancelled. How can it matter now?'

Because it would identify at least one dangerous councillor

who'd been in Appius's camp but had now turned against him. I did not say that, though. I thought quickly. 'I'm quite sure the commandant would like to know. He'd accepted an invitation, after all. He'd want to know who was really asking him.'

'Suppose the sponsor wished to be anonymous?'

'Then the commander should be disabused. He has been shown immense discourtesy if the banquet has been cancelled and he has not been told.' It was a ploy, of course. The legate was perfectly aware that Appius's promised feast would not take place.

But why had the cancellation taken place today? The argument had happened yesterday. If the councillor had decided to withdraw, why didn't he do so straightaway? What had altered since that heated argument? The fact that Appius was dead and the threat was over? And how could he know that, unless he had a hand in it?

I tried again. 'I wouldn't wish to take back news that His Excellence and the legate have been badly used, and not be able to explain by whom.'

It was enough, but barely. He took down the scroll again. 'Well, since it isn't going to happen now, I suppose that I could tell you. But we pride ourselves on our discretion, so please don't mention that you heard it here.'

'I won't,' I said, wondering how I would account for the information now. But I was in for a surprise.

'It was,' he bent forwards as if the walls might hear, 'a person called Titus Flavius. You might have heard of him.'

I had. I was carrying his letter of commendation at my belt. An alleged supporter and good friend of Marcus Septimus! 'Flavius?' I echoed, genuinely shocked. 'I can't believe it. That isn't possible.'

The slave rerolled the scroll and slammed it in its jar. 'Citizen, believe or disbelieve me as you wish; I assure you that's the information that is given here! Now, if you will excuse me, I have other work to do.' He shoved the container back on to the shelf and turned back to his previous work again.

'Pardon me.' I tried to sound appropriately contrite. 'Of course, if you say so, I accept it is the case. I simply meant it comes as a surprise. It's out of character, from what I know of Flavius, for him to have been planning a feast with Appius.'

He glanced at me. I thought he was about to insist again that Appius Limpnus had no part in this, but what he said was, 'You know the councillor, citizen?'

'He was a friend of my father's, and my patron's – or I thought he was. Assuming there are not two people of that name – or somebody was not impersonating him. I suppose that's possible. Would you recognise him? Has he been here before – in connection with other feasts, perhaps?'

'Not in my time, citizen, though I'm sure he has. Most of the curia do – and he is marked as a former customer. But I've only seen him once. I was here when he made the first arrangements for this feast.'

'But not when he cancelled it?' I was excited now. 'Could you describe him?'

He made a little face. 'I mostly noticed the toga and the purple stripe. But, otherwise, much what you'd expect.' He thought a moment. 'Thinning hair and middle height – so probably thirty-five or forty years of age . . .'

'Dressed impeccably and well-barbered too, though he often runs his fingers through his hair and tousles it?'

A nod. 'He did that several times while he was here.'

'It's clearly the same man. I wonder if Appius had some hold on him. Where was he proposing that the feast be held? In the victuallers' hall, no doubt, because that would hold a crowd.'

'Citizen,' he chided, 'I cannot tell you that. It is a matter of confidentiality.' But he did not deny it.

'Flavius would not mind you telling me. I'm carrying a letter from him, recommending me, at this very moment.' I began to produce it from where it was hanging round my neck. But suddenly, I realised, that was another thing! That letter! Flavius was supposed to be an ally of His Excellence. Why should his commendation have sway with Appius? You'd expect the very opposite. Unless, indeed, they were secretly in league.

The slave was looking expectantly at me. I showed him the seal. 'I'll undo it and show you, if you wish.'

He shook his head. 'I'll take your word for it. I recognise the seal. And since you carry that, I suppose I can tell you unofficially. But it's clear you know the man. Why don't you go and ask him for yourself?'

'Thank you,' I said. 'I do believe I will.'

I hurried out into the street. Unfortunately it had begun to rain, but I didn't stop to shelter from the shower. I wrapped my cloak about me, pulled the hood around my ears and hurried towards the block where Flavius's apartment was.

(Flavius, like Marcus, doesn't have a house in town, although, of course, he has a large country villa and estate. Here he merely has a lavish set of rooms, taking up the whole first floor of an apartment block, thus meeting the minimum area required for election to the curia. The upper storeys lack facilities, of course, and are increasingly overcrowded the further up one goes, but some first-floor flats are almost fit for emperors.)

I was drenched by the time I got there, though it had not taken long.

TWENTY-THREE

Flavius's block was almost opposite the baths and I was grateful to reach the cover of the entranceway. I went in, preparing to elbow my way through so I could climb the stairs. But as I shook the water from my cloak, I saw I was alone. Usually such places would be thronged – especially in the rain – and the stairways crowded with people of all kinds: residents, pie-vendors, soothsayers, gamblers, beggarmen and thieves (it pays to keep one hand upon your purse). Or, of course, official visitors, as I claimed to be.

No point in announcing it; there was almost nobody to hear. Only one young woman in a ragged shawl, who pressed herself against the wall to let me pass, and three old men on the landing, playing dice. They glanced up, ignored me and went on with their game. I stepped around them and knocked on Flavius's door.

It was opened – a fraction – by his famous Nubian slave: a handsome, dark-skinned man, all rippling muscle under his dark green tunic uniform. (Nubians are the latest fashion, since Severus – African himself – brought several to Rome. Marcus would have had one, almost certainly, if he were not afraid at present of servants being spies.) Meanwhile, this was the most expensive doorkeeper in town.

Certainly, he had a most impressive scowl. 'I cannot admit you, I'm afraid. Master's orders. But I could take a message. What's your business here?'

I had not considered, although I should have done, that there might be no one in. (Except, of course, for slaves.) I essayed a smile. 'I hoped to speak to Titus Flavius. Is he not at home?'

'He is, but he is not admitting visitors.'

'Not ill, I hope?' I said this doubtfully. I knew Titus had been at the victuallers' earlier today, but it was not impossible that he had caught the plague. It's said to strike extremely fast.

I was about to back hastily away, but then it occurred to me to be more sceptical. Simply taking your bed, in times like these, would offer an excellent excuse for keeping everyone away. If, for example, you had things to hide.

The slave surprised me. 'Not ill, but not receiving anyone – except on official business. Apologies. Another day, perhaps.'

He would have shut the door if I had not bleated, just in time, 'But I'm on official business.' That made him pause, at least. I burbled on. 'An errand from His Excellence Marcus Septimus . . .' I was about to add 'and the legate', but he interrupted me.

'Concerning?'

I hesitated. If I mentioned my suspicions I'd be turned away, to say nothing of risking a nasty fine for damaging a councillor's reputation. But I had to make Titus Flavius see me. I took a gamble. 'Concerning Appius Limpnus Corvinus. Would you be good enough to tell your owner so?'

The name was clearly familiar to the Nubian. He gave me an extremely doubtful look. 'I'll tell him, though I cannot promise anything. Who should I say is calling?'

'Junio, citizen and mosaic maker. He should recognise the name.' I had an inspiration. 'In fact, I have a letter from him here, commending me to Appius, written at the request of His Excellence himself.' I pulled the scroll-bag out. 'No doubt you can identify the seal.'

One look convinced him. 'Wait here, in that case!' This time he closed the door.

I sighed and settled for a lengthy wait. There was nothing to look at. Even the gamblers had now disappeared (from a hasty scuffling overhead, I guessed that they'd heard mention of high authority and swiftly moved to a landing further up).

I hardly had time to note this before the Nubian reappeared, opening the door now to its full extent. 'This way, citizen – he's agreed to speak to you.' He managed to sound insultingly surprised, but took my wet cloak and ushered me inside.

I'd expected to be shown to the reception *exhedra* that acts as an atrium in a flat like this. Instead, I was hustled through to a little study room where Titus Flavius was sitting at a desk, surrounded by slips of bark-paper, and scratching something on a writing-block. He looked up as I came in and put the stylus down.

'Junio.' He extended a ringed hand for me to bow over. 'This is unexpected.' His voice was not unfriendly, but it was hardly warm. He motioned the Nubian away, before he turned to me again. 'You have come with a message from His Excellence, I'm told, and bringing that letter which I wrote commending you. Tell Marcus it is polite of him to send you, and I can only apologise if Appius insulted you. I presume you didn't get the contract?'

I shook my head. 'Unfortunately not, I was on my way to see him, but—'

He gave a weary sigh. 'He wasn't there? I could have guessed. Perhaps it's just as well. If you'd got the commission he would only have tried to use you as a spy.'

(Past tense, I noticed, but remarkably similar to Marcus's reason for wanting me to get the work.)

Titus stretched out a hand. 'Let me have that letter. I will put it on the fire. It will be no use to you, or anyone.'

I havered. 'With your permission, Councillor, it is important to me still.' It was – it proved I had reason to want Appius alive. But Titus Flavius was instantly, and uncharacteristically, enraged.

'That is my communication. And my scroll-bag too. Give them back at once. I wrote the note as a favour to Marcus Septimus and it is worse than useless now. I don't want my name associated with Appius Corvinus.'

I still withheld the bag. 'And yet you planned to host a feast with him?'

He glared at me. 'You seem remarkably well informed!' But he'd turned ashen. He compressed his lips. 'How did you hear that? It was supposed to be a secret.'

'It's no secret at the garrison,' I said. 'The commandant himself was invited yesterday.'

Titus thumped the desk so hard the stylus jumped. 'That wretched Appius! So he did go in and ask the legate to attend? And mentioned me, it seems? Even after I said I'd not be part of it. I saw what he was up to, and I told him so. I didn't believe he'd dare to ask the legate after that, although he threatened to.'

'Among other things, I understand?' I said. 'The sentry on duty overheard it all. Including what appeared to be outright threats to you.'

Titus Flavius had risen to his feet, white with fury. I have never seen a man so roused. 'What's this? Common gossip? And now refusing to give my letter back? I don't believe you've come from His Excellence at all!'

I attempted to protest.

He paid no attention. 'Have you come for money? To try to blackmail me? If you were not a citizen, I would have you flogged. Well, I'll not be drawn. I should have seen that this would happen in the end. Well, let them accuse me openly. I shouldn't have been so cowardly before. If you hoped I'd pay for silence, you will have to think again.' He swung around to the brass gong hanging on a frame and seized the beating-stick – to summon the Nubian, presumably.

I gabbled desperately, 'I do come from Marcus. He was at the fort with me. I came to warn you about Appius . . .'

He looked at me sideways and sank back in his seat. 'Appius! I need no warning about him. That evil, traitorous snake. Untrustworthy as Celtic coin and slippery as a fish. Spying and prying into everything – and worse.' He spoke bitterly. 'When I think what he was trying to involve me in . . . and the means he used . . . I could have . . .'

'Murdered him?'

A sigh. 'That would at least save others from his devious ways. If he hadn't been so clearly in the Emperor's pay, someone would have done it long ago.'

'Be mindful what you're saying, councillor,' I said. 'That's what I came to tell you. Somebody just has.'

He looked oddly at me for a moment. 'Has . . . what? Killed Appius?'

I nodded.

'Huh!' He made a noise that might have been a laugh. 'Well, I can't say I regret it. I can't think of anyone who deserved it more.' He looked at me. 'So why has Marcus sent you to me? I hope no one expects me to attend the funeral. Though there might be something satisfying about doing so.'

'Appius is lucky to be having one,' I said. 'They almost put him in the common pit, as just another victim of the plague.'

'Plague? Dear gods. I thought you said that he'd been killed?' If the surprise was feigned, he did it very well.

'He was. Poisoned, I am inclined to think, then dressed in peasant's clothing and dumped beside the road. If someone had not stopped and recognised the corpse, the death-cart would have taken him, for sure, as just another victim of the pestilence.'

This time there was no doubt. Titus was grinning like a mask of comedy. 'A neat way to dispose of an unwanted corpse. But it didn't happen? Someone found the body and reported it?'

'I did,' I told him. 'I realised it was Appius because I'd worked for him before. Which is why your letter matters to me, Councillor. It proves that I had cause for wanting Appius alive. It might also be useful evidence for you – no doubt you were hoping for an introduction fee.'

His jaw had tightened, and I saw the colour rising in his cheeks 'What are you suggesting? That I had a hand in this?' He was already reaching for the gong again.

'I'm suggesting nothing,' I said hastily, and was relieved to see him drop the stick again. 'But others may. Circumstances are against you, Councillor. Yesterday you were seen to argue with him in the street. He threatened you with ruin. You storm away and this morning he is dead. But it's only then that you call on the victuallers and cancel the mutual feast you'd planned.'

'You can't believe this! You think I murdered him?'

'I think you know more than you are telling me. When I first came you said you "could have guessed" he wasn't home today. Which of course, he wasn't. But how did you know that?'

He seemed to be debating whether to reply, but finally he did. 'Because he'd caused me great offence. And inconvenience.

Deliberate offence, I thought, though from what you say, perhaps that wasn't so.'

'In what way offended?'

Titus gave a sigh. 'He'd prevailed on me to go with him to dine with one of his special cronies, Elvinus Posthumus, last night. You may have heard of him?'

I nodded grimly, remembering what Marcus told me in the lane. 'A friend of yours?'

Titus looked uncomfortable. 'Hardly that. I've never liked the man, but I've dined with him before, when Appius was at his machinations once again. This time, he said there'd be another guest as well – some man from Eboracum, who was a dreadful bore. I was to be placed beside him because he had no conversation except bees.'

Valerius, clearly. But I simply said, 'Not very flattering. But you did not refuse?'

He gave a rueful shrug. 'I didn't dare. Better bees than what might happen otherwise. And it could not be too bad. This man was a patrician, it appears.'

'So you've dined with Appius Limpnus several times? From choice – I hear the food is very good – or did he have some hold on you?' I saw a look of panic cross his face. 'I can't imagine what,' I added hastily. Titus had a reputation for being just and fair. 'But perhaps it hardly matters, now the man is dead.'

Titus Flavius gave me a sideways look. 'I think you could imagine very well. Though, perhaps, as you say, it doesn't matter now.'

'Something to your discredit, which he held over you?'

He ran a hand through his thinning tawny hair. 'He had a writing tablet he'd discovered at the provincial court, which somehow had got missed. Appius had ways of spying everywhere. It was a half-written message from our former governor, and was addressed to me, thanking me warmly for my letters of support, just as he was setting off to fight Severus for the throne.'

'And you had written such letters?'

'As a councillor I'd written several times and had letters in reply. Clodius was our governor, at that time, so my actions were no more than loyalty. But support for Clodius is called treason now. You know what it would mean. Expulsion from the Empire at the very least, being left to rot on some isolated rock or even execution. It's been done before. I was expecting a visit from soldiers in the night if I didn't meet with some convenient "accident" arranged by Appius. And now he's dead, though I suppose the letter might fall into other hands . . .'

There was nothing sensible I could say to that, so I merely made a sympathetic noise.

'Curses on the very name of Appius,' he said. 'Even in death he managed to cause me misery. He persuaded me to stand my servants down, and send my personal litter to collect him from his house.'

'But they did not return?'

'Not for hours, by the water clock. By which time they were chilled and I was ravenous. Appius had promised pork and duck, and I don't know what other things besides, all sent from London for his private use, while the rest of us in Glevum – ever since the plague – can find nothing fit to eat which does not come from someone's country estate.'

'He did not take your litter?'

'Oh, indeed he did. Asked for it to come a little before dusk, because he had some business in the town. He was going to use it to collect this boring guest and bring him here – the chair's a double one – then we would walk together to Posthumus's flat. It is not far away, and last night it was fine.'

'But that didn't happen?'

'Appius got the boys to drop him near the forum. For "business", he declared. Told them to come back for him when the sun had fully set. But he did not return, although they waited in the cold for hours. Eventually they came back home and I was forced to rouse the kitchen staff and have them make a meagre meal of bread and Roman cheese for me. I have never felt so insulted in my life.'

'I don't think you can blame Appius for the delay,' I said. 'But about this pork and duck. Did he leave it in the litter? Or was it all a myth?'

'Apparently he had some sort of sack with him and no doubt took it with him when he went. I assume it contained the treats that he described. It's no great distance from the forum to where Elvinus lives. Supposing that he ever went there, in the end . . .'

'I doubt it, from what I can deduce,' I said. 'I now must go back to the legate and report. But one more thing: did you ever have dealings with Craithaw, the miller near the docks?'

He frowned. 'The name seems familiar. I think there was a case – something about a rival who was contaminating flour? I found for him and handed out a fine. He actually sent me a gift of several loaves. And very good they were. Why do you ask me that?'

'Because Craithaw was found with Appius, on the road. Equally dead, and dressed in the same way.'

'So they were acquainted? Perhaps it was Appius who paid the advocate at court? I wondered at the time how a common miller could have afforded it.'

'Then he'd be indebted to Appius,' I said. 'I think you may be right. I'll tell the legate that. You have been most helpful. Thank you for receiving me.'

'And thank you for the news. It lifts a weight of fear—'

I interrupted him. 'Councillor, your troubles are not over yet. I shan't mention your correspondence with Clodius, naturally. But I fear you will be questioned over Appius's death. You would have had the motive and opportunity. But thank you for information as to where he meant to dine. I'll try to call on Elvinus Posthumus.'

'News of the death will be all over town by now. I hadn't heard it – I haven't left the flat today, since visiting the victuallers first thing. But Posthumus makes sure he knows the latest. Supposing he denies expecting me?'

'Why would he do that? If you and Appius did not appear, what does he have to lose? Unless you are suggesting that he's guilty of this death?'

'So you still suspect that I am?' He was furious again. This time he did reach out and strike the gong. The Nubian appeared like magic at the door. 'Show this man out, and don't admit him if he calls again.'

My damp cloak was round my shoulders in a flash and I was ushered firmly out. The door slammed behind me and I went slowly down the stairs.

TWENTY-FOUR

The rain had stopped by now and there were people on the street. But the afternoon was drawing on, and – though the sky was grey with cloud – a faint glow in the west suggested that sun would soon be set and I'd have to report to the garrison by then. Marcus would doubtless have gone home long ago.

But there were two things I wanted to do first. Titus Flavius said that Posthumus lived nearby.

I asked a passer-by, who looked at me suspiciously but directed me. It wasn't far, just further down the street. Another first-floor apartment. This time I fairly bounded up the stairs and hammered confidently on the door.

I was answered, finally, by an aged slave. 'What is your business here?'

'I am the citizen Junio,' I said, 'I come on behalf of the commander of the fort and His Excellence Marcus Septimus.' That should get me a hearing.

Something flickered behind the old grey eyes. 'May I ask what it concerns?'

'I merely wished to ask your master something about the dinner that he hosted here last night.'

He did not invite me in. 'Wait and I'll tell him that you're here.'

There was a longish wait, then – to my astonishment – I saw that Elvinus had deigned to come out to me himself. He was dressed in a dark-green synthesis, not unlike Marcus's, but that was the only similarity. The ex-councillor was as bald as a pig's bladder, with a face like an outsized turnip and a spindly beard. His eyes were cold as pebbles, and he held a wine goblet as if to indicate that I had interrupted him, but he spoke civilly enough. 'I'm sorry, citizen. You were enquiring about a banquet held here yesterday? There was no such thing. You've been misinformed.'

'Perhaps not a banquet. But you were expecting people for a meal? Appius Limpnus among them, I believe?'

A widening of the pebble-eyes. 'My good fellow, as you see, we're not admitting visitors, not while there is any danger of the plague. Otherwise, naturally, you'd have been invited in. Last night I spent here quietly alone, as my servants could doubtless testify. If Appius Limpnus dined away from home, it was certainly not here. Perhaps he's retreated to his country house again, for fear of pestilence. Either way, I'm afraid I cannot be of further help to you. Please give my best wishes to the commandant.' He gave a thin smile, raised his cup of wine, and softly closed the door.

A flat denial, as predicted! What should I make of that? How could Titus be sure what Elvinus would say, unless he knew there was no dinner here last night? And why was he so anxious and Elvinus so calm? One was clearly lying, but I did not know which, and neither was going to speak to me again. I'd hoped to impress the commandant by discovering where Appius dined last night – supposing he had actually appeared. What was I going to tell him now?

Nothing whatever, as it turned out. I presented myself at the gate of the garrison and explained my mission to the sentry there.

It was not the same man I'd seen earlier, who might have let me in. This one was younger, adamant and keen. He blocked my way with his spear. 'Impossible, townsman. The commandant is supervising the evening training drill. His instructions are quite clear. He is not to be disturbed, short of an official message from Londinium or Rome.'

'Or a serious crisis?'

'Like a civic riot or a rebel raid? Perhaps, but I do not think you qualify.'

I tried a little charm. 'There is a crisis of a kind. I'm here at his request. My name is Junio. I am a citizen and was tasked with taking some messages to town.' I gave no details. I wasn't sure what the soldiery were supposed to know. 'I came to tell him that it has been done, and I have information which might be of use. Merely possibilities, but I think he ought to know.'

Whether because he'd learned I was a citizen, or because I'd been on an errand for the commandant, his attitude relaxed. A little. 'I'll try to see he gets that message when they've finished the drill. I can't promise. He always watches training – since he decides what form it's going to take – then retreats to the praetorium to dine and does not like to be disturbed. Late morning is the best time if you want to talk to him. I'll do my best, but I suggest you come back and see him then. Tell the man on duty what you just told me. It won't be me by then.'

'And no doubt relieved to be relieved.'

He grinned wryly at my little jest. 'To tell the truth, I'm glad to be on sentry-watch right now. He's got them drilling with heavy weaponry.'

'Heavy weaponry?' I was envisaging battle-rams and slings.

'Weightier swords and shields, so the real ones feel lighter in a fight. Exhausting stuff. Much more pleasant simply standing here. Even in the rain.'

I laughed politely and thanked him for his help. But inwardly I was far from happy. I was going to have to spend the night in Glevum now. And Tenuis was waiting at the workshop all this time. He would be anxious by the time I got there.

He was. 'Master, what kept you? Problems?'

'More than you'd believe.' I took off my damp cloak and sat down on a stool before the fire. He'd found dry wood from somewhere so there was a cheerful blaze and the workshop was tidy, swept and warm. 'I had to report the death of Appius Limpnus to the fort, then I was sent to notify the households and ask questions round the town. It has taken me all afternoon. I see you've been busy too. You've done a good job here. No customers, I suppose?' Tenuis had found me a contract more than once.

He gave me a shy grin. 'Not so far, anyway. That's why I had time to clean the shop – it was very dusty, musty and cold without the fire. Fortunately I found some dry wood in the store upstairs. But no potential customers. At times like this, mosaics aren't the first things people think about.'

'Except for a thanksgiving shrine, perhaps,' I said wryly. 'But Appius is dead, and that won't be happening. Now, I'll have to stay in Glevum overnight. I need to speak to the commandant again and I've missed him for the day. It will have to be the morning. You ride Arlina home, and tell your mistress. Come back here tomorrow afternoon, and I'll return with you.'

'You'll be sleeping in the attic, master?' Tenuis sometimes stayed there overnight himself. There was a palliasse and blanket at one end, though the rest was mostly storage space. 'It will be damp up there, I fear.'

'I'll bring the blanket down and sleep beside the fire.'

'Have you eaten anything?' He gestured to the bench, where there was a bag. 'The mistress sent some food with me. A piece of bread, cooked turnip, an apple and some nuts. Not a feast, but something anyway.'

'I was given something at the mansio earlier, but I'll be glad of this,' I said.

'Shall I bring more water from the fountain for you too? There is not much in the jug.'

'Sufficient for my needs, for the moment anyhow. Now go, before you find yourself benighted on the road. We have no pitch-torch to light you on the way.'

Tenuis looked unhappy at the prospect of riding through the woods alone in the encroaching dusk. But he said obediently, 'Very good, master. I'll go and get the mule.' (I have an arrangement with a hiring-stables to mind her through the day.) 'Sleep well.' He put on his cloak and crept away.

I did not sleep well. For hours I did not sleep at all. I was feeling nauseous – perhaps cold turnip had not agreed with me – and I'd contrived to spill most of the water in the jug, so I was thirsty too, and I'd no chance to rinse my dusty feet and hands. My head was heavy but rest eluded me. So rather than toss and turn unhappily, I tried to make sense of the day's events.

The result was not inspiring. I had asked a hundred questions but was no further on. I still didn't know for certain where, and with whom, Appius meant to dine. And there was something niggling in my fuddled brain, a feeling there was something I'd missed or overlooked, but I couldn't work out what it was.

I felt befuddled – probably from stress and pure fatigue – but

I had to think this out. Someone had murdered Appius, and there'd be a price to pay for the whole of Glevum if a culprit was not found.

So, who would have killed him? Almost anyone of rank, if they had dared. He was the Emperor's delator, who sought out people to denounce. And almost all Glevum had supported Clodius. The question was, who had both special reason and opportunity?

Titus Flavius seemed the obvious candidate, though he'd been a friend of Marcus's. Or so Marcus thought. Yet Flavius had been close with Appius of late. Enough to feature on Sylvanus's list. Was that only because Appius held that letter over him – supposing it existed? Blackmail was sufficient cause to kill. And Titus had the opportunity. By his own admission it was his litter which collected Appius last night.

To bring the spy to his house, and walk elsewhere to dine? Wasn't that peculiar? Doesn't a rich men send a litter only for his *guest*? Titus denied the dinner had been his, but I only had his word for that – or that Appius didn't arrive at his house as arranged. And it would do no good to ask the litter-boys. Titus's staff would say whatever he required. Besides, he could have poisoned Appius, even if he'd merely called there on the way elsewhere. Any guest of rank would be offered refreshment of some kind.

The thought of refreshment made my stomach churn, and I turned my thoughts elsewhere. What about Elvinus Posthumus? Appius was supposed to be his friend, but in this town, who knew? Had Appius some power over him as well? Allegations of another letter, possibly? And there was something in Elvinus's glib denial that I did not believe. Or was I not thinking clearly?

I groaned. I had forgotten Craithaw in all this. Might he have been delivering fresh bread for the feast, wherever it was held? That batch I saw might not have been the only one. And he liked to deliver to the rich himself. Suppose he'd stumbled on something dangerous? What was planned for Appius, perhaps? If so, the murderer might need to get rid of him as well.

What was I overlooking? The peasant clothes! Of course!

Whoever killed Appius had evolved a clever plan for disposing of the body without raising suspicion that there'd ever been a crime. But there were two sets of clothing. Was that coincidence? Did that purple-striper buy both tunics from the stall to draw less attention to himself, and then find an unexpected use for the superfluous one?

Nonsense. Too glib, like Elvinus Posthumus. But what else could it have been?

The only person wanting Craithaw dead was Pulchra. She'd had a curse-tablet made to that effect. She had an ass and cart, which she could have used at night to take the bodies out. But it would be difficult. Craithaw was a large man; she'd have to disguise him under sacks of flour, and there was no hoist at the other end to help her get him down. She was strong, but surely not as strong as that? Hardly likely, either. A lone woman on a cart at night would have alerted the sentry at the gate, on suspicion of fleeing her husband's – or father's – legal tutelage. Besides, whoever bought the peasant clothes had been a man, and a patrician one at that.

Anyway, I thought dreamily, she had no reason for killing Appius – quite the opposite. He was a prestigious customer, who paid them handsomely. Not to mention the gruesome end one could expect for murdering the Emperor's special appointee.

I groaned again. My stomach was troubling me and I was getting more fuddled by the hour. I had forgotten Gaius Valerius and his bees. And his unlikely depiction of Appius as helpful and affable. That was, surely, quite impossible? So what had really happened? A quarrel Valerius was hoping to conceal? Afterwards, he'd sent Appius that wine. Appius had been scornful of its poor quality. Yet he had taken it with him to dinner, as a gift. According to his steward, anyway.

Supposing that he and Craithaw shared a glass of it? That would account for the death of both of them. But how? Appius would hardly have turned up in person to collect the loaves he had ordered; he would expect them to be delivered. And why would Craithaw be sharing wine at a patrician's house? No purple-striper would demean himself by including him, however much he was a citizen.

It was no use. I had to get up and go out into the chilly night and use the midden pile as an improvised latrine.

Perhaps the night air helped because – as I settled down again – it occurred to me that if that wine had poisoned Appius at dinner, why would the host not have called the watch at once? Anyone would be terrified, but there would be witnesses that he himself had brought the wine. Including his steward, who'd be 'questioned' anyway – though my father always said that information gained that way was unreliable. Under torture people will agree to anything.

And moving the bodies . . . why do that at all? Unless Valerius had arranged that already with his host? There had been peasant clothing on the market stall. I had only the stall-holder's word for when it had been sold – and he was anxious for me not to try to find his customer. Could Valerius have bought it on his way back to the mansio, after visiting Appius? Especially if the delator had not, in fact, suggested settlement but (much more likely) refused the claim outright? Clearly no other guest that night had drunk poisoned wine. Could this have been not one man, but a conspiracy?

Only one thing was certain. This was not an accident. Someone had planned it, and quite cleverly.

I sighed, and fell at last into an uneasy sleep.

TWENTY-FIVE

Dawn brought little comfort. The fire was out by now and I was cold and stiff, and feeling rather worse, if anything. My head was aching. There was not a drop to drink. And the lump of turnip that I'd kept in reserve turned my stomach at the very thought.

I wrapped my cloak around me, shivering, and managed to stagger to the midden heap. There I added to the mess by throwing the wretched half-gnawed root away, and a trip to the fountain filled my jug again. I drained it on the spot, though I attracted curious glances from the others waiting there. But it cleared my brain sufficiently to think of filling it again before I took it back.

I rued having sent my slave and mule away. All I wanted was to stumble home to the care and comfort of my wife and family.

But first there was the matter of the garrison. They would have been up and active since the bugle at first light. So, with a sigh, I locked up the workshop and set off unsteadily for the fort.

It was a crisp morning, with a touch of frost, and I had to watch my every step as I went in through the northern city-gate and found the colonia preparing for the day.

A few slaves and shopkeepers were taking shutters down and putting out displays of rugs and bowls. There was not much else on offer, and not enough of that for the piles to force me off the pavement as they used to do. But the town was recovering. I wished I felt the same.

It was a different sentry on the gate – of course! – and I had to talk my way inside, but finally an escort was grudgingly assigned to take me to the inner tower. I'd hoped to see the legate quickly, but there was no chance of that. I was left to stare wretchedly at my sandals in the waiting room downstairs for what seemed an hour while busy orderlies hurried to and fro, chalking up the day's rosters and punishment fatigues. None of them showed the slightest interest in me.

Finally a soldier came clattering down and told me that the commandant would see me now. I had to struggle to my feet and force them to carry me upstairs.

The legate rose to greet me, harassed and not entirely cordial. 'Citizen Junio, I am glad to see you here. We received the message from Appius's slave that the household there had been informed and we've arranged to bring the body back to them for the funeral. But Marcus assured me that we could hope for other news. I trust he is correct. This happened under my jurisdiction, after all. I must have something to tell authority.'

The governor and Emperor, he meant, with a warning that Marcus was still a suspect in his mind. And probably me too. Perhaps me most of all. Even in my fuddled state I understood the threat. It emphasised again what a huge risk there was, and what a powerful drive to find someone – anyone – to blame. I sincerely wished I'd never stopped to investigate that boot.

He sat down, leaving me to stand, swaying, like a nervous witness before a magistrate.

'I do have information,' I said unhappily. Despite the water, my throat was parched and dry. 'But it is not conclusive. And it does not explain why Appius should be found out by the road, dressed in such a fashion, and with the miller at his side.'

'Well?'

It took me a moment to arrange my thoughts. 'I discovered that he left his house that evening before dusk, dressed in fine clothing, and was going out to dine. He did not tell his household where. He never did, they say.'

'But surely a slave would have accompanied him? Even if he took a carrying-chair an attendant would have followed it.'

I sighed. If he was going to question everything, I was not sure I could continue. 'They swear not, Worthiness. It was not his custom to take a page with him. A private litter came to fetch him from the door.'

'Then we must discover who that litter belonged to.'

I shifted uncomfortably to keep myself upright. 'I can answer that, Commander. It belonged to Councillor Titus Flavius – the man with whom he was proposing to provide that civic feast.'

'I did not realise that was a joint affair. So, it might still happen after a decent interval?' The thought appeared to cheer him briefly, but then his frown returned. 'Unless this Titus proves to be the poisoner of course, which has to be regarded as a possibility, even if they were apparently good friends.'

I was so anxious to be out of there that I blurted out the truth. 'I don't think that describes it, Commandant. Titus was afraid of Appius, I think. And the feast will not be happening. Titus formally cancelled with the victuallers yesterday. He'd had a public quarrel with Appius over it the day before.'

'The day, in fact, when Appius was killed? The day before yesterday?'

Too late now. I nodded. 'Though it appears that they were still to dine together later on. Appius was heard insisting upon that.'

'And Titus admits he sent the litter as arranged?' The legate was positively beaming now. 'Then we have our culprit. It is obvious. Appius went to dine with him, but Titus was still angry and contrived to kill his guest. How else could he have known that Appius was dead – which he surely must have done – to cancel the feast that they had mutually arranged? You say yourself he was afraid, and Appius Corvinus was not a man to cross. This Titus must be questioned.' He raised his voice. 'Orderly, in here.'

The soldier who had been waiting at the door came in, saluted and began to mumble the password of the day. The legate cut him off. 'The decurion Titus Flavius is to be summoned here at once. Send an escort party and arrest him if required.'

'Immediately, sir.' The man saluted and was gone.

The legate turned to me. 'You have done well, citizen.'

I shook my head. 'Titus swears that Appius did not arrive. Says the litter-boys were told to drop him in the town, where he had urgent business, and come back for him a little later. But they insist he didn't come. And Flavius was not to be the host. They were going to dine elsewhere, and with another guest. Or so he declares, although the prospective host he named denies the claim.'

'So we do not believe it. Appius went to Titus's and met his death.'

'Which does not explain how the miller came to die.' I was feeling ghastly but I had to speak.

The legate looked at me. 'Supposing Titus was a customer, and this miller fellow was delivering fresh loaves to him that night? That would make sense, if there were guests to dine. I assume the miller does make deliveries himself? He does not send a slave?'

'He does not have one at the moment, Worthiness. Craithaw insisted on delivering to the rich himself. His widow was quite specific on that point. He got handsome payment, which she saw little of.'

The legate waved all this aside. 'So that would explain the presence of Craithaw at the house. And if he accidentally stumbled on what was planned for Appius, it follows that Titus would have to kill him too.'

'And what about disposing of the corpses by the road? Dressed in that way?'

'My dear fellow, Titus would have had no trouble doing that. He lives in an apartment somewhere, I believe; but, like any wealthy Roman, he will have a horse. Probably stabled in the courtyard at the back, where he doubtless has a kitchen block as well, where food could be prepared – and poisoned if required. With helpful servants he could load the bodies easily – and as for the clothing, this was obviously planned. It would not be difficult for him to purchase that, or obtain tunics from land-workers on his own estate, who would no doubt rejoice to have better ones instead.' He looked triumphant at his cleverness.

I had to admit that I hadn't thought of that.

That pleased him even more. 'It would explain the clothing. And the mutilation too. Hacking off the ring finger was no accident – the signet might have been observed. But it was made to look like wolves. Altogether, it was a clever plan. I admit a grudging respect for Titus for having thought it out.'

'But . . .' I began.

'I'm sorry, citizen, I see that you are anxious to defend the man – he was once a supporter of your patron, I believe – but I'm convinced that he's the killer. He will deny it, naturally, but denial won't save him when the facts all point to him. I have to say it is a great relief. Besides, what other explanation could there be? Did Appius have other enemies?' There was no mistaking the veiled threat behind the words.

I hesitated. 'There is another factor. A small flask of wine. Someone gave it to him, a few days ago, and his steward tells me that he was contemptuous of its quality. Sniffed it, rather than tasted it, I think. But it seems he took it with him in the litter, when he left – as if he intended to make a gift of it.'

'To whom? Surely not his host? That would be an insult.'

'Appius always contributed to feasts – Londinium ways, perhaps – and that's been welcome since the plague, I hear. Goods have been in short supply, while his were sent from the governor himself, and of the highest quality.'

He frowned. 'But this wine was not? It was a local gift? Are you suggesting it had been tampered with? And poisoned Appius? That might offer Titus a defence.' The legate did not like that, it was clear.

I was seriously struggling by now, but I contrived to say, 'I am suggesting it is possible, no more. But if Titus is right in saying they were going elsewhere to dine, I know the donor was to be the extra guest. He might have arranged that it was served to Appius alone.'

'With the so-called host as his accomplice? Who was that anyway? Another local councillor?'

'Titus says they were to dine with Elvinus Posthumus. A former member of the curia.'

'Who denies that he expected any guests, you say? I think we can dismiss him. And the donor of the wine?'

'Gaius Valerius, who is staying at the mansio.'

'The bee man? He seems innocuous. What has he to do with this?'

I was having difficulty thinking, but I managed to explain. 'He says he had a distant claim on Fortunatus's estate, and that Appius offered settlement, which seems improbable. I wonder if it's true, or if he's trying to deflect suspicion from himself.'

'So he might have a grievance against Appius too?' He sighed. 'I thought that this was simple, but I suppose we should investigate that wine. I'll have Gaius Valerius called and Elvinus Posthumus as well. Though I think we can imagine what they'll say. Thank you, citizen. The Emperor and governor will want a quick result.' He seemed to see me for the first time, properly. 'Are you quite well, citizen? You're looking very pale.'

'I have a headache, Worthiness.' An understatement, if I ever uttered one. Someone was banging rocks around my skull.

'And you are unstable on your feet.' He sounded angry now. 'I hope you have not come here carrying the plague.'

The thought, for some reason, had not occurred to me. Perhaps on account of the fuddle in my brain. I began to mutter something, but he interrupted me.

'Get out of here at once, and stay away, you hear? Soldier! Come and see that this man leaves the fort. At sword-point and as fast as possible. But cloak your mouth and keep your distance if you can, and ensure the sentry does. I think he may have the pestilence.'

I was dismissed in no uncertain terms. I tried to bow, but stumbled and was ushered out and marched ignominiously away into the street.

TWENTY-SIX

The fresh air was reviving, so after a moment leaning on the wall, I turned and began to walk unsteadily back towards the town.

But I got no further than a pace or two before a curtained litter passed me, going the other way and at alarming speed. I took a startled backwards step and, to my astonishment, it stopped. The curtain was pulled back and someone called my name. For a moment I didn't recognise the voice.

'You! Of course! I might have known that I'd have you to thank for this!' It was Titus Flavius, huddled in a blue fur-trimmed cloak and looking furious. He signalled to his slaves to put down the carrying chair and gestured me across to speak to him.

I shook my head. 'I may be carrying the plague.'

'Nonsense. Yesterday you were in the peak of health.' He gave an exasperated sigh. 'But I suppose one must be careful. I'll get out and the litter-boys can wait for me around the corner there.'

Once they'd gone, he stood at a distance, holding the corner of his cloak around his mouth. It muffled his voice, but he raised it sufficiently for me to hear. 'I see you are not well – a judgement from the gods, perhaps. I hope you're proud of what you've done. I risk my life attempting to keep your patron safe and this is my reward. My fault, I suppose. I was not brave enough. I would have been better to defy Appius and taken the consequences!'

I said stupidly, 'My patron? I don't . . .'

He waved the words away. 'Your father's patron, then. Though if you are not officially Marcus's *cliens*, he behaves as if you are. He had me write that letter recommending your services to Appius. Which you have no doubt handed to the authorities as evidence that I had connections with the wretched spy?'

'I've done no such thing.' At least my mind was clearing, though I still felt very weak. 'And I don't believe Marcus knew that you were friends.'

'Friends? With Appius? I would trust a serpent first.'

'But you were going out to dine with him last night – and planning to co-host a feast with him. That speaks of friendship.' I don't know where I found the energy.

'Or intimidation. Which is what it was. Oh, he was courting me – seeking me out to talk to at the baths, inviting me to dinner and being as charming as he could – in public, anyway. He held that incriminating letter, so I did not dare refuse. At first, I thought he was simply hoping for my vote, and my help in swaying other members of the curia. But I got more and more suspicious.'

'Of what?'

He looked around as if he feared he might be overheard. 'Has it occurred to you how many people who stood somehow in his way are now conveniently dead?'

'Of course, he's had ex-supporters of Clodius exiled . . .'

'As I am only too aware. But that's what he was sent for. That's not what I mean. First Fortunatus and his household chanced to die, just when Appius was looking for a townhouse to fulfil the residential requirements for candidature to the curia. Fortunatus was very much against his standing, I recall – he thought it was in order to spy on members of the curia.'

'But he caught the plague. As I may have done myself,' I said pathetically. I was still leaning on the wall, but I dared not walk away from somebody of Titus Flavius's rank.

'Did he? It's true there was already pestilence about. But it was elsewhere in the town, and it spread from house to house extremely fast. Fortunatus – and his household – were the only victims in that area for weeks. Another day and he wouldn't have been there. He was planning to escape out to his country house – then, suddenly, they all fell ill and died.'

'You think Appius had a hand in it?'

'I began to wonder. He went to visit Fortunatus a day or two before – allegedly bearing conciliatory gifts in an attempt to win him round. He was fussing about it in the forum, next day, saying he'd almost caught the pestilence. Nobody thought anything of it at the time – just supposed that he'd tried to bribe the old man into supporting him, and—'

'You can't suppose . . .'

He cut me off. 'And there was Rufus too. Another one who was openly opposed to Appius's candidature. Another one whom Appius visited.'

'But I thought . . . the supperating rash . . . the hasty funeral?'

'I made enquiries . . . And guess who began that rumour about disfigurement – and – in the absence of local family – appears to have bribed and bullied the household slaves and undertaker to put him on the pyre that day – with dreadful threats about what would happen if they talked? Then, suddenly there was this plan to host a feast – though in my name, of course.'

I stared at him, appalled. 'You think he was planning something for that night?'

'I've become convinced of it. I thought, at first, he only wanted me involved so that the rest of the curia would be sure to come. He even made a formal contract out of it – he would pay for everything, provided the most senior magistrates were there. But it occurred to me, if anything went wrong – if Marcus, for instance, were to die – who would be legally responsible, according to the records at the victuallers?'

'You think Appius meant to murder Marcus at the feast?'

'Not personally, of course. Arranged some kind of accident, I expect – or contrived for someone to put poison in his wine. So I cancelled yesterday, and called on him that morning to tell him so. But he wasn't there, of course.'

The blue-cloaked visitor! Of course! That tallied with what Sylvanus said. What would the legate make of that – a visit the next day? Probably declare it was a ruse, to suggest he didn't know that Appius was dead.

The thought of Sylvanus stirred something in my befuddled brain. 'Wine, I wonder! Did Appius leave anything in the litter, that night, when he got out of it?'

Titus frowned. 'What has that to do with anything?'

'A great deal, possibly. Appius had a flask of wine with him when he left home. And a bag of other delicacies for the feast. It has not been found?'

'Not as far as I'm aware. I'll ask the litter-boys.'

He whistled, and they reappeared at once, but the enquiry produced a determined shake of heads.

'He was carrying something when he got into the carrying-chair. His steward told me so,' I said, finding the strength to think, from somewhere. 'What did he do with it?'

The lads exchanged a glance, and then the largest spoke. 'Took it with him when he left, I suppose. But I couldn't swear to it. He had a cloak around him, and we were more concerned about his instructions to return.'

Anxiety acted like a tonic cordial on my brain. I turned to Titus. 'Perhaps he was really intending to come back? Do you suppose he'd poisoned it himself, and meant it to be used for someone at the meal? Yourself, for instance?'

'I doubt that. Appius wanted me alive, at least until the feast. Though possibly it was meant for someone else. But what are you suggesting? That he somehow drank it by mistake? That makes no sense – if he'd poisoned it, he would not have touched a drop. Unless . . . it was tampered with by someone else?'

'That's possible. The flask had been a gift.'

Titus was so startled that he almost dropped the cloak from round his face. 'Then why didn't you say so earlier? It gives me at least a shadow of a plea. You don't know who gave it to him, I suppose?'

'I do, as it happens,' I replied. 'Valerius, the tedious bee man who was to dine with you. He had a claim on Fortunatus's estate – or thought he had. I ought to have suspected him before. His account of meeting Appius should have alerted me. He spoke of him as courteous and offering settlement.'

'Doesn't sound like Appius Corvinus to me. Much more likely to send him off with a rebuke. Which might give Valerius a grudge – enough to send a gift of poisoned wine.' Above his muffler, Titus was looking visibly relieved. 'Something, at least, I can plead in my defence. Though much good it will do me, if that letter's found.'

'Supposing that it actually exists?' Something had suddenly occurred to me.

'You don't believe it?'

'If an incriminating message had been found, wouldn't it have been used against you long ago? I think Appius made a clever guess. Letters between you and the provincial governor – I imagine that you used the Imperial post?'

'Naturally! Being on the curia!'

'Then it must have been known that Clodius sometimes wrote to you. Of course, the fort was manned by a different legion then, but not all the relay stations in between. A man of Appius's skills . . .'

'You think he may have invented the whole thing?' Titus Flavius looked as if a heavy rock had been lifted from his shoulders. 'When I think of the fear I've been under all this time . . .'

I said hastily, 'We can't be sure. He may have been withholding it just to blackmail you. But I think it's probable.'

'Citizen,' he said, 'you give me hope.' The voice was warmer now. 'It would be ironic, wouldn't it, if Appius was poisoned by a gift to him, instead of his gift poisoning someone else? But why would he have drunk it, at that time of night, when he was expected out to dine? Hardly with the miller! Appius would not have deigned to call on him, even if he'd ordered bread. He'd want it delivered.' He shook his head. 'It's a mystery. But I must go and see the legate before I anger him still more. Could you arrange to have the bee man sent across as well? I'll willingly pay you for your services.'

I did not say that he was being summoned anyway. 'Of course.'

'I won't hand you the money, just in case,' he said. 'Though you don't look like a victim of the plague to me. If you were, you'd be deteriorating fast, but you seem a little better. Have you eaten recently?'

I shook my head. 'Some food from home last night. But nothing since. I think it must have disagreed with me.'

'Then use this to buy breakfast. But no point in risking plague – especially if I'm likely to be dragged to Rome in chains or exiled to a barren rock somewhere.'

He tossed something at my feet. I stooped, rather dizzily, to pick it up and was surprised – and delighted – to find I was holding a half-denarius.

I turned to thank him but he was already gone. I stood for a moment, looking at the coin. Quite enough to buy myself some food – and something to take home a little later on. But I had no appetite. The very thought of a hot pie, or anything from a hot-food stall, made me feel nauseous.

What I wanted was something plain. A hunk of bread, perhaps. A pity that Pulchra would not be baking anything today. Or even selling flour. Not until her husband's pyre at least. Until then she would be funesta – connected with a body awaiting funeral – and socially forbidden from doing anything. Any bread would be rejected anyway. Once news spread about Craithaw's mutilated corpse (and it would certainly be all over town by now) no wealthy Roman would want to be defiled by anything connected with the mill.

But I was not a wealthy Roman, just a queasy one. I thought about that batch I'd seen cooling yesterday. Spoken for, she'd said. If it was a single order, as it appeared to be, it would be for a wealthy household, and so good quality. But, being funesta, she could not deliver it. The buyers wouldn't want it anyway. So, what happened to the loaves? It was worth a try, I thought.

They might be a little stale by this time, but good bread lasts much better than the common stuff – and these would be much cheaper too. And, though Pulchra now had Craithaw's purse, she might be glad of a few extra coins. Besides, I confess I was not averse to seeing her, to tell her what I'd learned.

I was feeling a little better, to my great relief. With plague, they say, you just get worse and worse until you die. It must have been that cold turnip after all. Comforted that I was not contagious, I stopped at the fountain outside Minerva's shrine, and drank from my cupped hands. And knew at once that this had done me good. Perhaps I had offended Jove by failing to make a cleansing ritual last night. I must remember to offer an oblationary morsel of what I ate today, wherever I managed to obtain it from. Supposing it was fit to sacrifice.

Which made me wonder suddenly. Was that bread fresh yesterday? Or was it left over from the day before? Appius, after all, had come to order bread – presumably as one of his presents to his host. And Craithaw always delivered personally to him. Did that explain how the two came to be together later on?

But I was being stupid. The loaves were still there yesterday. Obviously Craithaw had not taken them and Appius would hardly have come for them himself. If they'd not arrived, he would have sent a slave, together with a stinging reprimand. And Pulchra wouldn't cross her husband by delivering them herself – at that time she did not know that he was dead.

I crossed the road, using the raised stones which kept my sandals dry. I wanted to look respectable when I arrived. Which reminded me of Appius that night. Dressed formally to dine. Why would he want loaves? He was not the host. I had lots of witnesses to say he'd gone out to dine. And taken that flask of wine which Valerius gave to him. Had he shared that with Craithaw – and it had accidentally killed the miller too?

That was ridiculous. Appius would never have drunk with Craithaw in someone else's house. Had he gone in person to the mill, after all? To cancel the delivery, perhaps, or alter the delivery address? To that of his intended host? Much depended on who that really was. Everything suggested Titus. The sentry heard Appius insist that they'd still meet that night – as though it were a threat. And Titus sent his litter – as if for a guest. And there had been that quarrel earlier. Had Titus decided not to host the dinner after all, so the venue was altered? That made a kind of sense.

Pulchra might know. Craithaw never told her anything, but if Appius came again . . . and it was there he shared the poisoned wine? Socially unlikely but not impossible. As a woman she wouldn't have drunk with them, of course, but she would have found the bodies.

And almost died of fright. The punishment for killing Appius would be terrible, and no court would believe it was an accident. They needed a culprit, and having made that death-curse for her husband would not help. Of course she'd try to move the corpses somewhere else. And it would explain the undelivered loaves.

But I was back to where I started. How could she have done it – even with the cart and hoist? Or pass the sentry at the gate without being questioned at that time of night? Or, for that matter, have provided that disguise? Those peasant costumes had been pre-prepared; these murders had not been an accident.

I was going round in circles, and the street was slippery. I tried to concentrate on simply getting to the mill.

TWENTY-SEVEN

I was not surprised to find a barrier. The rope across the entranceway, loosely tied between a large stone either side, was just what you'd expect – like the chalked notice on a board against the wall announcing they were shut, 'until further notice'. No one expects the funesta widow of a citizen to trade. A bunch of cypress was nailed to the board, a usual courtesy, warning potential customers to keep away from an ill-omened place. What I'd not expected was to see a glow, showing that the oven was still hot. Pulchra must be active and about, at least.

The door to the building was firmly closed, and another bunch of cypress nailed to that, but I ignored the double warning and – without much difficulty – climbed across the rope into the milling yard.

That baking oven was the only sign of life. The rack of loaves had gone – from the smell they were probably what was burning in the fire. Not surprising really – they could not be sold and certainly Pulchra couldn't eat them all herself. There was nothing in the mixing vat. Even the starting-mixture bowl had disappeared. Pulchra may not have been wholly sorry at her husband's death, but she was taking her public mourning seriously. Wise of her, though obviously I'd have to buy my bread elsewhere.

However, I was here now, and I wanted to report, and find out if Appius had called again that night. I went up to the door, and – conscious of ill-omens – spat upon my hand and rubbed it behind my ear, before using it to knock. But there was no reply. She was not receiving visitors. I rapped a little harder, then stepped back and called her name, reassuring her that it was only me. No response, and no face at the upstairs window-space. I was alarmed now. I hammered on the door, with no result. At last, I put my shoulder to the gap and pushed with all my might.

It did not give at once, but when it did I was appalled at what I saw – or didn't see. No donkey in the stall, no sacks of grain, no cart. Only a few limp leaves left in the storage vat, and all the extras in the cupboard behind the lid had disappeared.

Shock acted like a dose of cold water on my brain. I found I was thinking far more clearly, suddenly.

I shimmied up the ladder, but it was the same up there. The storage chest was open, revealing a neat pile of Craithaw's clothes, and one of the floorboards had been lifted to reveal a hole, but there was nothing here of Pulchra's own beyond the stained and tattered tunic she was wearing yesterday. Not so much as a blanket on the palliasse.

Dear gods! I hoped my earlier theory wasn't right – that Appius had brought the poisoned wine with him and shared it with Craithaw. But it rather looked like it. Pulchra found the bodies and disposed of them (though how she could have passed the guard and where she got the peasant clothes was still a mystery). She'd have no proof of innocence. The penalty for mariticide was a frightful one, and that for killing Appius still worse. At present there was nothing to link her to the crime, but by fleeing she was admitting guilt. There'd be a search for her.

Not because of Craithaw. His death was unimportant in the scheme of things, and though there would be a pretence of seeking her for that, it would not last long. But Appius! The whole army would be on high alert, at every bridge and crossing, every inn and staging post, throughout Britannia. And when they found her – as they almost surely would – I could not bear to think about the fate that lay in store.

I sat down on the bed-straw and tried to think it out. But I came to the same conclusion every time. Appius had been here in the morning – I had Pulchra's word for that. And more than likely he had ordered bread – a special order, as he sometimes did. No doubt he intended to give it to his host. It would explain his dismissing the litter-boys that way. He would not wish anyone to know he had demeaned himself by calling, in person, to collect his purchases.

Had he shared the wine with Craithaw – offered it in part payment for the bread, perhaps – and been induced to take a cup himself, not realising that it was poisoned? The miller would be thrilled to entertain a man of rank and would not recognise inferior wine. It was the only explanation I could find.

Valerius, I began to think, had much to answer for. But he was with the legate, so I could not talk to him. And I must find Pulchra, if I could, and persuade her to come back. I'd promise, if she was accused, to speak on her behalf.

I slid down the ladder, and – remembering to push the door so it looked closed again – I managed to get across the rope and out into the street. Unobserved, I thought.

But a voice came from behind me. 'Don't you understand plain Latin? The mill is shut, and probably for good.' I whirled around. The bald-headed slave again. 'Craithaw's dead,' he said, 'in case you hadn't heard – rumour says he killed himself because he couldn't pay his debts. Certainly his goods were confiscated. I saw them being driven out of there myself.'

'By his widow?' I was convinced now that my guess was right.

He looked at me as though the moon had struck me mad. 'Well, naturally not. Someone had sent a man for it. I saw him driving off. Just as day was dawning. And clearly in a hurry to get out – before the ban on horse-drawn transport, I suppose. No sign whatever of the wife, or anybody else.'

I frowned at him. 'What sort of man?'

'Two arms, two legs, a body and a head. What else?' He was derisive. 'Or I imagine so. I couldn't see; he was wrapped up in a cloak.'

'So, it might not have been a man at all. It might have been a woman, simply dressed like one? Especially in the half-light . . .?'

'In that case she had enormous feet and very hairy legs!'

'There was light enough for you to notice that! What were you doing at that time of day?'

'Full of questions, aren't you? But since you ask, my master heard about the miller's death and wanted me to be the first man in the queue elsewhere. But other people had the same idea, and though I waited I had no success – for which, no doubt, I shall be whipped when I get back. I wasn't thinking about carts until it nearly ran me down – I told you townsman, it was certainly a man.' He frowned at me. 'What business is all this of yours, in any case?' His face cleared. 'Unless perhaps he owed you money too.'

'Something of the kind,' I said mendaciously. 'The money in his purse was owed to friends of mine.'

'Too late for that, I fear! All gone – just like the flour I was supposed to buy, So you'd better go and tell them so – while I go home and take my punishment.' And he slouched off morosely back the way he'd come.

I couldn't help feeling sorry for the slave, but his news disturbed me very much. I'd assumed that Pulchra left here of her own accord and taken all her goods. But it seemed that she had not. Had she been kidnapped? Was she dead herself? And was it true that Craithaw had fallen into debt? He might have done. Attempting to live the high life with his 'fancy friends' and doubtless gambling. But his death had been no suicide.

One thing was certain, I had to find that cart. I began by calling at the gates – I wanted to know if it had left the town, or if a major local creditor had really seized the goods, as he would have been entitled to. In which case, where was Pulchra?

No news at the northern gate – the road which leads you to Londinium. No information at the west. The eastern gate is more or less abandoned now, leading only to a muddy path, a swamp and a stream where watercress is grown. The southern gate – the one that lies on my way home – is very close beside the mansio and fort, so if this was a criminal escape, I did not hope for much.

I was not mistaken. The guard on duty had just come on watch, and there'd been no unusual reports. I sighed. I was no further on – indeed I had now another mystery to solve. I was about to turn dispiritedly away, and go to wait for Tenuis at the shop, when someone behind me tugged sharply at my cloak.

I turned. It was Decima, the woman with the ox. The cart was parked nearby, and she was smiling now. 'Citizen, I hoped I might see you come this way again – I knew you hadn't passed us yesterday. I was looking out for you. My husband says we should be grateful to your patron – I've forgot the name – but I know it was you we have to thank. You made him promise he would pay us, if we stopped the death-cart from collecting up those dead, and he kept his word. You can't imagine what a difference it has made.'

I was embarrassed by this gratitude – and a bit impatient too. I had other things to think about. I tried to wave her gracefully away, but she clutched my cloak again.

'The thing is, citizen, we're wondering if you could do the same again. After you had left us there on guard, the children were playing – and they found this in the ditch.' She held out something in her palm for me to see. 'It isn't gold, I think. But it might have some value, possibly?'

It was a signet ring. It wasn't gold. In that case, she might have hoped for a significant reward. They are worn only by the very rich, or civic officers. (My own father had one, when he was on the curia.) But this was not a poor man's iron one, either. It was bronze, and finely made – probably belonging to an artisan, and used to mark his work or seal his documents. I glanced at the engraving and heaved a disappointed sigh. It was the symbol of the bakers' guild. Found by the bodies – so most likely Craithaw's own.

I explained this to the woman. 'You might find someone at the guild who would give you something for it. But I think the owner was one of the corpses that we found. Taken off to hide his identity, no doubt.'

She looked doubtfully at me. 'You mean that miller? It couldn't be the other one – from the fuss they made of taking him away, you'd think he was the Emperor himself. He would not have worn a thing like this.'

'Craithaw's, almost certainly,' I agreed. 'But you won't be getting anything from him. Even if his widow wanted it, which I rather doubt, his goods have all been taken – to pay his debts, they say.'

She was still frowning. 'But surely, citizen, it can't possibly be his. He was well-fed and stout. When the funeral guild collected him, they struggled with the weight. This would never have fitted on his hand. A woman's ring, perhaps?'

TWENTY-EIGHT

Pulchra? For a moment I flirted with that absurd idea. But, of course, that could not be. Few women had a personal seal in any case – what would they use it for? They could not make legal contracts of their own. A few rich individuals – like Julia, Marcus's wife – might have a stamp to seal the wax on messages, but not generally a ring.

'Signet rings are usually for men,' I said to Decima.

'I'm sorry, citizen, I didn't know. We don't read or write, so we don't have documents to seal. But one thing is certain: this would never have fitted that miller's hand. Besides, his ring finger was missing.'

'Ever since a milling accident,' I agreed. 'So it could not be his.'

She was ahead of me. 'Unless it was worn on a cord around his neck?'

'Perhaps,' I said. 'It couldn't be a woman, anyway. Females can't join that guild, however much they bake.'

'I don't know why they shouldn't,' she said indignantly. 'They're in lots of other guilds, these days – though, naturally, they don't have the same rights as the men. But it does ensure a proper funeral. We'd join the cutlers if we could afford the dues.'

'The bakers pride themselves on exclusivity,' I said. 'There was a time when a baker's son must be a baker, and could not escape, except to public office.'

She ignored my little homily. 'Speaking of funerals, do you know when these two are to be?'

'You are not expecting to attend?'

She coloured. 'Of course not, citizen. That would be impertinence. But when the undertakers came to put the rich man on a bier, they brought some finery to dress him in. They let us take the cloth that he was wrapped in, and his boots and clothes. The army were there, guarding, and they did not object. Those things will be very useful to my family. We'll do a purifying ritual, of course, but it's safer not to use them until his spirit is at rest. I don't wish to bring a curse on us.'

I understood. 'Craithaw's pyre will be this evening, I presume. The guild will see to that. His widow arranged it yesterday. But Appius will be cremated at the town's expense, with a procession and paid mourners, and a memorial feast. All that will take a day or two to organise. Longer still if he is laid in state – though the undertakers will have to hide the mutilated face while people pay respects. No doubt most of the councillors will go, and make sure they are seen.' (Even Marcus, I thought regretfully.)

She clicked her tongue impatiently, 'A lot of fuss for someone who was generally disliked. Don't look at me like that – we've been here at the gate, and you can't help hearing people murmuring. It's clear that everybody's relieved that he is dead – but terrified of what might happen next if the authorities don't find the man responsible.'

An observant woman. It gave me an idea. 'You've been here, just outside the gate, throughout? You haven't seen a donkey cart go by, very early after dawn? Driven by a man dressed in a hooded cape?'

She shook her head. 'I'm sorry, citizen, I cannot help you there. There was a donkey cart, but that was a man and wife. Travelling people by the look of them – or moving out of town. They seemed to have their whole life piled on that little cart.'

I gulped. 'A woman, did you say?'

'I said "wife", or that was my impression anyway. It might have been an adult daughter, or a female slave. Or his mother, even. They both wore hooded cloaks and I did not really look. Is it important?'

A whole new possibility had occurred to me. 'Very important, if my guess is right,' I said. 'I only wish I had my mule with me. I'd like to catch them up – but that's impossible on foot. No doubt they were moving fast?'

'Not so fast as to be suspicious, citizen, though they urged the ass on when they'd passed the gates. As anybody would.'

She glanced at me sideways. 'You think those people were the murderers?'

'I don't know. Until this moment I thought it was an accident, and the woman moved the bodies afterwards, though I couldn't understand how she managed it or provided that disguise. I was concerned she might be blamed for everything, and the punishment would be simply terrible. But now . . .' It had occurred to me, at last, that Pulchra had talked of her husband's body being 'near the forest' when I'd simply said 'beside the road'. She'd been deceiving me. 'There are two of them, and I am not so sure . . .'

'So how would your catching them improve things?' she enquired. 'Seems to me it would only make things worse.'

'I meant to persuade her to come back,' I said. 'And plead her innocence. Even now that might be possible.'

Decima snorted. 'Mere tradespeople? Some chance there'd be of that! The authorities would have them put to death by sunset, simply to appease the Emperor.' She grinned at me. 'Admit it, citizen. You cannot save them, but you'd like to know the truth.'

'Perhaps,' I acknowledged with a sigh. 'But every moment they are moving further on, and there's already little chance of catching them. There's a hiring-stables down the road – they know me, they pasture my mule when I'm at work. They'd let me have a horse. But by the time I got there, it would be far too late. I would never catch the cart – or find which way it went.'

'My turn to help you, citizen!' I thought for an instant she was going to suggest the ox-wagon, which would be much too slow. But she surprised me. 'My eldest boy runs faster than the wind. I'll send him on for you, with a message, and they'll have the horse prepared by the time that you arrive.' She raised her voice and shouted to her brood. 'Sanus, come here – I have a job for you.'

He was a sorry figure, with his tattered clothes and grimy face, but I had to take the chance. I told him what was wanted. 'Tell them it's for the citizen Junio,' I said. I was about to add that there might be a reward, but he was already halfway down the road. Decima was right, again. He ran, if not exactly like the wind, a great deal faster than I could myself. I thanked the woman and set off after him.

The horse was waiting, ready-saddled when I reached the gate, and my name already chalked up as the hirer on the board. So after exchanging the formal words which bind a contract, I was on my way.

I'm quite adept at riding on a mule. A horse is a different matter. It is higher for a start, and one's legs dangle at some distance from the road. I was glad of the Roman saddle to wedge me into place. I clamped my knees against him and he moved into a trot, which left me clinging desperately to his neck and reins. For a few moments I was sure that I would fall, but I managed to cling on and gradually learned to get the swing of it.

I dared not urge him to any greater speed, but at least I looked more like a horseman now, and certainly we were moving faster than a donkey-cart. All the same I feared I'd lost it by this time – there are several turnings where the road meets ancient lanes (including the one that leads down past my house). But I needn't have worried. There was the stricken tree, and stopped beside it on the verge, the donkey-cart.

As Decima had said, it was piled high with goods – flour sacks among them. The ass itself was tethered to the tree. There was no sign of a driver, or a passenger. I contrived to slow my horse and slithered down. I was so impatient I almost failed to tie him up, but I recalled in time, then went across to see what I could see. Pulchra was kneeling, with her back to me, scrabbling in the ditch. The cart had hidden her from view.

'Pulchra?'

She looked up, terrified. 'You! I might have known . . .' She was not wearing mourning clothes, but a neat ochre tunic with a *birrus* – that long, hooded, woollen British cloak – over it. She looked like any travelling tradesman's wife. 'What do you want? It isn't what you think . . .'

'I'd like to believe you, Pulchra,' I replied. 'Tell me I guessed aright. It was an accident? Though you should not have tried to dispose of the bodies in that way.'

She was staring at me, still on her knees, fear shining in her eyes. 'I don't know what you mean.'

'Oh come,' I said. 'Of course you do. Just as I know what you are looking for. Unlucky that your friend should chance to lose it in the dark.' I held out the signet ring.

She went to snatch it, but I pulled it back.

'You recognise it? I was sure you would. That is what finally convinced me that you brought the bodies here – and that you weren't alone.'

'How did you guess that?'

'The ring, in part. It suggested Loftus came and helped you dump them here.'

'You are mistaken, citizen. Loftus doesn't bake. The ring is mine. My father was a guild member, by right, and when he died with no surviving son, it came to me. Not that I could wear it openly – I could never join the guild – but I wore it on a cord around my neck, under my tunic.'

'And what did Craithaw say to that?'

'He never knew. He would have beaten me. He strove so hard for his.'

'But surely, as your husband . . .'

A scornful laugh. 'He hardly ever touched me, and even then he was usually drunk. I hid it under me. It was the only thing belonging to my father I could keep – and it has his initials engraved around the rim. Any guild member would know whose it had been. That's why I made Loftus stop and search. He was unwilling, but I thought it might be found and prove that I was here. I didn't imagine anyone would follow us so soon.'

'So I was right! It was Loftus! I couldn't believe you'd moved the bodies without help. Even passing through the gate would draw attention from the guard. But a couple – with the corpses hidden under sacks of flour, no doubt – would raise no suspicion. Loftus is well-known to the garrison – he supplies them now and them – and he has a daughter. In the dark, and hooded, you could pass for her. When you returned, the cart was emptier. Nothing remarkable in that.'

'But what made you think of Loftus?'

'A piece of gossip that I heard long ago, before the plague.

Craithaw had him fined for contaminating bread – and no doubt it was Appius who paid the advocate, or bribed the magistrate. He had friendly dealings with your husband, even then?'

'If it hadn't been for you,' she muttered bitterly, 'no one would have suspected anything. But you come along and find the corpses – and apparently the ring. Why didn't you tell me about that yesterday?'

'I hadn't seen it then. It was found by someone else. But why did *you* not mention that Appius came that night to pick up loaves you'd baked for him? He did so, didn't he?'

She was sullen, but tears stood in her eyes. 'If you know all about it, then you know he did.'

'And shared a flask of wine with Craithaw?' I waited for her nod. 'That was meant for Appius alone, so you could not be blamed. Whose idea was it to use the peasant clothes, and hope the bodies would be picked up by the cart?'

There was a flash of puzzlement across her frightened face. 'Why, Appius's of course. He brought the clothing too. He had it in a sack. He'd contrived to exchange it at the marketplace for the two unwanted tunics that our slaves had used. I heard him and Craithaw gloating over it. They must have been planning this for half a moon.'

It was my turn to be baffled. Appius and Craithaw had planned to murder? Yet they had ended up victims themselves. My brain was scrambling to keep up. 'But if they both were poisoned by the wine . . .?'

A voice behind me interrupted us. 'Leave her alone.' I whirled around. Loftus had approached us from the forest edge, but I'd been too engrossed to notice it.

He was not a big man, but he was sinewy and strong. A miller has to be. He was looking grim and he was carrying a carving knife. He held it like a weapon. For the first time, I was terrified.

'I'm a friend of Pulchra's . . .' I gulped.

'I know who you are. You buy your flour from me. You're Junio. A friend and client of Marcus Septimus, the senior magistrate! And seeking to have us dragged before him, I can see. Are they offering some kind of a reward?'

They would be, certainly. I tried to murmur something, but he shook his head.

'Get on your knees. Your hands behind your head.' He gestured with the knife. 'I'm going to tie them with your belt.'

And there was nothing I could do, except comply.

TWENTY-NINE

Loftus spoke over me to Pulchra. 'What's he doing here, by all the gods?'

'I wanted to persuade her to return.' It sounded feeble, even to myself. 'Her flight will just create suspicion. There is nothing otherwise to connect her with the deaths.' I was burbling with fright.

'You seem to have made a connection, citizen.' He came around to face me, tapping the knife handle against his palm, as if assessing what he might do with it. 'Get up, Pulchra. And don't worry. This is unfortunate, but I'll deal with him.'

'You knew him already?' She was incredulous. 'This is the man I was telling you about, who came into the mill when I was clearing up and frightened me by asking lots of questions. On behalf of the authorities, he said.' She scrambled to her feet.

As she did so, she revealed both her arms.

'Your wound has made a marvellous recovery,' I said. 'No bandaging, I see. And no sign of a scar.' If I was going to die, at least I'd do so having learned the truth. 'So, it wasn't your blood on that cloth I saw?'

She did not deny it. 'I damaged Craithaw trying to lift him with the hoist onto the cart. And even then I could not manage it. I had to risk fetching Loftus to come and help. He said the gouges would look like claw marks of a bear or wolves, especially if we did it to the other body too. It might even help, if it disguised the face.'

'And because you couldn't move the seal ring, you cut the fingers off, and made that look like the work of animals? Then put him on the cart as well and covered both with sacks?'

A nod. 'As you seem to have guessed!'

'Pulchra! What are you saying? Now we can't let him go, or he will have us traced and executed, for sure.'

'But he knows what happened. He knows they were poisoned, so he must have wondered why there was blood, at all. I was washing it away when he arrived. I tried to hide, but then he started probing at what was in the niche. I had to stop him, and there was blood on me, so I wrapped the washcloth round my hand and told him I had hurt it on the hook.'

That humbled me. I was so proud of having noticed there was no wound today that I hadn't considered where the blood was from. 'Appius's ring. What did you do with it?' I asked. 'You could not hope to sell it within the Empire.'

'I put it the oven fire, of course. The finger too. And all his fancy clothes. Together with the pottery wine flask and the other poisoned loaf. The sandals were the worst. I thought they'd never burn, although I made it very hot – and there was such a smell. I put a pot of stew on top, and let it scorch to help disguise the stench. No one seemed to notice anything amiss.'

Including me, I thought. 'And Craithaw's clothes?'

She glowered at me. 'I burnt those, too, of course. They were stained with blood and vomit. Except his sandals. I just took them upstairs. Where else should they be? Then we dressed the corpses in the peasant clothes that were hidden in the stall. It wasn't easy, but we managed before the bodies got too stiff.'

'The thing that I don't understand . . .' I made to rise, but a sharp blow on the arm dissuaded me. I stared at Loftus. He hadn't used the blade, but this was serious. The penalty for assaulting a citizen on the public road is death. I was unlikely to get out of this alive.

I tried appealing to him. 'I know that showing disrespect to a patrician's corpse is an offence. But not a capital one. My testimony may be of assistance to you yet, as to the rest of it.'

He frowned at me. 'What do you mean?'

'That wine was meant for Appius alone – and I know who sent it to him. His steward knows he took it when he left home that night. That could be sworn in court. If he shared the wine with Craithaw, and it killed them both, then – despite appearances – it's not your fault. A magistrate might be persuaded of the truth – that the donor poisoned it – but he's a rich patrician and can afford defence. By running off, you only attract suspicion to yourselves – and to the fact that you, Loftus, had a grudge against both victims . . .'

I was rewarded by another rap. 'There was nothing the matter with the wine. Pulchra discovered what they planned for her – and for some hapless relative of Fortunatus's – and swapped the loaves, that's all.'

'The loaves?' I said stupidly.

'Let me tell him, Loftus. He knows half of it.' Pulchra turned to me. 'I told you I'd returned home for a water jug earlier that day. When I did so, Appius was still there. His litter-boys were not.'

'Still on that errand that you spoke about?'

'Probably fruitless, to get rid of them. Appius and my husband were sitting in the store, on stools beside the table, murmuring in low voices. I was astounded to find Appius there. They were so absorbed they didn't notice me, and I didn't interrupt – I was afraid of Craithaw's anger, so I loitered in the yard. But then I heard my name, so I sidled up behind the door and listened carefully. If I hadn't, I would certainly be dead.'

'What?' I was appalled.

She went on calmly. 'They were going to poison me – and this other person too – by putting something toxic in two different loaves. Craithaw was to mark them from the rest of Appius's order by the little round doughball on the top – you know how loaves are decorated in that way sometimes? The poisoned loaves would have a slightly oval one. No one unsuspecting would ever notice it.'

I was trying to take in this new idea. 'And what was Craithaw to put into it? Some of that special flour from Londinium, I suppose.'

'That, of course,' she said. 'But that's not poisonous. It was the flavourings. For my loaf, it was to be the herbs. Hemlock among them, this time, I believe. And for the other . . .'

'That white powder in the jar?' I was a fool, I thought. 'I thought that was chalk.'

'It was,' she said. 'Though Craithaw claimed it was a raising agent to improve the bread. The poison was the salt. Heavily laced with something called arsenicum, and supplied direct from Rome. Until I heard them gloating, I'd no idea of what it was. Craithaw said it would improve the taste, but it was vital that you used exactly the correct amount, so he insisted on doing it himself – just as he always did the flavourings. Didn't trust me to get it right, he said. He kept the cupboard locked, and it was only after he was dead that I could use his keys and open it. And you were just about to put your finger in the jars. I had to stop you – you might have tasted it.'

I had. A pinch of it in fact, and it was on my fingers too. I licked them when I ate with unwashed hands last night. It would explain why I'd felt unwell today.

'I heard them discussing how they'd eat one of the harmless loaves made with Appius's flour themselves that night – on some excuse – and gift me a poisoned herbal one which looked just the same. "Dead in ten minutes," Appius said. I was so shocked I made a noise, so then I had to go inside. I pretended that I'd just come back, because I'd broken the water jug.'

'And Craithaw, for once, did not punish you?' I said.

She shook her head. 'Too satisfied with what he had in store for me. But I knew now what the marker was, and when he'd set the loaves to rise a bit – and gone out to drink with members of his guild – I swapped the oval markers to two harmless loaves, but substituted a little knife-point marker of my own on the two poisoned ones.'

So that was the agreement! Titus was correct. Appius had been poisoning people for his private gain, and Craithaw had agreed to help, in return for money to sue Loftus with, and a chance to rid himself of a wife he didn't want. Together with a handsome payment for his bread, to ensure he didn't talk. What an unlovely pair! Perhaps divine Juno had arranged the breaking of that jug! 'So when Appius came that night, you gave them a poisoned one?'

A wry smile. 'I allowed them to select it. And they drank some wine he'd brought. That was so unusual I'd have been suspicious anyway, I think. But it was a celebration, Craithaw said, for a huge order to supply a feast, and for Appius's candidature for the curia. They didn't expect me to eat with them, of course. I was only there to serve. They told me to bring the loaves, and Appius bestowed one of those with an oval ball on me – a reward, he said, for all of my hard work. They didn't look at theirs too carefully. I'd put the loaves with the knife-point markers on the top, and they tucked into one. And he was right. Within a short time both of them were dead – though they had frightful cramps and sickness first. I had to clear that up before I moved them anywhere.'

'So Appius brought those peasant clothes . . . for you?'

'And for his other victim. That man would die within the hour, he said. He himself would feign a stomach ache and their host would offer him somewhere to lie down, and later help him to dispose of both of us. It was a risk of course. If there was any question, people would blame the host.'

'And who was that to be? Not Titus Flavius?'

'Titus Flavius? Never heard of him. Someone called Elvinus something, I forget. Craithaw was to deliver the remaining loaves to him, courtesy of Appius, and Elvinus would see the right man got the other poisoned one. Appius had bribed him handsomely. I heard him say as much. And he had information that ensured the fellow's help – and silence afterwards. Appius was to offer to "take the man safely to the mansio", in front of other guests and slaves, but actually he was to be brought back to our mill for a change of clothes. I'd be given one as well, and then we would be taken out and left beside the road. Two dead peasants to be thrown onto the cart. I only did to them what they meant to do to me – and others. And he did select the poisoned loaf himself.'

'You dressed Craithaw in rough clothes. What prompted you to leave the purse with him?'

'We thought the soldiers on the death-cart would help themselves to it, and be all the more concerned to throw them in the plague-pit with no questions asked. Appius didn't have a purse of course – he'd set out to dine, and he was not a man to tip the servants anything. He'd left payment for Craithaw in the sack, he said, and we found it later on. Besides, my husband had a special knot that I could not undo, but there obviously weren't many coins in the purse. I didn't realise two were silver ones, until you gave it back.'

'Part of the bribe, no doubt.'

'A down-payment, rather. Appius paid more handsomely than that,' Loftus interrupted. 'We found a money chest beneath the floor. And there was money in the sack – together with some fine cooked meats that we have brought with us. We've enough cash to live on for a good few years. Or would have done, if you'd not interfered. Appius and Craithaw conspired to kill, and it was only justice that their crime turned back on them. That I don't regret. But now I'm faced with having to dispose of you. Why couldn't you have stayed at home, and let the matter rest?'

'Couldn't you just tie him up and leave him here?' Pulchra asked. 'Someone will find him and it would give us time to flee.'

'Not now you have told him everything. We have done nothing wrong . . .'

'Except defile the patrician's corpse,' I said. 'And conspire to let him kill himself.'

'You see?' He heaved a heavy sigh. 'He knows too much. We cannot let him go. Perhaps we should have stayed at home ourselves, as he suggests. But, thanks to him, the trap's now tightening.' He turned to me. 'Citizen, you can hardly regret this more than I do myself. I will try to make it quick and merciful. The knife is sharp. If you lie down it will support your head and make this easier. Otherwise, I shall have to behead you where you are. I'll try to stun you first. Pulchra, go out onto the road and make sure there are no witnesses.'

I thought of making a run for it, or putting up a fight, but he would have stabbed me before I gained my feet.

This way was quicker. I hoped the edge was sharp. I lay face down in the muddy grass and braced myself to die.

THIRTY

It was chance that saved me – the sound of carriage-hooves. The donkey moved sideways, alarmed at its approach.

Pulchra came darting back around the cart. 'Loftus, wait – there's someone coming. A fast gig by the sound of it. You don't want to be discovered in the act.'

I opened my eyes and rolled onto my side. Loftus was standing over me wielding the knife, as if about to plunge it in my neck. He lowered it and clapped his free hand round my mouth. 'Don't move,' he said to me. 'Make a sound, and I will slit your throat.' He turned to Pulchra. 'Go round and soothe the ass. That gig will soon have passed. Nothing visible here to draw attention from the road.'

I looked around for ways to make a noise, but Loftus had too firm a grip on me. I simply lay there, frozen to the spot, and listening to the sounds of wheels and horses thundering by. And slowing. Stopping?

A pause, and then the sound of footsteps on the road. Loftus let go of me, and whirled round, as if prepared to kill the interloper too.

The footsteps paused beside the cart, and after a moment a young man appeared around the back, peering cautiously at us. A handsome young man: dark-haired, athletic, strong and dressed in a slave-tunic of sombre blue.

Loftus took one step forwards.

'Callidus!' Relief had torn the word from me. 'Don't touch him, Loftus – this is the personal page of Marcus Septimus.'

The slave's eyes widened in surprise. 'Citizen Junio! It's you! The master sent me to find out what anyone was doing here, stopping at this spot . . .' He saw the knife and paled. 'I'll tell him you are here.' And he was gone, quicker than an arrow.

The two conspirators exchanged a look of horror.

I found my tongue. 'Cut free my arms! Before His Excellence arrives. Quickly, or you've sealed your death warrant for sure.'

Loftus looked doubtful, but Pulchra seized the knife. It was sharp, as promised, and she cut swiftly through the belt, muttering to Loftus, 'I told you it was dangerous to flee.'

I flexed my arms to ease them. 'Why did you?'

'Because of you, of course. You knew that Appius had dealings with my husband, and had come in person to the mill that morning. I had to tell you that. You asked so many questions, I knew you would find out. You had only to speak to the neighbouring businesses.'

'And it's because of you that we've been discovered now.' Loftus scowled. 'No one expects to see a recent widow in the street.'

'Or at the funeral?'

'Not all wives attend, without a slave or male relative for support. And I spread a rumour in Glevum that Craithaw was secretly in debt, so there was no surprise to see his goods removed. It very nearly worked.'

'And you had Pulchra hiding in the cart?'

'Until we found a quiet alley where we were unobserved. Then she got out from underneath the sacks . . .'

'And horrible it was, after what was there before. I kept begging him to let me up before I drew a curse.' She scowled at me. 'Though I already had, it seems. Loftus wanted me to stay there till we were out of town, but I couldn't stand it. And it was hard to breathe.'

'I let her up to silence her and we drove through the gates. If I was challenged, I was prepared to say that I was taking her to a kinsman who'd offered her a home. But the sentry hardly glanced at us. Thought she was my daughter, probably. She was hooded and it wasn't fully light.'

'Hush!' Pulchra interrupted. 'That patrician's coming. I hear footsteps. Put that knife down, Loftus. You'll only make things worse. It's all over; we'll never marry now.' She turned on me. 'And it's all because of you . . .' She tailed off as Marcus and his slave appeared.

'Junio!' He extended a ring for me to kiss. (I did not have

to bow, I was already on my knees – and so, by now, were the fugitives as well.) 'I'm told that these wretches have kidnapped you. And I hear there was a knife. I assume they're the killers? Were they about to murder you as well?'

They had been, but I did not answer that. 'Not kidnapped, Excellence.' I took a chance. 'I hired a horse and came here of my own accord. It's tied up by the road. This is the miller's widow. She'd paused here to make a purifying offering to the gods.' I opened my hand in which I still held the signet ring.

Pulchra let out the breath that she'd been holding and Loftus stared at me.

'After she had killed him, and doubtless Appius too?' Marcus thundered. 'But you intercepted them! Junio, we have much to thank you for.'

I shook my head. 'Appius and Craithaw killed themselves unwittingly,' I said. 'And it's these two you should thank. They prevented the same thing happening again, first to Valerius—'

'Valerius? Who's that? I've never heard of him.'

'The bee man who is staying at the mansio. He is a man of rank. Appius planned to poison him at the meal that night. Assisted by Craithaw and the host.'

'And who was that?'

'I believe it was to be Elvinus Posthumus, Excellence, though he denies it now. I think he panicked, realising that something had gone wrong, and swore he knew nothing of the whole affair. He was to see that Valerius got a poisoned loaf of bread. But it did not happen, because Appius was dead. And so was the baker.'

'By unhappy accident? I don't believe a word. This woman killed them.'

'All she did was give them bread that had been meant for her.' I explained about Appius's order, the 'additives', and how Pulchra had changed the marker on the poisoned loaves. 'Appius often took presents to a feast. It was his idea to leave the bodies here, dressed as peasants – he had acquired the clothing and brought it to the mill, which, incidentally, proves that he had planned this in advance. It seemed a clever plot, and she adopted it.'

'It would have worked too.' Pulchra was bitter. 'If it hadn't been for him!'

Marcus ignored her. He was looking stupefied. 'You are sure of that? Why would Appius want to kill this visitor?'

'Because he was a relative of Fortunatus's.' I outlined the story. 'Appius made promises he never meant to keep. He was the Emperor's delator, but he was more than that. He had a line in private assassinations too.' I repeated what Flavius had said about people who stood in Appius's way being suddenly 'conveniently dead'.

'Fortunatus and his family, and Rufus too?' Marcus was shaken.

'And probably that old friend who wrote to warn you and then died. At the civic banquet the commander talked about, it was intended to be you – and probably Flavius himself, since Appius had no further use for him.'

Marcus was more than shocked. He was positively grim. 'Me? Is there any evidence for this?'

'Titus Flavius suspected it, that's why he cancelled the thanksgiving feast. And I believe these two still have the poisonous ingredients. Sent direct from Rome at Appius's request.'

The woman shook her head. 'I put them in the fire. We could not leave them there. Someone might have tasted them and died. I do have the arsenicum jar. There might be traces there. I did not have time to clean it properly.'

Marcus looked at me. 'You're quite convinced of this? Appius has been poisoning people with his gifts of bread?'

'Not consistently enough to bring suspicion himself, but from time to time,' I said. 'I thought at first it might have been the special flour he boasted of. But the poison was in the flavourings he supplied.'

'And he fell victim to one of them himself?'

'Most of the bread was excellent, of course. It always was if Appius supplied the flour. So superior that people vied for it. The different poisons took different times to work, and caused differing symptoms too – so there was no pattern, and men did not suspect. Nor did I, to start with. I thought it was something in the wine. But he and Craithaw ate a poisoned loaf.'

'Which was intended for Valerius, you say?'

'Not that one,' Pulchra said. 'He intended that for me. Craithaw wanted to be rid of me, to gain the mill and be free to wed again. Appius was to come and share bread and wine with him – not a thing he'd ever done before – on the pretence that it was a celebration for them both, and make a present of a poisoned loaf to me.'

'A celebration?' Marcus was abrupt.

'Appius's nomination for the curia, and Craithaw's major contract for a civic feast. It was only a fiction anyway. Appius supplied the wine and asked for one of the loaves he'd ordered. I let them choose their own – making sure that the ones from which I'd moved the oval markers were on top, though I'd substituted another marker of my own. Appius and Craithaw selected theirs, and Appius graciously bestowed an oval one on me. I didn't poison anyone; they did that themselves. It is true that we desecrated Appius's corpse by leaving it here for the death-cart to collect, but – as Junio says – it would have otherwise happened to the bee man. And to me.'

'And very soon after, I'd have died as well. I see. You won't convince the legate about this.' Marcus stroked his chin. 'The governor – and Rome – want somebody to blame. And to make an exhibition of.'

'But you believe it?' I enquired.

'I suppose I must. I'll see that Elvinus Posthumus is questioned, certainly.' He turned to Pulchra. 'Why did you leave your husband's body in the ditch, rather than nearer to the woods, with Appius? If that boot had not been visible, this citizen would never have stopped to look.'

Pulchra made a helpless gesture. 'We meant to – hoping the wolves might really find them before the death-cart did, and render them entirely unrecognisable. But Craithaw was too heavy and it was getting light. We heard a wagon coming from the town and it had torches lit. They would have noticed us at once. We just dropped him in the ditch, then got back in the cart and trotted off. As it was, we just got back before they shut the gates to wheeled transport for the day. There were lots of wagons queuing up to leave, but we managed to slip through in time. I took the cart home and was so exhausted I collapsed on to my bed. I was just clearing up the mess when you arrived.'

Marcus looked at me. 'What are we to do with these two?' he enquired.

'I suggest you let them go,' I said. 'You're right. The authorities will be looking for somebody to blame, but they have saved your life. And rid the world of two unpleasant men. You can tell the authorities the truth. Craithaw accidentally poisoned Appius with his own hemlock bread.'

'The army will want these two anyway.'

'But if the alarm is not raised until tomorrow, you'd still get the praise – and doubtless a reward – and they would have a better chance. But where are they to go?'

'The first thing to do is lose that furniture.' Marcus was suddenly in control again. 'I suggest they take it somewhere and set fire to it. A place where it could be taken for a private pyre. No one will be looking for an empty cart. And we must find some other clothes for them, in case they were noticed at the gate. I may be able to help in that regard. I have some slave-tunics which are not in use. Junio, lend Callidus your horse. He can ride back to the villa and say I sent for them. Now, once you have finished your rituals here, I suggest you get swiftly on the road again. Callidus will find you with the uniforms. In the meantime you can let me have that jar. If there are traces in it, that is evidence. And give me Craithaw's keys – if it's proved he kept the poison locked away, it might help your case if you are caught.'

'But they will have nothing, Excellence,' I bleated, 'if they burn it all.'

'Not quite nothing.' That was Loftus now. 'We have Craithaw's money. Appius paid him well.'

'But that is forfeit, surely . . .' Marcus said. 'The profit from a crime.'

I saw Pulchra wince. 'Not all of it – on most occasions there was no crime at all,' she said. 'Mostly it was simply payment for our bread, and if Appius chose to make the contract generous, that's not against the law.'

I seized on this. 'So it was Craithaw's money and part of his estate? Which goes to his widow, since they had no family?'

'No wonder she was content to lose the money in his purse!' Marcus sighed. 'I should issue a hefty fine, at least.'

'And prove that you have met and talked to them? That might raise questions, and lose you the reward. Which – given Appius's value to the Emperor – might well be more than all the money Craithaw had.'

Marcus looked thoughtful. 'Perhaps you're right. Though if they're caught, the money will be damning evidence.'

'But with your help, they won't be caught,' I said. 'No one's going to question two slaves in a cart – on a mission for their master, if anybody asks. And if they go to Aquae Sulis, I have a contact there, a friend of my father's, who might take them in. Though not as millers, for a year or two at least.'

Marcus grunted and turned to Loftus. 'Speaking of milling, what will happen to your business in the town?'

'It can be run by my daughter and the slaves. I've told her what happened, and it's a relief for her. Craithaw had been pressing me to let him marry her – he talked of divorcing Pulchra, who was a faithful wife – but that way he'd have lost the mill that he already owned, and wouldn't have qualified for membership of his precious bakers' guild.'

'So he planned to murder her instead?'

'Exactly, Excellence. And I was likely to fall victim soon. Appius would nominate a guardian to my girl, and arrange for Craithaw to marry her forthwith.'

I thought of Trovatus.

'And now?'

'There's a Celtic freeman who is fond of her.' Loftus gave me a sideways look. 'Honest and hardworking, as you'll know, Junio, because he works for you. Anylan Trovatus, I believe he's called. Perhaps the courts could name a guardian who'd give consent to that.'

Marcus said, 'I'll see it is arranged. Now, Junio, you can ride to town with me and wait for Callidus to come back with the horse.' Not to mention Tenuis and the mule, I thought.

'I will write a letter to my contact,' I replied. 'If I could trouble you to send it with your fastest courier. It will take me some time to explain all this, but with luck it will arrive before the cart.'

And that is what I've done. I hope this explains everything.

EPILOGUE

Thank you for your courtesy in reading all of this. You know Anylan Trovatus, and will be pleased that he and the miller's daughter are to wed, which loses me a partner, but gives him a good trade. I am training Tenuis instead.

So far, the fugitives have not been caught, but Marcus is in favour with the legate. He has received rewards for giving information, and for bringing Posthumus to court. Elvinus will be exiled, I hear, but the army are still searching for the cart – though the description they have of it is not accurate.

So, if this reaches you, and so do they, I wish you joy.

Farewell.